Praise for Christina D

'Intelligent, suspenseful, provocative, and disturbing – everything a great novel should be.'
LEE CHILD

'A fast-paced, twisting thriller that left me speechless.'
DAILY MAIL

'[Dalcher] knows how to hit the emotional buttons . . . this is a compelling, fast-paced read.'
GUARDIAN

'Razor sharp and terrifyingly plausible. Extraordinary.'
LOUISE O'NEILL

'A novel ripe for the era of #MeToo.'
VANITY FAIR

'The book of the moment!'
MARIE CLAIRE

'Thrilling and provocative, you'll be flipping through the pages at breakneck speed.'
OK!

'A truly compulsive novel.'
STYLIST

'A dazzling debut.'
GOOD HOUSEKEEPING

'A sharply written and terrifyingly plausible tale . . . I devoured it in a single day.'
LOUISE CANDLISH

Christina Dalcher is the *Sunday Times* bestselling author of *VOX*. She earned her doctorate in theoretical linguistics from Georgetown University, specializing in the phonetics of sound change in Italian and British dialects. *The Sentence* is her fourth novel.

Also by Christina Dalcher

VOX
Q
Femlandia

THE
SENTENCE

CHRISTINA DALCHER

ONE PLACE. MANY STORIES

HQ
An imprint of HarperCollins*Publishers* Ltd
1 London Bridge Street
London SE1 9GF

www.harpercollins.co.uk

HarperCollins*Publishers*
Macken House, 39/40 Mayor Street Upper,
Dublin 1, D01 C9W8, Ireland

This edition 2023

1
First published in Great Britain by
HQ, an imprint of HarperCollins*Publishers* Ltd 2023

ISBN: HB: 9780008559472
TPB: 9780008559489

This book is produced from independently certified FSC™ paper to ensure responsible forest management.

For more information visit: www.harpercollins.co.uk/green

This book is set in 11.6/16 pt. Adobe Garamond by Type-it AS, Norway

Printed and Bound in the UK using 100% Renewable Electricity at CPI Group (UK) Ltd, Croydon, CR0 4YY

This is for the falsely accused, the
wrongfully imprisoned, the unjustly burned.
You know who you are.

Death is different . . . Death is final. Death is irremediable. Death is unknowable.

—ANTHONY G. AMSTERDAM

I shall ask for the abolition of the death penalty until I have the infallibility of human judgment demonstrated to me.

— MARQUIS DE LAFAYETTE

Death Row Inmate #39384

If I wasn't going to die, this story would end here. There wouldn't be no beginning and there wouldn't be no end, nothing interesting to talk about, only another self-published prison diary that would sell lots less copies than Lord Jeffrey Archer's memories of being a guest at various stone hotels. My name would be forgotten, instead of on the lips of newscasters and parents and schoolchildren. I'd be a number, a series of digits on an orange jumpsuit, a man whose face and name no one remembered.

Except for Emily. Emily would remember me. And so would Jake Junior.

One of the last times they came, after spending almost an hour in the security line, after Emily had to remove her underwire bra and trade her best shoes (the ones with the pretty buckles I bought for her last birthday) for a pair of too-large slippers with no metal adornments, we didn't say much. Jake Junior, cranky after being forced to leave his precious Legos in a plastic bowl with one of the screening staff, gave me a quick kiss and went all quiet. I hated them for taking his toys. As if I was gonna build an escape staircase out of a bag of plastic bricks. Jesus wept.

I still had contact visits then, and Emily hugged me just long enough for the hug to feel good, to get some of my old motor purring under all that orange polyester, just short enough to silence any alarm bells about to sound off in the watching guards posted at each corner of the room. She sat down and stared at me through baby-fine lashes. No mascara that morning; she was probably worried about it running if our conversation took the wrong turn, or even if it didn't.

Jake took in my jumpsuit and said it looked like a mechanic's work uniform, except the wrong color.

'Mechanics always wear blue,' he said.

I reached across the broad table and ruffled his hair, freshly cut since the last time I saw him, sticking up a little on the crown as if he'd slept on it wrong. 'Yeah. Hides the grease and stuff,' I said.

And then we didn't say anything for a long time.

We didn't say, for instance, 'When will you be coming home?' or 'The boys at the shop are throwing a keg party when you get out.' or 'I can't wait to have you in our bed again.' That sort of banter is for the C Block men and their families. Not for me. Not for Emily and Jake.

When we did talk, we said different things.

'The papers for the house need to be signed by Wednesday.'

'Mom and Dad have cleared out the spare room for me and Jake Junior.'

'Marty Kray from down the street bought your Ford. Less than you were asking, but at least it was something.'

It was all business. The business of getting ready for the end, an end that would come all too soon.

I tried not to count the remaining visits in my mind. One, two, three more times of regular visits, if anyone could call sitting across a wide steel expanse of table, constantly under the eyes of three armed guards, prohibited from more than a casual touch, 'regular'. And then the next visit. The last. I tried not to think of what we would talk about – or what we wouldn't talk about – at that final reunion.

I saved those thoughts for night, when I was alone. When Emily couldn't see my tears.

Someday, I'll meet them again, my darling Emily, with those eyes of hers that see all the way to the bottom of your soul, that see the lies and the truth. My little Jake – although by then he'll be a grown man instead of a six-year-old. Maybe a college graduate, maybe married, maybe a rock star or a writer. Who knows where his life will take him? None of us can ever know that. But I sure as shit hope he ends up better off than his old man.

I'll meet her, too, the woman who wrote the ending to my own story. Maybe I'll put a hand out to push her away. Maybe I'll forgive her. The first is more likely. I won't be sure until the whole tale's told. As for her, the first time she meets me again, I'll be no more than a bunch of words on paper.

I've had a lot of time for writing words these days. But time is running out.

CHAPTER ONE

Two words buzz around my head as I sit in Judge Petrus' chambers this afternoon. One is 'murder'. The other is 'certainty'. The lawyer in me doesn't much like either word on its own. In combination, they're even worse.

'Well?' Petrus looks at her watch. Carmela Petrus is a scarecrow of a woman. Too many facelifts have turned her into a Picasso painting, all hard lines and angles. She's living evidence that you can't judge a book by its cover. Underneath, Petrus is a fair woman. Sympathetic. She knows what I'm going to say and why I'm going to say it.

She's not the only one waiting. Outside, the reporters started gathering over an hour ago, and the family has been there even longer. Families, really – one who will cheer and one who will hiss when I deliver my decision to them. The rest of the public has neatly divided itself at the foot of the courthouse steps, milling around with their handmade signs, half of which want to send this one down, all the way down, down to a kind of locked basement from which the odds of escape are less than zero. The other half carries signs saying *Execute Justice, Not People!* and

Execution Is Legal Homicide! and *Why Do We Kill People Who Kill People to Show That Killing Is Wrong?*

I'm thinking that if I've ever seen a case with an overabundance of damning evidence, it's this one, the case that will end with a unanimous verdict of guilty after five minutes of jury deliberation. The defendant confessed, for Chrissake.

But.

There's always a 'but'. There needs to be one. There needs to be that final, lingering hesitation, that unanswerable question in a prosecutor's mind. Now more than ever.

What if I'm wrong?

Petrus again, impatient but not unkind. She knows the stakes. 'Well?'

My ears register the form sliding across the desk and flapping lackadaisically as the current from the ceiling fan catches its edge, a little extra punctuation from the somber environment in the judge's chambers. I don't need to look at the form, to read the few terse sentences of legalese, to see the underlined spaces waiting for a signature and a date. The text was on the front page of every newspaper in the country after the State Remedies Act was passed.

Future headlines, unwritten but possible, flash through my mind.

DNA EVIDENCE REVEALS FATAL ERROR

APPEALS COURT REVERSES CONVICTION

POSTHUMOUS PARDON FOR VICTIM

VIRGINIA PROSECUTOR SENTENCED TO DEATH

'They're waiting, Justine.' Petrus again. I hear the click of a polished nail on the wood of the desk, tapping the form. 'You need to decide.'

They're all waiting. The public, the press, the family of the seventeen-year-old honor student whose murder is the subject of the upcoming trial, and the family of the woman who killed him. The hundreds of students and teachers who had taken a day off from their daily routine behind the serpentine walls of Virginia's most prestigious public university to wait out my decision.

They'll hate me. Well, half of them will hate me. But a woman can survive hatred. Hatred doesn't kill you. Hatred isn't on the same plane as a lethal cocktail working its way through your veins or two thousand volts of electricity stopping your heart. Or, maybe worse than that, a lifelong shadow of guilt.

I take the single sheet of paper from Petrus' hand and read the text.

I, Justine Callaghan, lead prosecutor in the case of The People v. Charlotte Thorne, hereby seek the death penalty. I affirm that in the event of future exoneration of the defendant, I shall myself stand in her place, and this will serve as full and fair reparation of the wrong as stipulated by the State Remedies Act of 2016.

The two words continue their circuit in my mind. *Guilt. Certainty.*

Charlotte Thorne is guilty of murder. And I'm certain of it.

CHAPTER TWO

With two exceptions – and one of those exceptions I don't care to think about – no prosecutor in the Commonwealth of Virginia has called for the death penalty in seven years. That's a drastic reduction from the seventy-some people who were executed in the 1990s. After the Remedies Act was passed, every man and woman in my line of work was scared shitless. Same in a few other politically divided states – Florida, North Carolina, Nevada.

If he'd stuck around, my husband would be proud of me.

Petrus clears her throat. 'I don't envy the position you're in,' she says. 'They're going to eat you alive this time, Justine.' She rubs her eyes, stops, and then her fingers move to her temples, starting to move in small, deliberate circles. At this point, Petrus looks less like a judge and more like a barfly recovering from a weekend-long bender. 'Fucking Remedies Act. Why couldn't they leave things as they were?'

She's talking about the state's ban on capital punishment. And the exception to that ban known as the Remedies Act.

Virginia hasn't been one state for decades now, not functionally. Look at any election data, and the lines are clear: progressives in the northern suburbs of Washington, DC, in the college towns of Charlottesville and Williamsburg, in Richmond and the southeast; God-fearing, lifelong conservatives in plenty of other places. Almost a straight fifty-fifty divide between the blue and the red, a cataclysm waiting to happen. It's a near-perfect analog of the entire country. As I stand here, twenty-seven states utilize the death penalty; the other twenty-three don't. Sixty percent of voters want an alternative punishment – life without parole, for instance – but a healthy third are fine with the way things are.

I've never understood that third of the population. I expect it's mainly ignorance of some hard facts that keeps them sticking to their opinions like glue. They don't know how often mistakes are made – an average of four death row inmates are exonerated every year. They don't realize executions have shit to do with lowering homicide rates. And as much as they yell about the expense of keeping every first-degree murderer in prison for life, they don't have a clue that a death penalty case in Texas costs over two million dollars – three times what it would cost to put someone in a single cell for forty years. So they want to see a man in a chair. Or a man on a gurney. Or a man in a gas chamber.

It's all about the emotion.

What I always want to ask those thirty-three percent, those staunch death penalty advocates, is simple: What are your emotions going to be if the man in the chair, or on the gurney, or in the gas chamber turns out to be innocent? But I know the answer. *There are procedures. They had opportunities to appeal. The law doesn't allow for mistakes.*

'I mean,' Petrus says, waking me up from my statistical nightmare, 'I hate this goddamned "We have a ban, but . . ." crap. You want to get rid of executions, fine. Great. I agree. Get rid of them. It would make my job a hell of a lot easier. But don't open a back door a few years later because of some shithead who was the spawn of Hannibal Lecter and Charles Manson. Christ on a pogo stick. What the fuck were they thinking?'

'They were thinking they wanted to keep their seats in the legislature,' I say. 'And the right case came at the right time. The Remedies Act was supposed to make everyone happy. The third of the population that cried for justice got what they wanted – a reinstated death penalty. The rest of us got what we wanted – an insurance policy that would prevent any prosecutor from asking for it. You don't really want to revisit that now, do you?'

Once more, her fingers move to her eyes, either to rub the hurt away or to prevent herself from seeing the evidence photos again. My bet is on the latter, and I close my eyes involuntarily against the images of small bodies that want to present themselves all over again. She waves at me as if swatting away an insect. 'No. I still have nightmares about that trial. Anyway,' Petrus says, nodding towards the window where a crowd waits outside, 'maybe they'll go easy on you since Thorne is a woman. You know how reluctant people have always been to execute females.'

'Very. Chivalry isn't as dead as we think.'

In fact, chivalric treatment of murderesses has always seemed to be alive and well. Something about the system was hesitant to put women to death – unless, of course, the crime was perceived as 'unwomanly'. Of the fifty-odd women who sat on death row in recent memory, most of them were what society would call bad girls, in for rape-murder, infanticide, or the killing of other women. In other words, you had to be a true femme fatale.

Not so with men. When we still had the death penalty, if a man killed, he was sent to die. No jury or prosecutor ever weighed the convicted's manliness when making the decision.

Maybe that's why there were always fifty men for every woman on the row, even though they only outnumbered women by a factor of seven when it came to taking a life.

Like I said, chivalry isn't all gone. Except when we're talking about a bad girl. And Charlotte Thorne is a classic bad girl.

'In this case, I don't think they'd be so reluctant, Carmela,' I say. 'No one who looks at Thorne sees a woman. They see a cold-blooded killer, a monster, like that truck-stop hooker down in Florida twenty-five years ago.'

Petrus makes a sound of pure disgust, then says, 'Monster. Right.' She stares at the form in my hand, the slip of paper that can turn a life sentence into a death warrant in the Charlotte Thorne case. 'If you ask for death, Justine, I know we'll get there. I'm sure of it.'

As am I.

But.

I let the form float back down to her desk, unsigned.

Petrus' thin lips become even thinner. 'I understand.' Then: 'I know what happened with that other case, and you weren't yourself then. I know you're cautious and I know you're conservative, and most of all, I know you've got a rare sense of integrity. But I need to know, between us girls.' She takes off her glasses and lays them on the desk next to the form. 'If they hadn't passed the Remedies Act and made the exception after that – you know – that other case, if everything were as it was before, what would you do now?'

It's a complicated question, but my answer is simple.

'Considering the nature of the crime, the state of the deceased's body, and the complete lack of remorse Thorne has displayed, I still wouldn't ask for Charlotte Thorne to pay with her life.'

'Okay. Personal question, Justine. Why not, if the evidence is golden?'

'You know why not. Because I can't take it back if I'm wrong.'

She nods, and on her face there's both understanding and disappointment. 'Well, I guess you're covered when you go outside to make a statement. You know how it works, Justine. The Remedies Act sort of covers your ass, doesn't it?'

'Yep.' I know exactly how the Remedies Act works.

After all, I helped draft it.

CHAPTER THREE

Telling Petrus is one thing; telling the crowd waiting outside is another. But I'm covered by the law. I can't be spat on or shouted at or threatened. The law will do what it's designed to do. It will protect me.

Or so I think.

I gather up my things – purse, briefcase, the light coat I needed this morning when early April's chill hung in the air – and start down the long corridor toward the main hall of the courthouse. It hums with the usual activity. Security equipment sounds off occasional beeps when a forgotten set of keys or a few coins at the bottom of a pocket trigger it. Ambulance chasers scramble to beat each other to the clerk's office to file their civil suits. Men and women crowd around wall-mounted dockets to see where they need to be and when they need to be there.

With each step toward the main doors, I review the evidence against Charlotte Thorne. It's solid evidence, the kind you can almost wrap your hands around and feel. Its corners are sharp and well defined, its weight like a chunk of lead. Charlotte had – and I know this because I've had the case material to study for over a year now – called her student to an afternoon meeting. Nothing spectacular about that. Plenty of high school teachers meet with their students. They discuss grades, performance, attendance. Sometimes they shoot the shit like old colleagues rather than teacher and student.

What made Charlotte Thorne's meeting with Robbie Forrester different were three things. The meeting took place at Thorne's house. The topic under discussion was sex instead of Shakespeare. And Charlotte didn't shoot the shit.

She shot a .45 into Forrester's groin. Twice – one shot for each testicle. She waited an hour and fired a final bullet into Forrester's head. Then she called 911, told them what she'd done, and gave herself up, probably to clinch an insanity plea, which didn't work in the end.

I step out into the sun and give my eyes a moment to adjust. When they do, I see the eyes of the crowd on me. They all seem to settle on my skin simultaneously, like brazen flies, unafraid. My next words will either bring relief or rancor to the waiting crowd, depending on which side of the ideological fence they sit, which moral pole they adhere to.

A microphone waits on the podium, and I walk up to it, adjusting the height.

Now the flies on my skin seem to crawl, seem to bite into me, turning from a mere nuisance to something more sinister. I have to remind myself they aren't flies, only eyes. Only eyes passing judgment, incapable of doing actual harm.

'In the case of The People versus Charlotte Thorne, the city will not be seeking the death penalty.'

At the bottom of the courthouse steps, the eyes become words, and the words sting like a swarm of wasps whose nest I've disturbed in a moment of carelessness. There are cries and shouts and hoots worthy of a lifelong back-row heckler. At least a dozen people in a circle hold hands and chant lines from the Bible. Exodus, maybe. An eye for an eye. A tooth for a tooth. A lash for a lash. A life for a life. A bright line separates the right and left halves of the crowd, a bright blue line of police, their hands poised on nightsticks, ready to intervene should right and left decide to close the gap and rumble. It's happened before.

An object flies from somewhere ahead of me, a white sphere describing an arc against the blue background of the sky. I think, *Golf ball? Something worse than a golf ball?* before my overworked brain recognizes it as not a sphere but an ovoid. An egg. It hits my forehead an inch below the hairline and cracks, dripping sticky albumen and yolk over my eyes, spattering bits of broken shell on the linen of my blazer, where they stick like tiny mosaic tiles.

A cheer ripples through the crowd.

'Should have been a fucking grenade!' someone yells from the masses.

'Serves the bitch right. He was a kid,' a woman calls out. 'Just a kid!'

'Maybe her kid'll be next,' another voice says. It's met with a collective agreement so enthusiastic I can't help but think of Jonathan, of that age-old conversation stopper: *So, you're against capital punishment? Well, suppose it were your son who was murdered. Your daughter. Your husband. You'd change your tune then, wouldn't you?*

I shut my ears to all of it, but the words still sting like wasps.

Suddenly there's a pull, or a sensation of being pulled, a gravitational force from my left side. I blink to clear my eyes and recognize the source.

Daniel. Thank Christ for Daniel. He has a firm grip on my arm, and one hand pressed into the small of my back, steering me up the stairs, returning us both to the shelter and relative safety of the courthouse.

He sits me down in one of the hard chairs next to the security screening tables, and his clear British speech, softened by a few years in the States, has a calming effect. 'Stay here. Don't move. And for the love of God, don't speak to anyone. I'll get my car and come back for you in less than ten. Just quote the Act if they try anything, okay? You're covered.'

I don't respond.

'Okay?' he says again. 'Ten minutes. Tops.' Then he bends toward me and gently wipes my face with his sleeve. 'Bloody bastards. You'll be fine.'

I watch him retreat to the far end of the hall, toward the bank of elevators that carry hundreds of passengers each day, either up or down. Up to the courtrooms to either preside over or await fates; down to the parking garages. After Daniel disappears into one of them, six uniformed guards escort a handcuffed Charlotte Thorne to the last set of steel doors. They form a human shield around the woman.

The murderer, I think.

The system isn't supposed to work this way. There are safeguards in place to keep the convicted from coming face to face with anyone from the district attorney's office, either before or after a decision is taken. Separate entrances, separate elevators, separate levels in the subterranean parking garage. But earlier in the month – *just my luck* – the service elevator failed, the replacement parts arrived three weeks later than scheduled, the union guys decided to strike, and now here we are, opposing numbers in close contact. Closer than I'd like.

Charlotte Thorne looks across the hall at me, smiles, and says two words: 'Thanks, honey.' Christ, if the woman doesn't look cheery. No. Cheery isn't the right word. Victorious.

'What's the matter, counselor? Lose your nerve?' Thorne says. The guard closest to her repositions himself and speaks to her, a warning, possibly. If it is a warning, Thorne ignores it. The woman knows what she's doing, knows they can only send her to prison once, and that any potential death sentence was taken off the table as soon as I addressed the waiting crowd. She's untouchable, and she knows this. 'Not quite sure enough, eh? Fucking coward,' she says, and the words, like arrows now, fly across the hall in my direction.

She's taunting me, and it doesn't make sense at first. Humans are hardwired to survive. But then I remember Charlotte Thorne has lost some of her humanity. She's a psychopath, after all.

Coward.

Daniel could tell me to sit tight and stay quiet. It's easy for him. He's from a country that hasn't seen an execution since 1964 – and hasn't seen a woman executed since the mid-Fifties when Ruth Ellis was hanged for murder. Also, he never gets the hard cases. Daniel works for a swanky private firm dealing with international bank fraud, not homicide, and who in the public gives a shit about bank fraud? No one, that's who. His cases go largely unnoticed, unreported, and unsensationalized. No electric chair will ever dangle in the prospective futures of the men and women Daniel helps send up to plush stone hotels with low security and even lower press coverage.

'COWARD!' Charlotte screams again.

This single word forces me to my feet.

Coward.

The same word may be hanging on the lips of the outside

crowd, the Bible-thumpers who chant chapter and verse of Old Testament judicial philosophy at the top of their lungs, so loud I can hear every word from here inside. I wonder, in my shoes, who among them would act differently?

I backtrack to the main doors of the courthouse and once again step out into the bright afternoon sun. I don't bother wiping the rest of the egg from my face and suit.

A dozen microphones appear in an arc around me, heavy, monstrous-looking things, like pointing fingers, accusatory and cold. For a moment, I'm back in the northwest corner of Harvard Yard, twenty-five again, surrounded by a different set of microphones but speaking the same words I speak now.

'Listen to me,' I say.

A few cries of 'Shut the fuck up' and 'Who cares' ripple through the crowd below me, then all goes quiet.

'This afternoon, I had to make a decision. I had to decide whether to send a human being to her death.'

'You decided wrong,' someone shouts.

I ignore this, then look directly at the speaker, a stout woman in a too-tight suit and a silk scarf that has a chokehold on her. 'Okay. Let me ask you, then.' I keep my eyes locked on the woman. 'Are you sure enough to put your life on the line?'

'She did it,' the woman says. 'You know she did it.'

I continue. 'You say you want a life for a life. Fine. But you all know what the stakes are now. I've got a kid at home. A young boy. I can't risk it.' The likelihood that Thorne will ever be exonerated approaches zero on the Kelvin scale, but still. I'd be insane to put my own life on the line for Charlotte Thorne's brand of shit.

The woman in the scarf says nothing. Her stare, stony and sure when I began talking, softens.

'If you're going to send a human being to die,' I say, feeling buoyed by the response, 'you have to be sure. You have to be dead certain. There's no do-over in this game. There's no take-back, no *Sorry, I made a mistake,* no reset, no start again. Not anymore.'

I've got them now, I think. They're listening. And then one of the Exodus-chanters calls out, ending this brief illusion. 'You're sure enough to send her to prison. You should be sure enough to send her to the chair. She killed a kid, Ms Callaghan. A kid. Someone needs to pay for that.'

A cry of 'That's real Christian of you' comes from the left side of the police line, and it's met with an equally loud cry of 'Go fuck yourself, you leftie moron' from the right section. It's as if a random sampling of America, in all its red-and-blue divisiveness, has shown up at this courthouse to drive home the ugly truth about our country. Not so long ago, the cheers and boos came from opposite sides, with the conservatives backing me up and the liberals shooting me down. That's the real world, I suppose, being able to please some of the people all of the time, all of the people some of the time, but never all of the people all of the time.

Then, to my horror, someone raises a baseball bat. And that's enough. The sides draw together, the blue stripe of police between them, effective at keeping an uneasy peace, not so effective at keeping five men from running up the courthouse stairs. Towards me. The cops manage to herd them back down, but they leave a wide swath of unprotected granite, a no-man's-land that only serves as a reminder that everyone is on one side of two.

A younger woman, much younger than the one in the silk scarf, threads her way to the front of the crowd. I put her in her mid-twenties, tops, but her thinness makes her look like a young teenager. She's got a kid with her, a small boy with a smear of dirt on his cheek and a miniature toy car clutched in one hand. She stops at the yellow tape of the police line, now temporarily unguarded, and looks up at me with watery eyes.

'You talk about how there's no take-back. You stand there and tell me there's no way to start over.' Her voice breaks, the soft southern drawl of western or southern Virginia trailing off. Then she collects herself and continues. 'I wish someone had said that seven years ago, Ms Callaghan. My boy wishes it, too.'

She could charge up toward me, maybe get close enough to slap or at least spit, but she doesn't. She only stands in place, one hand holding on to her boy, the other tightly wrapped around the straps of a scuffed brown purse.

I know who she is.

She's Emily Milford, and the last time I saw her was seven years back, on the day Carmela Petrus sentenced her husband to death.

Now the reporters have started a stampede down the stairs, away from me and toward the woman with the purse. It's a chum-fest, twenty-five sharks all smelling blood at the same time.

'Mrs Milford, do you—'

'How do you feel about the Remedies Act, Mrs Milford?'

'Do you think your husband deserved to die?'

'What would you do if new evidence came to light?' The reporter asking this question isn't looking at Emily Milford, but at me.

And then another woman pushes her way through the pack of camera- and microphone-wielding predators. She's in a smart red suit and hat, same as all the Vita activists, same as I used to wear, although this one looks too well turned out to be one of the original flock. She leans close to Emily Milford and whispers something in her ear.

Emily's eyes widen.

'I said to wait for me, not to start a war.' Daniel is at my side again, and this time the pull is stronger as he turns me back into the building.

I steal a last glance over my shoulder. Two burly cops have succeeded in wrestling one of the charging men to the ground – no small trick, the charger leading the group is a mountain of a human being. Cries of protest rise up from the rest of the crowd – some directed at the apparent police brutality, others at me.

Emily Milford, her son, and the woman in the blood-red suit are gone.

CHAPTER FOUR

'I can't believe you let her off.'

They're familiar words. They should be, since they've been pouring out of Susan Stewart's mouth at least twice a year for the past decade. The only variable is the pronoun. Usually, it's 'him' instead of 'her'. The rest is the same old song, a snippet of shitty music you can't get out of your head.

I open the door wider, and the boys run in, passing me by with a brief 'Hi, Mommy' and 'Hi, Aunt Justine' on their way to the back room where the television and PlayStation wait. Before I can dump my briefcase and purse on the hall table, the first chords of the Star Wars theme music have started up, and the cousins are busy light-sabering Lego Darth Vader and Lego Han Solo and Lego whatever-his-name is. I tell myself it's only pretend violence, perfectly suitable for six-year-olds after a half-day of school. You can't really harm a virtual Lego.

Part of me believes this. A small part.

'I mean, Jussie, what the actual fuck? She killed that kid. She screwed him and then she killed him – grotesquely – and then she basically admitted it all in front of God and everybody. So don't give me that moral high ground crap of yours.' Susan pulls out a stool from the kitchen island, letting its legs squeak unnecessarily on the floor. 'Got any wine?'

In response, I take a single glass from the rack above us and open the fridge. 'Not if you're going to be a bitch.'

'Come on, sis. The kids are having fun. They like each other, and Tommy doesn't have Lego Star Wars at home. Let them play for a while.' Susan smiles one of her best smiles. 'I'll be nice. I promise.'

'No, you won't.' But I take a second glass down from the rack and uncork a bottle of Syrah. 'Oh, I almost forgot.' On my phone, I transfer another five hundred dollars into Susan's account. 'For this week, okay?'

'It's too much.'

'No, it isn't. Jonathan's better off spending his afternoons with you than in some shitty after-school program, and you need the money. Besides, like you say, he and Tommy get along.'

Susan doesn't protest again. We both know she can use every penny, even if we usually avoid the subject of her runaway husband and focus on mine. 'All I'm saying is, that Thorne woman is bad news. No one wants to pay for her to watch cable television and work out on Pelotons for the next fifty years.'

'"No one" covers a lot of ground. Besides, you said you'd be nice,' I say, pouring the wine, a half glass for Susan and barely a finger for myself.

Susan sips hers. 'I did. I didn't say I'd be silent.'

'I couldn't sign the thing.'

'You mean you wouldn't.' Susan's sips turn into long swallows, not quite gulps, but she'll get there soon enough. I know the routine, the seven steps of my sister-in-law's grief.

Anger always comes first, along with the accusatory questions.

How could you do that? How could you let her get off so easily? There will be a brief tour through niceties, a quick promise to be civil (for the boys' sakes) following that. In a few minutes, Susan will start matching drinks two-for-one, and then the tears will come. Eventually, unavoidably, our conversation will shift to Ian.

We get there a little sooner this afternoon than usual.

A lot sooner.

Tommy and Jonathan run into the kitchen, the Star Wars music temporarily on hold. 'Can we have popcorn, Aunt Justine?' Tommy asks.

Jonathan beams a smile that's all his father, none of me. 'Please, Mommy?'

A couple of peas in a pod, I think. Same grayish eyes, same Cupid-bow smiles, same timbre in their voices. Even their writing is nearly identical. I turn to the fridge, where a pair of what-I-did-on-my-spring-break drawings are stuck with alphabet magnets. 'My God, they're alike,' I say to Susan. 'You think it's because they're in the same first-grade class?' But I know it isn't. Maybe you inherit handwriting like you inherit eye color and curls and Cupid's bows. Maybe they get it all from Ian.

I can't say Susan is like Ian, not really. Looking at her, I see that she's much shorter, the nose is different, and she doesn't have her only brother's off-color sense of humor that can send me into almost uncontrollable fits of laughter until my stomach hurts.

Correction: sent.

'Mom?' Jonathan says. 'Earth to Mom.'

'Sure. Popcorn.' I put the bag in the microwave to nuke and shoo the boys out. 'Go back and play, kids. I'll bring it in when it's done.'

'Two bowls?' Jonathan says. 'Because Tommy always takes big handfuls.'

'Two bowls. Now scoot.'

They leave just in time. Susan has started up the waterworks, and by the time the Star Wars music is playing again, she's full into her sixth stage of endless grief.

I brace myself. Time to talk about how I sleep.

'How do you sleep?' Susan asks. 'How do you sleep knowing the assholes who killed people have been sitting down to dinner and a movie every night for the past seven years? Playing hoops out in the goddamned recreational area with a pack of other murderers? Getting in some gym time? Hell, maybe they're even going for a degree. I hear they do that now. So tell me. How do you sleep?'

'They're still locked up, Susan. Disen-freaking-franchised, with or without three meals a day and workout rooms.' As for her questions about how I sleep, the answer is easy: I don't.

Susan drains her glass and pours another. All the way up to the rim. 'The evidence was always there, Jus. It was there in every single case. Prints, hair, gunshot residue. A full confession.' Now the glass is half empty again, Susan's voice rises to a soprano, the first bars of the goddamned Star Wars theme seem to be on endless repeat, and a toxic smell is coming from the microwave over the stove. Nothing quite like the aroma of singed corn and smoked fake butter.

Shit.

'Ian wouldn't have wanted it, Sue,' I say. 'You know he wouldn't have.'

'You always say that.'

'Because it's the truth.'

We don't ease into this last part; we never do. Susan takes another swallow, and I brace myself for the freight train of guilt she's about to roll toward me.

'What if Charlotte Thorne's student had been Jonathan?'

'It wasn't,' I say.

'But what if it had been?'

There's no answer I can give Susan that would satisfy her. If I say I still wouldn't want Thorne sentenced to death, she'll come back with the usual, 'You can't know that. Not until it hits close to home.' If I say otherwise, she'll lay into me for hypocrisy, for having one rule for me and one for everyone else. I can't win, so I shut up, pretend to sip more wine, and blink back tears.

The sour smile on her lips fades, and Susan lays a hand on my arm. 'I'm sorry,' she says. 'I shouldn't have said that about Jonathan. I know he's all you have left.' She draws circles around the rim of her glass instead of looking at me. 'I get emotional when I drink. Are we cool?'

'Yeah. We're cool, Sis.'

'I miss Ian, too, you know.' She pulls me close in a tight hug. 'I guess every time I hear about another murder, it opens that old wound again. Know what I mean?'

I know. 'Stop it. I don't want to start crying while the boys are here.'

'Okay. Okay. But I wish we didn't have the Remedies Act. I know how you feel about the whole irrevocability thing, but I still wish we didn't have it.'

I pull away, not abruptly, and look Susan in the eyes. 'We had to. They were going to bring back the death penalty after the – that other case. The one with the kids. We only wanted to keep legal executions to a bare minimum.'

'You still haven't told me all the details about that case.'

'About Toby Barrett? No, Susan. I haven't. And I'm not going to.'

'Why not?'

'Because it was a thousand times worse than the one I tried this week.'

CHAPTER FIVE

Toby Barrett came at the right time. Ten children in all, kidnapped, starved over a period of months, kept alive on water and saline until he grew tired of it. The bastard showed about as much remorse as a rattlesnake.

Barrett wasn't my case, but I followed the trial, and I took a few personal days so I could attend the closing arguments, verdict, and sentencing. When Petrus condemned him to ten consecutive life terms (far too short, in my opinion), Barrett stood there, baring a set of crooked, tobacco-stained teeth. I remember wondering how someone so small – he couldn't have weighed more than a hundred thirty pounds soaking wet – could contain so much evil. Even his court-appointed defense attorney seemed to want the greatest distance between them as the courtroom setup would allow. Maybe he thought close proximity might prove infectious, and the guy on the right side of the law would find himself waking the next morning with an irresistible urge to copycat his client. Petrus' nightmares were well warranted. Still are.

The crime had been heinous, so ugly, I thought Merriam-Webster should list it under the dictionary entry for 'evil'. The man was a rat, rabid and vicious. But it was the words he said after Petrus sentenced him that changed our part of the world.

Barrett stood silent for a moment, just silent enough to make his outburst all the more of a punch to the collective gut of the courtroom. Then he did something. He laughed. Threw his head back and actually cackled, paying no attention to Petrus' gavel or calls for order. His laughter had the sound of a thunderclap and the shape of a mortal wound.

In the front of the courtroom, the victims' families sat huddled together, mothers leaning on their husbands or on each other, fathers steadying other fathers with a firm arm on their shoulders. I counted seven couples, two single mothers, and one sandy-haired man on his own. There had been eight couples in the earlier days of the trial. The sandy-haired man's wife had come along with him. Then she stopped coming. Toby Barrett might have been behind bars, but he had still managed to take another life.

My heart sank as he laughed. One of the mothers in the front collapsed with all the grace of a rock tumbling down a jagged incline. The sandy-haired man close to the aisle darted to his left and made for Barrett as the other fathers leapt to restrain him. It was a shit-show. And it was about to get worse.

A whole lot worse.

Petrus' cries for order continued, but Barrett's voice drowned hers out. He spoke in a deep baritone that demanded attention. I mean, you couldn't not listen to him. You couldn't prevent his words from seeping into your ears like evil little worms.

'Thanks very much, your honor,' he said. He stretched out the last two syllables until the word 'honor' almost broke into two separate pieces. Barrett turned to the jury. 'And thank you, my fine fellow citizens, my peers.' Again, 'peers' morphed into something palpably evil as he spoke. 'Thank you, ladies and gentlemen.' He nodded toward the victims' parents, winking at the sandy-haired man who was still writhing in the grip of three others. 'And thank you to that governor who made this fine state death-penalty-free back in good old 2016. And the reason I want to thank all you lovely sons of bitches,' Barrett said, 'is that I'll be getting my three squares and a free bed and cable television for the rest of my natural-born life.'

He bowed then. The man actually bowed. 'You can't touch me now, can you? I know my rights. I know every single one of you politically correct weenies would love to see me get the death shot or ride the lightning. And you can't touch me. I can't imagine how much it must hurt to know that.'

Petrus slammed her gavel down, and it skipped off the bench, landing in a dead thud just short of the bar. A hundred pairs of eyes locked on it, including my own. I know what the minds behind those eyes were thinking. *Smash the motherfucker's brains out.*

The crowd only stared as he spoke. From the bench, Petrus called for the bailiff. Unfortunately, the court-appointed peace officer weighed in at even less than Barrett. He shook the bailiff off as one might shake off an annoying child.

'You weak-kneed liberal weenies! Gotta ban the death penalty for votes, right? Gotta be all soft and tolerant and understanding. Gotta be good Christians. Well, you got what you wanted, and I say again, thank you. Thank you, Mrs Judge; thank you, jurors; and thank all you taxpaying fools for setting me up for the next forty years. I'll be smokin' and jokin' with the boys by tomorrow night, watching me some football on a big screen you're all paying to keep lit up.' He winked again. 'Maybe even some kiddie porn, too. Ain't exactly approved viewing material, but everyone in stir knows how to get anything he wants.'

A woman in the front stepped onto the wooden bench, making herself taller. 'Make him stop!' She screamed it at everyone and no one. 'Make him stop!'

In came the backup, a team of four burly men. There were a few seconds that seemed like an eternity as each took one of Barrett's limbs, and the murderer was stretched on an invisible plane while they carried him away. He looked like Jesus in the hands of the Romans.

There was a wail from the group of parents, a drawn-out vocalization of pain that belongs in one of the inner circles of Dante's hell. I heard it. And I hear it all over again this afternoon as I sit in the kitchen with Susan.

Psychopath, I think. Not so different from Charlotte Thorne this afternoon.

But they aren't all like that. I've seen trials where the accused sits quiet, where there aren't any outbursts. Jake Milford was one of those types, if I recall. As the sentence was read out, he did nothing more than stare at his hands.

Death Row Inmate #39384

I've learned there are two different kinds of people who work in prisons. Mostly, they're guys who need a paycheck. They go about their jobs in a mechanical way, locking doors, unlocking doors, bringing food trays, taking away food trays. I don't think they much like their work but, like I said, some folks need a paycheck.

Then there's the other kind. The sadists.

Mr Lively and Mr Coombs are that other kind.

'There are things people don't get right,' he said when he brought me back to my cell on the afternoon of my last day. 'Like jumping. Your body don't jump, Milford. It sorta seizes up the way an engine might without oil. The only difference is engines don't feel pain.'

Coombs disagreed. 'I've studied up on electrocution. Some say it's instantaneous, and if they're right, then that's a damn shame. For kid-killing scum like you, there shouldn't be any instantaneous shit, only lots of pain drawn out over a good long while. The good news is some say it ain't so instantaneous. You remember that, Milford. You remember that while you're taking your last walk.'

I kept my mouth shut. I might not be smart, but I'm smart enough to know Coombs and Lively still had the power to make my final hours a living hell. They'd only have to tell the warden that I slipped and fell. Real shame.

'See,' Lively said. 'The folks who come to sit behind the glass and watch all think they know what's happening. They think seeing is believing, and if they're actually there, they have all the facts and they believe those facts. Thing is, those people can only see part of the story. They can't see you up close; they can't see all the fear. They can't smell you when you shit your pants, and they can't hear you when you whimper like a little girl. Believe me, Milford, you're gonna feel a lot of fear.'

He laughed. 'Last frying I saw was eight years back, but I remember it like it happened yesterday.' He leaned toward the bars of my cell right after they locked me in. I was still cuffed to the bars, and they left me that way while they talked. Coombs leaned in closer, the stench of his tobacco chew heavy on his breath. 'You'll have to shuffle-walk from your cell to the room with the chair, Milford. Like a little baby who hasn't learned to be steady on his own two feet. You'll be tied up like a wild hog, just in case you get any ideas.

'Not many ideas to get in a hallway about twenty feet long with three locked doors. One back to your cell, one to your killing, and one to a whole 'nother world of fences and towers and search lights,' Coombs said, spreading his hands wide as if to show the expanse of this other world. 'Beyond the fences, even if you could get over or under them, there's a town about the size of a city block. But we'll truss you up anyhow. Don't want to see you hurting yourself on the way.'

36

Stupid, I thought. All he had to do was look at me to see I no longer had the strength to hurt myself or anyone else.

Coombs seemed to read my mind. 'After you eat and after you wait, your body's gonna go numb, like you been shot with some strong kind of medicine. Seen it before.'

'Yep,' Lively said. 'Sometimes, it's all they can do to bend and crouch the way they're supposed to while we put all the gear on.' He forced my head to turn towards him. Like Coombs, Lively chewed tobacco, and he made sure I got a good whiff of it when he spoke. More than that, though, his eyes told me he was looking forward to tonight. 'Walking is gonna be hard, Milford. Hardest thing you've ever done in your short life. Ain't only because of the leg shackles.' He pointed toward the tile floor in the hallway. 'That floor's gonna turn into one long glue trap. You'll feel like you gotta peel up each foot before taking a step.'

We had a mouse problem once. Emily didn't want me to set traps because she thought it was cruel. I guess I agreed at the time, but changed my mind after I found the first baby mouse stuck on the surface of the Tomcat mat. The little guy was trying so damned hard to get free, and the more he struggled, the more he stuck. I didn't think that was so humane after all. After that, I took care of those critters the quick way. It seemed a kindness.

Coombs rattled his keys, and for a second I thought they were done torturing me, that they'd unlock the cuffs and let me go lie down.

I was wrong.

'Ain't that strong a glue, Bill,' Coombs said, arguing the point. He was talking more to Lively now than to me. 'Sonofabitch will finally make it to the room with the chair.

The first thing that'll hit him is how clean it smells, like my kitchen after my wife finishes up one of her super-cleans. Then they'll tell Mr Kid-Killer Milford here to sit, and he'll sit. He'll feel like about a million hands are on him, all working on something different at the same time. Someone will cut the plastic ties around those scrawny wrists, and another two will get his arms strapped to the chair. Same thing with his legs.' The tobacco stink vanished for a second as Coombs crouched down. 'Yep. That leg. The left one. They'll shave it bare as a newborn babe. Gotta cut the pants off at the knee first.'

Now Lively was down there, too, lifting up the cuff of my prison trousers. 'Look at that lily-white skin, man.'

I looked down. My skin was white. I don't think I ever realized how white it was until Lively put his hand on me, stroking up and down at the coarse hair that would be gone in a few hours. His hand was brown and tanned from days working out in the sun. I used to be like that. Emily would laugh when I came in from a side job, telling me we'd never get into the country club if I didn't stop looking like a redneck. But now I was pale as paper. Bleached. After so long inside, I looked like a sick man.

The guards stood up again, and Coombs started working the keys to my cuffs. He was speaking to me again, his breath hot in my ear. 'By the time we got your sorry self all strapped in, you might be able to lift two fingers on each hand.'

My left hand was free and I brought it around in front of me, studying it. Those fingers that had turned wrenches at work and played along Emily's soft skin in bed were useless now. They won't turn any more wrenches, and they won't ruffle my boy's hair, and they won't caress the woman I'm crazy in love with. Not ever again.

A sloshing sound inside the cell brought me out of my thoughts. I wasn't worrying about my fingers anymore because a new thing was happening. Lively was at the sink, running water over a towel. He stepped over to me and put his hands on either side of my face, holding my head steady. For a stupid moment, I thought he was gonna kiss me. Then my head was wet and cold, and a heaviness pressed down on that spot they'll shave this afternoon.

I've never liked wet or cold. It brings back a memory so ugly I wish I could burn it from my mind.

'That's what the sponge is gonna feel like, Milford. And my hand right now is what the cap'll feel like. It's gonna force you to look straight ahead, right into the eyes of the twelve people sitting behind the glass. Mr and Mrs Church are gonna be there, and a few reporters scribbling on their notepads, but they won't actually be looking at what they're writing. They won't want to miss what comes next.'

'What comes next,' Coombs said, like he was musing on some riddle. 'What comes next is gonna happen fast and slow. There ain't gonna be no way you can separate out the sounds and the pain. It just happens. At a quarter to midnight, you're gonna be alive.' He unlocked my right wrist and pushed me into the cell. I fell onto my cot, head soaked, trying not to show them how scared I was.

The cell door slammed shut and the bolt turned.

Coombs got philosophical again as they walked down the hall. 'Yep. At a quarter to midnight, you'll be alive, Milford. Then you won't be.'

CHAPTER SIX

The mailman arrives early today. His truck's motor grows louder and higher-pitched as it pulls up the drive, taking less care than usual to avoid coming too close to the rows of neatly trimmed boxwood on either side. I hope it's all letters today, no packages. Nothing that will force me to open the door and stand face to face with another human being.

So, naturally, the doorbell rings, and a package the size of Texas is pushed into my arms. The mailman holds a signature device out, waiting for me to take it, possibly with a third hand that I'll pull from the pocket of my suit. In my rush to retrieve the signature pad, I drop the Amazon package. It sounds like a crash box in a shitty radio play as it hits the brick at my feet.

Jonathan appears in the front hall, followed by Susan and Tommy. He checks out the cardboard box, and his face lights up. 'Oh, boy! Is this what I think it is?'

Not anymore, I think, remembering the box hitting the bricks.

Jonathan and Tommy wrestle the package through the door while Susan and I pick up the rest of the scattered mail. Bills, letters, half a dozen glossy postcards alerting me to which million-dollar-club real estate agent sold which million-dollar house this week. As if I care. The only real estate I'm interested in right now is the kind for sale on some other planet.

'Aw, jeez,' Jonathan says from the hall inside. 'It's all broken.' Surrounding him are a few hundred pieces of what used to be twin sets of Star Wars china – one for him and one for Tommy. The boys look up at me and speak at exactly the same time. 'You dropped it? How could you drop it?'

I say the first thing that comes to mind. 'It's complicated.' My heart feels like the plates on the floor.

'That's what you have on your Facebook relationship status,' Susan says, laughing. Then she ushers both boys into the kitchen and does her Susan Thing, magically making everything right with a few words.

Like Ian used to do.

When I turn to shut the door, I see her at the bottom of my driveway. The same woman in red from the courthouse steps. I know who she is and why she's here.

The problem with Vita, and I suppose it's the problem with any movement or any population, was that the group eventually divided. What we all believed was one single-cell organism split itself in two, giving birth to a more extreme version of itself. I think of the woman on the courthouse steps, the one who whispered to Emily, the one who's now watching my house, and I understand which side she's on.

Twice in one day, I think, and draw the blinds closed.

I shouldn't be surprised at her presence. It's something I've been expecting every day for years now, maybe even waiting for. Most of the time, I'm able to bury the expectation in little things. Waking up. Showering. Dressing Jonathan for school. Turning the coffee machine on; turning the coffee machine off. Work.

Driving. Oil changes and clothes purchases and Star Wars plate orders from Amazon. But, like all the things we bury, it never completely disappears. Which is why I'm not surprised to see Emily Milford's letter in today's stack of mail.

I get quite a lot of mail without return addresses. All of it contains the same flavor of bile from victims' families and friends, sometimes co-workers or neighbors. This one doesn't need a return address; I can tell from the light blue envelope and the careful printing of my name, identical to the dozens she's sent over the past two years. I almost don't want to open it, but today's hate-fest has started strong, and I might as well let it pile up. Sometimes it's easier to deal with a storm of hate than with a slow drip.

While Susan lectures the boys on the fact that broken Star Wars dishes by no means signify the end of the world, I go up to Ian's office, sit in the chair by the window, and slit open the envelope with the letter opener I gave him on our first anniversary. It was the paper anniversary according to all those wedding websites. Still, I bought him silver, thinking I'd skip ahead twenty-five years, not knowing we would never get there.

Emily's letter is one page of tight, perfect printing. The date in the upper right corner doesn't match the postmark on the envelope – it's off by a day – and I wonder if she had second thoughts or simply ran out of stamps. We do that, I guess, or at least we did back when we wrote letters instead of WhatsApping each other. We take pen to paper, and just when we're about to look up an address or hunt for that elusive Forever stamp in the bottom of a junk drawer, forgotten in its near-obsolescence, one of life's little distractions interferes. A boiling kettle, a kid home from school and hungry, the telephone. From the handwritten date, Emily wrote this the day her husband was executed. So, Wednesday.

I'm surprised she could keep a steady hand. I wasn't able to.

There's sadness and grief in the words, and I know she's as ripped apart as I was, that her life has been tilted like a bad carnival ride. But it's the last few lines that I keep reading.

I don't know much about the law, but I'm not stupid.
I know about the Remedies Act. I'm talking to
a lady from the Oversight Committee next week.

I think the time has come for us to meet.
I'll be at the Broad Street playground this
afternoon at three. Please come.

The Oversight Committee. Full name, State Oversight Committee for Prosecutorial Responsibility. It's the watchdog organization, the small clique of prosecutors recruited after the Remedies Act passed, the ones who realized they could make more money working wrongful death cases than they ever had standing on soapboxes at anti-death-penalty rallies. After all, what use is an organization once it achieves its end goal? Their job isn't very different from mine, except that instead of bringing murderers and rapists to justice, they focus on people like me.

In Ian's old chair, even though I'm drenched in sunlight, my entire body goes cold.

'So,' Susan says when I head back to the kitchen. 'The boys have decided they'll live another day. And you've got mail.' She takes the envelope from my hands and examines it more closely. 'I thought I told you not to open these.'

While she reads, I pretend to look for a corkscrew. It's right here in front of me, its curlicue tail sticking out from between bottle openers and toothpicks, but I keep looking all the same. I know what she'll say next. She'll ask if I'm going to meet Emily Milford today at three.

It turns out I'm right.

'Here,' I say, holding up the corkscrew that was always at hand.

'Well? Say you're not going, Justine.'

'You're not going, Justine.' It's a stupid joke, but it serves a purpose. It buys me time.

'I'm serious.' The bottle of white she's been working on opens with a definitive plop, punctuation for the two words. Susan holds up both hands. 'Look, girl. She's sent you almost a hundred notes since the trial. I've been around when most of them arrived. Every time you get one of these poison pen letters, you end up sick. Every single time. I can't stop you, but I'd be in the running for world's worst sister-in-law if I didn't give it the old college try. So this is me trying.' She hands me back the letter and opens the drawer to the recycling bin. 'Put this thing where it belongs.'

My hand hovers over the container of bottles and newspaper and junk mail. 'She's never wanted to meet before, Susan. All her other letters have been – I don't know – venting, I guess. Some form of one-way therapy for the woman. This is different.'

'The only thing different about it is this time you'll be within spitting distance. Or worse.'

'Emily Milford weighs a hundred ten pounds soaking wet. I think I can defend myself,' I say. But I let the envelope and its contents fall into the bin.

'Good,' Susan says, shutting the cabinet. 'Good.'

I look away from her and glance out the front window. The

day has rapidly changed from sunny to drizzly, the sort of grayish wet that makes April look more like November and tricks us into thinking spring is only a cosmic joke. In the colorless palette, the woman in red is still there, watching from beneath her umbrella.

CHAPTER SEVEN

It's two-thirty and sunny again when I leave the house and start driving into the city in Susan's ten-year-old Volvo. The car might be safe, but it's a pig on wheels, groaning and chugging its way along the road. But if there's a chance of Emily Milford seeing my ride, I'd rather be in a clunker than in my Mercedes. I even worked hard at dressing down, throwing on a pair of faded jeans and one of Ian's old sweatshirts.

I still look richer than I'd like to.

She'll notice my nails. She'll see that my hair is professionally colored and highlighted, and that my sneakers aren't from any store that ends in '-Mart'. She'll try to match my face to my age, and even though she can't know which labels of toner and night cream are on the shelves of my vanity, she'll know I look younger than I am. Funny how you can buy years. For a while, anyway. Eventually, the rich and the poor end up equal.

We have as much in common as we don't, Emily and I. We're both slight, although she's lost even more weight since the trial, the same way I did after the incident that shattered my life seven years ago. Our children are the same age. We're husbandless, and our boys are fatherless.

Emily lives in the south part of town, not far from Ian's sister's place. It's a neighborhood of cheek-by-jowl postwar bungalows with neatly trimmed lawns and ugly chain link fences. There isn't a car on the street younger than ten years old, no hybrids, no German imports, mostly Chevys and Fords. A blue-collar, little-pink-houses kind of a place. I live somewhere else, in a suburban-rural development where you need a telescope to see your neighbors, and there are more Land Rovers than schoolchildren. People call it The Village because no one who owns property in this enclave is comfortable calling it The Village at Wolf Rock Pointe. Stupid name. Emily's area is just 'the south part of town'.

And I don't expect she's got a sheepskin from Harvard Law School hanging in her hallway. Or from anywhere.

But I think we were very much alike on the day after, and I imagine her walking around her south-part-of-town house, doing the same things I did up in The Village.

It hadn't sunk in, Ian being gone. I woke in a daze, then fixed a bowl of cereal for Susan and a mug of coffee for me.

'I'll get it,' Susan said when I poured almost a quart of milk onto the kitchen counter. 'And you need to eat, too. I could close one eye and thread you, Jussie.'

It was the kind of thing I'd heard her brother say a million times, and it always made me laugh. Except today. Today it made me fold over and bawl.

Susan dropped to her knees, started mopping up the milk, and gave up on trying to force-feed me. She had come over right after I called the night before and stayed through to morning. I expect Emily had someone do the same. A sister, maybe. Or a sister-in-law. I know Jake Milford had a brother, and I know the brother was married, but I tried not to wade too deeply into his personal life. In my line of work, boundaries are necessary. Boundaries keep you sane.

After Susan shooed me out of my own kitchen, I wandered around Ian's upstairs office, touching things he had been working on, reading whatever he had been reading the day before. Maybe Emily did that, too, although not in an office. Maybe she went out to the garage and opened a toolbox, running her fingers over the cool metal of ratchets and sockets.

There's no maybe about it. I'm sure Emily did these things, in the same way I'm sure she went through his pockets and his laundry and the bathroom drawers, looking for scraps of paper with his writing, cloth with his scent, a comb with a few strands of hair. I'm sure of what she did because I did the same, and I can't imagine anyone spending that first day doing anything else.

I found things. Stupid things. A wad of chewing gum neatly folded up in its paper wrapper. A Starbucks lid lost under the front seat of Ian's Benz. A receipt from the Orapax Greek restaurant dated a year ago, which made me want to both scream and never eat another gyro again. What I didn't find: love letters to other women, traces of lipstick on a collar, a burner phone with secret sext messages. If I had, I can't say whether I would have been angry or whether I would have treasured these as much as all the other pieces Ian left behind when he left me.

What I know is that I was broken, and I stayed broken for a long time. No one but a broken person would have done what I did when Jake Milford's case landed on my desk.

But all that was seven years ago. Emily's grief is only two days old.

CHAPTER EIGHT

I swing the Volvo into the first free space I can find, cursing the perfect spring weather that has dragged every man, woman, and child out of doors. There's a ball cap in the back seat, one of Susan's, and I put it on with the brim far down on my forehead. It's not the sun I'm worried about as I walk the two blocks along Broad Street toward the playground. We live in a world where everyone carries a video camera.

Emily is sitting on a bench on the far side of the fenced-in area. She doesn't see me; she's busy doing the spit-on-a-hanky thing that seems to be encoded in the DNA of all women. The target of her attentions is a small boy, the same one who was with her on Friday outside the courthouse. At her side, on the bench, is her purse and a packet of Kleenex.

I stop behind a tree and turn around, my back against the bark, and I think of all the things.

The boy is Jonathan's age, but out of school for the day, so maybe there was another of those half-days; maybe he's still in kindergarten. The woman, like me, is a single mom. Our husbands are gone for different reasons, but we both hurt and we both hate and there's nothing anyone can do about it.

Of course, there are differences in our stories. Emily's

mouse-brown hair and shabby clothes, for instance. Or the fact that her boy attends a public school in one of the shittier districts, while Jonathan sits in a private Montessori class thanks to an annual tuition fee approximately the price of a small car. Two small cars, really, since I pay for Susan's son as well. And then there's that indisputable, if ugly, fact: my husband, unlike Jake Milford, didn't kill anyone.

I peek around the tree and watch as Emily pats her boy on the behind and sends him off to the play area. There might have been woodchips here once, maybe even the same tire shreds we have in our gated, only-for-residents playground up at The Village, but now the ground is bald. This is the place where regular kids play. The underprivileged. The poor. The fatherless.

She takes up the book again. Her eyes, barely visible over the top, track the boy as he tries to decide between the swing set and a recently vacated horse on a spring. He chooses the horse, and bobs back and forth, side to side, while his young mother looks on and smiles.

If I go over to them now, I'll interrupt this temporary peace.

I've been telling myself ever since Emily's letter arrived that she only needs an outlet. She needs another human to hear her screams and see her tears. Maybe we all do. Maybe our screams and tears aren't really there if there's no one to perceive them.

I won't allow myself to think she's found something.

At five minutes past three, I make my decision and start walking toward the bench on the far side of the park. Emily looks up from her book when I'm close, and I brace myself for the onslaught.

She doesn't say a word at first, only pats the empty seat of the bench and closes her book after dog-earing the page. She's stopped smiling.

'That's my son,' she says. 'Jake Junior.'

I nod.

'He's supposed to be in the first grade now, but they wouldn't take him. Principal said he has some kinda emotional development problem. So now he's in kindergarten, he'll be the biggest in his first-grade class next year. You think people are gonna think he's one of them dummies? Like he got held back 'cause he's stupid?'

'Kids all learn differently,' I say, wondering why the conversation has started out like this and why I'm opining about early childhood development to a woman who probably wishes I were dead.

'Yeah, I guess they do.' Emily's voice is soft, with a tinge of southwestern Virginia in it. It's also flat, and when she opens her purse to put the book inside, the bottle of pills gives me all the explanation I need. 'You got kids?'

'I have a son. He's about Jake's age.'

'Jake Junior,' she corrects.

Emily's head bobs up and down slowly and automatically, more evidence of the pills at work. I hope she and Jake Junior took the bus. 'Fact is, Ms Boucher, we ain't – we aren't – doing so good.'

I don't know why I haven't thought of money before. I've thought of everything else. 'Is there some way I can help you?' I open my own bag and take out a pen and my checkbook while Emily stares as if I've pulled a dinosaur out. Which, I suppose, I have. Ian used to laugh at me for carrying around a checkbook when ApplePay and GooglePay and Venmo were all a click away.

'Put that back,' Emily says. 'We don't need your charity. I got a roof over my head and three square meals a day thanks to my folks.'

Okay. So not money. I put the checkbook into my purse and fold my hands over it. 'You wanted to meet me. I thought—'

'I don't actually care all that much what you think, seeing as the kind of thinking you lawyers do almost always ends up either killing people or bankrupting them. I got something to say to you. That's why I wanted you to come.'

I came here prepared for a rant. But Emily doesn't seem to want to rant. As we sit in silence watching her son move from the spring-mounted horse to a spring-mounted cow – there's a difference in six-year-old land – her hands clutch the cotton of her skirt, then let go. Clutch. Let go. Clutch. Let go. The material where her hands have been is dark with sweat.

I really hope she isn't driving today. Honestly, I'm surprised the woman can even walk. I wasn't in any shape to do more than curl into a ball in the days after Ian left me. On the other hand, Ian's sudden absence was a shock. The woman sitting next to me had years to prepare.

Finally, Emily speaks. 'I found a piece of paper.' She whispers it and keeps her focus either on Jake Junior or on the patch of skirt that looks as if it might start protesting the torture. 'I was in my parents' attic going through a box of Jake's old stuff the other day, and I found a something tucked into a notebook that I never saw before. I don't know why I started rummaging – I guess I packed everything up so quick when we had to sell the house and I thought maybe there were some pictures or something. You know, for little Jake. I wanted him to have some memories of his daddy that weren't all behind bars or in a prison outfit.'

She smiles the kind of smile with no joy in it. 'We were high school sweethearts, you know. My dad tried to break us up because he didn't want me going with one of those grease monkeys. That's what he called the auto shop boys. Grease monkeys. Kinda funny how people make fun of mechanics like that. Jake always said it was a good job. Not a very clean job, but a good one, 'cause as long as folks are driving cars, guys like him have work. Can't say the same for a lot of other jobs. I used to be a waitress, and I'll tell you when the money bombs drop, my pay drops. Don't matter if it's a mortgage scandal or a virus. But mechanics always get paid because folks always need to be driving somewhere. And let me tell you, we ain't in the land of the 1970 Volkswagen Beetle. Most people don't even know where the battery is.'

Most of Emily's armchair economics, sound as they are, go in one ear and out the other. The last full sentence I heard was *I found a piece of paper.* My hands start to sweat, and I rub my palms on my jeans.

She looks me over, taking in my nails and my hair, the matching Bally loafers and handbag that still shine like they did in the shop window when I bought them. Women like Emily Milford might not know the brand, but they know if it's better than what they're carrying around and wearing. 'I suppose women like you don't ever gotta worry about where the next paycheck's coming from.'

'We worry about other things,' I say. *Things like 'I found a piece of paper'.*

'Anyway, Jake was some kind of handsome. And he treated me like gold.' She turns the ring on her left fourth finger. 'Not that we ever had any gold. This is just steel. But the day he put it on my hand was the happiest day of my life. Besides, Jake always laughed and told me to say it was platinum. That's what the rich people buy, but it looks exactly like stainless steel, so I never knew what the point was.'

The words chug along in my head. *I found a piece of paper. I found a piece of paper. I found a piece of paper.* These six words, strung together, are all I can hear until she says the next thing on her mind.

'He always said he was innocent,' Emily says. 'I told him no matter what, if he had an alibi, he should tell it. But he kept on saying he didn't remember where he was that day when the little Church boy was killed.' She opens her purse again. The clasp is broken, and she fiddles with it nervously until a piece of brass-colored plastic finally breaks off. Then she takes out a small square of folded white paper.

I hold my breath.

Whatever is in Emily's hands could be the end of everything. A simple gas station receipt. The telephone number of a man or woman who saw Jake Milford in another town and came forward a few days too late. A letter from a mistress.

The paper she's holding isn't a paper at all, only a Kleenex.

'I begged him to tell me. I said I didn't care if he was in some sleazy motel banging five waitresses from the highway truck stop. Or men. All I wanted was my baby back home with me.' She sniffs into the tissue. Automatically, I move my arm toward her. I don't know why – maternal instinct, maybe. This woman is only a woman on the outside. Inside, she's a tiny young thing who has seen more shit over the past six years than anyone should. Emily shrinks away from my arm, blows her nose, and stuffs the tissue into the cuff of her sweater.

She stands on wobbly, stick-thin legs, smooths down her skirt, and calls her boy over. 'I have to go now. It's hard for me to be out of the house, but I gotta try for my Jake Junior's sake. I only wanted to tell you that I found something in a box of my husband's old stuff.' Before I can answer, before I can ask what she found, she continues. 'I haven't decided exactly what I'm gonna do with it. Not yet.'

Jake runs up and stops short in front of me. 'Are you my momma's new friend?'

I don't know what to say, so I say nothing.

'She needs a good friend,' Jake says. 'So I think you should be it.'

As if that's going to happen.

With a curt little nod and a 'Come on, Jake Junior. We gotta get home and cook up some lunch before you fade away,' Emily starts walking toward the gate closest to us, holding her little boy's hand.

I stay on the bench with those words stuck in my head like a bad song lyric until I feel steady enough to get to my feet. Then I walk through the park back to the Broad Street entrance. Only when I'm through the gate to the park do I turn around for one last look.

And I see the woman in the red suit approaching Emily. She's nodding and smiling.

Death Row Inmate #39384

People say death is different. They can't know this, but they're right. It's different when it happens, and sometimes it's different before it happens. For me, the change started long before the day of my execution.

I've spent the last six years of my life in a state of differentness. Different color clothes, different cell block, different rules.

Maybe it would have been better – no, not better, there is no sense of better in this man's mind anymore. Maybe it would have been less awful, slightly less awful, if I wasn't the only one. If I wasn't the sole occupant of a twelve-cell block for six years.

Time and numbers are such funny things. Take the number six. Six sounds small. A man can put up with six of pretty much anything. Multiply it by 365, and I reckon it's still something you can rationalize. Two thousand one hundred ninety – about the same as high school and an associate's degree. Multiply that by hours, and we're getting somewhere. Six becomes a few thousand becomes 52,000.

we haven't even gotten to the minutes yet. All three million of them.

Over three million minutes ticked by while I've lived in that state of differentness. Some flew, some crawled, most lingered.

I want you to imagine a parking space. Walk its perimeter, counting out your steps, stopping a stride or two short of each corner. I want you to imagine an area only a smidge larger than a king-sized bed. Or roughly the same dimensions as one of the kennels in your local SPCA. Pace out eighty-four square feet. Get comfortable in them, know them.

They're your new home.

They're your bedroom and your living room and your dining room and your toilet. They're your meditation space and your exercise space and your oh-Christ-I-wish-I-were-dead space. Those eighty-four square feet are your world for over twenty-two hours each day.

Now imagine craving to return to them, as I've done.

On the days I saw Emily and Jake Junior, I never wanted to go back to those four walls. On the other days, I couldn't wait.

Being alone was more tolerable when I was really alone. The rest of the time, not so much. Maybe I can explain it to you.

Imagine an exercise yard, a vast and vacant plot of land with a few handball courts along one end and a line of basketball nets, frayed and brittle, but still things you could toss a ball through and play a game of horse. Picture a rack of bleachers, the old pull-out kind you knew from high school assemblies, the ones that rattled as they slid from the wall and turned into seats for hundreds, as if by magic. They overlook a grassy area defined by soccer nets at each end.

The thing of it is, you can't play a game of horse without a ball and a mate. You can't sit in the sun and swap stories on a bleacher bench when there's no one to shoot the shit with. And I can't see the sense of defending a goal net from a team of invisible players.

I think that's what got under my skin most, what made me understand death was different, and that all the days before death were different. For the one hour out of twenty-four I spent in that exercise yard, I was the star in a warped kind of last-man-on-earth show.

For the five-minute walk out and back inside to my cell, things were worse.

My turn outside came immediately after lunch, from half past noon to half past one. Half the guys from C Block – I guess there were about a hundred fifty of them – got the hour before me, and the rest got the one-thirty to two-thirty slot. They all wore dishwater gray uniforms with numbers on the back. Some were short; some were tall. Some were blond, and some were dark-haired. And that's all I knew of them. I never saw their faces.

When my hour was up, four screws called me over. They were assigned to watch me as I walked from one end of the yard to the other and back again as many times as I could in sixty minutes. Watching a guy walk was a job I thought had to be shit-boring but tonight, I'll learn there are shittier alternatives.

'Face the wall, hands behind your back,' one of them said. The steel of the cuffs clanked around my wrists, the leg irons around my ankles, and the tether chain held it all together. Behind me, the voices of the C Block inmates quieted.

'C Block prisoners turn to the wall!' It wasn't one of my guys who bellowed this, but one from C Block. My guys had formed a small human cage around me. Whether that was to keep me from seeing or from being seen, I still don't know.

And then my slow shuffle home began, a shot-by-shot reverse image of the earlier march from cell to outside.

'Dead man walking! Dead man walking!'

I didn't know why they had to shout it so loud. Hell, I didn't know why they had to shout it at all.

And then I figured it out: I've been a rarity, maybe a once-in-a-lifetime event. A story they can pass on to their grand-children or their buddies, embellishing it with every retelling.

Most violent man I'd ever seen.

Nearly killed me, he did.

And you know what? He was a coward in the end. Bawled like a baby.

Pissed himself as soon as we got him into the chair.

Fessed up at the last minute. Said he killed that little boy.

I'm more than the only man they have on death row. I'm even more than the last man some of the older ones would see there. With the way things are going, I'm possibly the last man ever to be executed in the state. Maybe in the country. I'm movie material, a modern Gary Milford with a different name. Too bad Tommy Lee Jones got too old and wrinkled to play me, but maybe those special effects guys could do something about it.

So that's another way I'm different. And I got double reminders every day, one at half past twelve and the other an hour later.

Now, on my last day, I think I'd still return to all of it.

I'd still go back to six years (three million minutes) of hell, repeating them over and over. There was so much I didn't have, a junkyard of life's trivial comforts they had taken away from me, but at least I would still be breathing. I'd still have my memories of my beautiful Em and my boy.

And they were right to take it all away from me, I expect you'll say.

But you might be wrong.

When the Supreme Court – or, as Emily calls them, the 'Supremes', which still makes me laugh – brought back the death penalty in 1976, it took seven years or so to get things rolling again. Then, for another decade, the total executions in America bounced around the low teens and twenties. Not a very big number – unless you happened to be one of those numbers or were unlucky enough to be in the great state of Texas. I'll tell you, when it comes to firing up the execution engine, Texas wins every time. And there are other ways you can be unlucky. You can be in the South instead of the Northeast. You can be black instead of white. You can be a man instead of a woman.

But there are ways you can be lucky. You can be one of the almost two hundred people who got released from death row because – get this – they were innocent all along. That's about four every year since the early Seventies. Sometimes it's because a witness lies. Sometimes that witness ID's the wrong guy. Sometimes the public defender ends up being fresh out of a fifth-rate law school, wet behind the ears, and barely more literate than the person he's supposed to be defending. There's also a hell of a lot of what's called official misconduct, which I guess means nothing more or less than bad cops doing bad things for bad reasons.

I think about the number four a lot these days, about how I might have been one of those four lucky ones. That thought never left me in all the three million minutes I spent waiting. It was one thing they couldn't take away.

My dad used to say you can't rob a man of the shit you can't see. But until today, I held on to my hope. Thin as it was, I had that, at least. Up until this last day.

CHAPTER NINE

By the time I'm back at the house, Susan has dipped too deep into my wine stash to be driving anywhere. Which means she and Tommy will be spending the night. I make dinner as hurried and perfunctory an affair as possible: veggie nuggets for the boys; a plate of spaghetti with sauce from a jar for us girls. Every second I draw the meal out is another opportunity for Susan to needle me with questions or throw a few of her word darts my way. I don't want to be needled any more today.

I glance at the clock on the wall. Daniel should have been on his way here by now, having wrapped up another day in the life of chasing down white-collar criminals, but he's stuck in arbitration up in Fairfax Country until late, and I encouraged him to get a room instead of making the hellish drive back on I-95.

I think of the first words he would say to me – would have said if I were alone tonight: 'Bath, back rub, or booze?'

All three, baby. All three.

Well, at least I've got the booze. I pour myself a glass of wine, draining the bottle. Susan flew through the second one as if it were water. So no Daniel, no bath, no stress-relieving sex. Instead, another night with Susan snoring in the guest room and the kids in their superhero sleeping bags on the rec room floor. And the dreams, of course. Always the dreams.

After Ian died, the ghosts started to come. Mostly, they come at night, and, mostly, they're not friendly ghosts.

June Whitcomb comes, her face a partially caved-in mass of skull fragments and strawberry jam from the last blow her husband delivered, the infant in her arms a limp bag of bones.

Five young women come, bleeding from their eyes and from between their legs, mouths forming an unanswerable question, a chorus of *Where's our justice?*

The victims – too many to count – of the seemingly uncatchable parking lot killer who finally fucked up last year. They come, too, slipping into my room and invading my dreams.

They all come, either one at a time or en masse, in shadowy groups of three and four. In my sleep, I try vainly to banish them, waving the dead off with one arm, repeating empty threats into my pillow. Tonight, they're joined by seventeen-year-old Robbie Forrester, all-around good guy, honor student and high school senior, five months from starting his freshman year at Stanford. Robbie's only crime was being high on hormones and low on sound judgment.

But it's always the last ghost who does the most harm.

Ian is here. Again. Ian, with the broad smile and the tiny entry wound, only a pinprick in the blue cotton of his polo shirt.

He turns around, heading out for the night. No matter. Ian will be back tomorrow. And the next day, and every goddamned day after that. Before he leaves, I see the stain on the back of his shirt, the dark patch of blood from the exiting bullet slowly blooming, turning the blue cotton to black. I've been seeing it for seven years.

If I had done things differently, the ghosts would still come.

Only their names would be different, and that wouldn't really be different at all.

They would all be Jake Milford ghosts.

They wouldn't come with gunshot wounds or caved-in skulls. They wouldn't come with broken bones or broken hymens. They would visit with nooses around their necks and needle pricks in their arms. They would limp in, their ankles and wrists bound with leather straps, their eyeballs bulging from the force of a deadly current. They would reek of rot or charred flesh, but they would still come.

I know this because Jake Milford made his first appearance two nights ago, right after he was executed.

You don't have to be physically present at an event to be there. On Wednesday evening, I put Jonathan to bed after a supper only one of us ate, scraped my plate into the garbage bin, and poured enough vodka to put five large men under the table. Then I sat in Ian's office chair, spun it to face a blank patch of wall, and watched as a series of images flashed through my mind.

In the story I imagined, Jake Milford ate a meal he chose himself for the first time in over six years and for the last time in his life. He ordered pork barbecue, the Virginia kind with that thin, vinegary sauce, asking to round it out with coleslaw, biscuits, and baked beans. The prison provided a single can of his favorite root beer – something that, as a free man, he had only allowed himself on special occasions because it cost too much for regular drinking. Jake also got himself a shave, but not in the usual places men get shaved. And then he walked, flanked by five guards, to the death chamber. There, on that blank white wall in Ian's office, I watched the straps go on and the sponge get soaked, and the leather cap get placed on his head. I watched the rough cloth of the shroud cover Jake Milford's face and felt my own body jump when his did.

I thought, at the time, that I would be seeing this movie again, and I was right. It plays every time I close my eyes, and if it isn't Jake Milford who comes, it's Ian. If it isn't Ian, it's one of a hundred other victims. I've gotten used to lying in bed with my eyes open.

Around three in the morning, I get tired of watching the clock tick off its bright LED numbers.

Tonight is worse than most; the nights after I make the really tough decisions are always worse. I pull my body out of bed, tiptoe down the hall so as not to wake Susan – if I have to deal with Susan for one more goddamned minute right now, I'll find myself on trial for murder – and I creep upstairs to the third-floor room that used to be Ian's office.

Sometimes it helps.

I sink into the easy chair he used for reading and grading papers, the one by the window that catches the morning light. The desk, Ian always said, was for the monkey-work administrative shit that was the bane of every working academic.

'What do you say, Jussie? I quit my job, become the world's youngest professor emeritus. I even have the pipe already.'

I laughed when he asked. Every time.

The office is a mess; it has that shabby look of a workplace belonging to a man who lived more in his mind than in the physical world. Notes scrawled on the backs of gas station receipts poke out from under Ian's keyboard. Books lie open, upside down, their spines protesting the indecency. Strands of pipe tobacco decorate every flat surface and stick to the fabric of the chair.

I still haven't worked up the courage to put the room in order.

Oh, I promise myself every New Year, and then it's Christmas again, and Christmas is no time to be screwing around with the detritus of the dead. If it isn't Christmas, it's Ian's birthday, or Jonathan's birthday, or fucking Arbor Day. Always an excuse. In all these years, I've become an expert at conjuring up excuses. Not so good at the moving-on business.

At my elbow is a stack of law review articles waiting to be read. I pick up the top sheets, paper clipped together, and let my eyes work over Ian's almost illegible handwriting.

The writing ends on page three. No matter how many early morning visits I make to this office, his notes always end on page three.

I don't know whether I like it when he seems to come back, when he stretches his long legs out through the desk's kneehole and claps his hands behind his head, fingers laced together.

I don't like it, but I'll take it. I'll take any moments with Ian I can get, one more conversation, one more touch of his hand, one more kiss.

'Thoughts?' he asks, nodding at the article in my hands.

I finish reading it, pretending I've never done this before, and lay the papers back down on top of the stack. 'I don't think you should publish it.'

'I can't not publish him just because I don't agree with him.'

'I was kidding.' I wrinkle my nose. 'Sort of. First, it's the closure argument I don't buy. Yeah, sure, I get that a victim's family – some families – think they need that. But the argument falls apart when we consider the possibility of wrongful execution.' Ian starts to speak, and I silence him with one hand. It's a complete reversal of the power play I remember from our first meeting at a faculty house in the Cambridge area of Boston, a time long ago in some faraway galaxy called youth. 'What kind of closure does that guy's family get? Second, there's the certainty issue. This author seems to be saying that if we're not a hundred percent on board with the guilty verdict – in other words, not certain enough to execute, then how can we be certain enough to sentence the defendant at all?'

'And you disagree because—'

I blow out a sigh. 'You know damned well why I disagree. Because death is forever. A prison cell isn't. Remember what the Supremes said.'

'Stop in the name of love?' Ian said with no trace of humor in his voice.

'The other Supremes, you charming idiot.'

'Oh.'

'They said, "Death is different." That's it. Different. Honestly, this whole paper sounds like it was written by your sister.'

Ian rocked back in his chair. 'Let's go back to the first argument, the part where he's talking about closure. Here's a hypothetical for you, baby. Say some jumped-up sociopath breaks into the house, shoots me in the gut, and I die a drawn-out, painful death while you're at the office. Assuming they catch the bastard, how do you know you wouldn't want closure then?'

'I know. I love you more than anything, but I know,' I said, and rose up, leaning over the desk to kiss him on the lips. 'And don't be silly. That's never going to happen.'

'Why not?'

'You forget we live in a gated community, darling.'

It's a conversation we'd had a thousand times, always ending in the same way, always hypothetical.

An hour later, my answer wasn't hypothetical.

CHAPTER TEN

After breakfast, Susan takes Tommy home. We have a long hug at the door, Susan's wordless apology for last night's bitchiness, and an enthusiastic 'See you on Monday morning!' She ruffles Jonathan's hair and pauses. 'On second thought, how about you call that man of yours and tell him you want to have a date night? I can come back this afternoon and fetch Jonathan.' Then, to the boys, 'Sleepover at my place?' It isn't a question she needs to ask twice.

They leave, and I brace myself for another hour or two of John Williams' never-ending space opera music, but Jonathan stays with me in the kitchen, drinking a second cup of cocoa and watching me wash dishes.

'Did that lady teacher really hurt a boy in her class?' he says. It isn't the conversation I want to start Saturday with. I wish my kid would ask the crucial questions: Do snakes have nipples? Why do spiders run away when I fart? How come you get to use bad words and I don't? Things like that. Some simple, some hard, but I have better answers to them than to the question Jonathan just dropped on me.

'Who told you that?'

'Me and Tommy heard you talking to Aunt Susan last night.'

'That's called eavesdropping, and it's not nice. Don't let me catch you at it again, Jonathan.'

'But you were kinda loud,' he says, staring at his shoes.

I toss the dish rag aside, literally throwing in the towel. 'We don't know, honey,' I say. 'Lots of people think she did.'

'Why?'

'Why did she hurt him, or why do people think she did?'

He pauses a moment and inspects the cocoa in his cup. 'Both.'

'Okay. You get these two questions and then you need to go play something non-electronic. Deal?'

Jonathan nods.

'I don't know why people do bad things to other people. Some of them are sick and some of them are angry. As for why people think she hurt that boy, well, I guess they have good reasons.'

'Like evidence?'

So much for the two-question limit. I dry the last of the breakfast dishes and give Jonathan the damp towel to hang up on the oven handle. 'Yes, like evidence.'

He folds it into perfect thirds, the way Ian always did, although Jonathan couldn't possibly know that particular – and very un-Ian-like – display of anal-retentive behavior. 'Like the kind of evidence when my daddy got hurt?'

'Exactly like that,' I lie. He couldn't know that, either. Unless someone was helping him along. Susan.

'Do you think if I ever found the man who hurt Daddy I could do something?'

'Such as?'

'I don't know. Punch him in the nose, maybe. Real hard.'

'You think that would be a good idea, honey?'

Jonathan's lower lip pooches forward in a childish pout. 'Aunt

Susan says I could. Because no one else will. And she says it would probably make me feel better.' A swift, but not total, change of subject, and he says, 'Anyway, I wish I had a daddy.' Then he's off to his room to pick out jigsaw puzzles or books or whatever non-battery-operated time-passer he can find in a wall-to-wall sea of electronic, noise-making shit.

'I wish you did, too,' I say to the kitchen walls.

Thanks to my six-year-old son, I've started my Saturday in pain. Might as well go full-out, pop in the video of Ian's last will, and make it really hurt.

I bring Ian back to life again, this time on the flat-screen television in the living room, as soon as I'm sure Jonathan is busy constructing Lego monsters down the hall. My husband's face fills the screen, surrounded by a mane of shoulder-length dark hair with curls of gray at his temples. He never was one to adopt the lawyerly look; Ian didn't give a damn.

He states his name and the date, says he is of sound mind, leans forward to adjust the screen of his tablet. Then he sits back again, pipe in one hand, a legal-sized folder in the other.

'I won't bore you with the specifics of my will,' he says. 'If you can't wait out the mystery, I'll say this: Justine gets everything. Except my old Doors albums. Those I'm taking with me to the other side.'

'Damn fool,' I say to the television screen.

'I think you all know what I'm about to say, and I think you also know that I mean every word of it. We've all heard the arguments in favor of capital punishment. In my career, I've heard them more. Take that old tit for tat chestnut, a technical term I'll casually translate as "do unto others as they do to you". Those of you who know me well, know that I think that's a load of

73

bullshit, so let's move on to argument number two: arbitrariness. You also know exactly what I think of that one. Same accused, same crime, different prosecutors. So what's the thin blue line between life and death? The prosecutor.'

An unexpected smile creeps across my face. I remember the first time I heard that. It seems like yesterday, and it seems like forever ago.

'Lastly, closure,' Ian says. 'Listen closely here, people, because this is one near and dear to my heart.'

I pause the video and look at my husband, knowing what comes next.

'Closure is a fictional opiate, a dirty seven-letter word. It's a lie told to suffering family members by politicians. Let's look at a few numbers. One of them is twenty, the other is two-point-five.' He paused, took a slow drag on his pipe, and went on. 'Twenty percent of victim's families report that the execution helped them heal. That's a significant number, but far from a majority. On the subject of closure, we dive down into the low single digits: only two and half percent of victim's families report achieving this Valhalla of emotional reprieve. That's one in forty. In other words, not much.'

He goes on, citing facts and figures, scientific journal articles, and law review papers. He's got all the numbers right there, right in his hand, and he feeds them to us, one by one.

'I've been a lucky man,' Ian says. 'I've done work I'm proud of, and in Justine I have a partner who sees the world as I see it, who sees that the myth of execution is just that. A myth. I'm proud of you, girl. I always will be.'

It's pure masochism. And I love every minute of it.

'One last note, and pay attention because this is the real

clincher.' Ian points a finger toward me from the screen. 'Even if I could wipe out the biblical nonsense – and I'll remind you all that Christianity starts with Christ, not with that fucking leg for a leg and eye for an eye crap; even if I could abolish the arbitrariness of prosecutorial discretion; even if I could know that one hundred percent of victim's families would magically cease suffering – that their pain would disappear with the pulse of the perpetrator. Even if I could do all that, I could not live with myself if I sent a human being to death and one day discovered I was wrong.' He punctuates these last few words with that pointed finger, stabbing the air after each syllable.

Then Ian is Ian again. 'So, in the immortal words of Lynyrd Skynyrd, if I should leave here tomorrow – or next month or next year – if I should ever be the unfortunate victim of the kind of crime I'm talking about, the worst crime and the ultimate crime, here's what I want. I want a promise from you all that you will do your level best to see justice done without resorting to any form of execution.' He stabs at the air again with his finger. 'You may not believe in the afterlife, and I may not believe in it either, but I can't rule out the possibility that we'll meet again someday, and if we do, I'll have questions. Of course,' he says with a chuckle, 'if the Vita movement ever gains ground, maybe we won't have anything to talk about. Also, darling Justine, put me somewhere with a bunch of trees. I like trees.'

I'm proud of you, girl. I always will be.

The screen goes dark, Ian is gone, and I spend the next hour sitting here wondering how proud he would be of me if he knew I'd sent Jake Milford to die.

CHAPTER ELEVEN

Change always has to start somewhere. For me, it started the first time I walked into Ian Callaghan's living room on Ellery Street. The room was warm, almost stifling after the five-block trek over icy pavements from my third-floor bedsit in Mrs Munson's drafty Victorian. Boston Januarys were shitty, but this one was particularly shitty. It didn't even snow, only rained down ice that would melt and refreeze until the streets were mantled with a slick coat of winter.

The wood fire contributed to some of the room's warmth; the conversation took the temperature up another few notches. Callaghan stood in the center of a group of six or seven people who were strangers to me, probably all Three-Ls, law school speak for third-year students. Ted wasn't here yet.

'You coming in or not?' Callaghan said, not looking toward the door. He had the manner of a tenured professor, not a third-year law student. 'If you're coming in, close the goddamned door and take a seat. If you're not, close the goddamned door and don't bother coming back.'

Ted, the Three-L I'd been dating off and on for the past year, had already warned me about Callaghan. 'He hates wafflers. So whatever you do, don't waffle. Act like you have your shit together.' Ted had paused. 'No. He'll see through that. Get your shit together before you come over.'

So I did, or I thought I did. I spent an hour in front of the small medicine cabinet mirror in the shared upstairs bathroom of Mrs Munson's house pulling my shit together, rehearsing what I would say and what I wouldn't say. I lost that shit about a second after opening the front door. Callaghan had a take-no-prisoners look about him. As a One-L, I'd never had to share space in a lecture hall with the man, but when it comes to reputations, law schools are like high school cafeterias. Anyone who tells you different is lying.

Decide, girl.

I shut the door behind me, walked into the living room, and took the empty chair closest to the fire and farthest from the editor of the *Harvard Law Review*. Part of it was fear, but I'd be lying if Callaghan's smell didn't have something to do with it. The guy reeked of Scotch and sweet pipe tobacco.

'Yeah,' Ted had agreed a few days ago. 'But he's a genius. People put up with stink when it's wrapped up in genius. Look at Steve Jobs.'

'Just don't decide to emulate him on the booze and tobacco front,' I'd said. 'Or you'll be making a renewed acquaintance with your right hand and a tube of K-Y.'

'You wouldn't do that. Not to good old Ted.'

'Don't overestimate my tolerance for stink. Sugar-coated in genius or not. And he wears a Mickey Mouse watch. He's twenty-five, Ted. Not six. I can't take a grown man who's still into Disney seriously. And the pipe is stupid.'

'He says it's his grandfather's. Like the rest of the junk in this house.'

I frowned. 'Okay, only slightly stupid, then.' I no longer thought it stupid at all, but a little endearing.

In the living room, Callaghan turned toward me. 'Do you have a name?' The power in his voice seemed to reach out and grab me by the throat. No wonder the rest of the group was enthralled with him. Or cowed by him.

'Justine.'

'Justine what?'

'Uh—' I might have looked at my shoes. I might have started counting the frayed threads in the carpet. Damn Ted for not getting here earlier.

'Come on. It's an easy question. The five-pointers come later.'

'Boucher.'

He smiled. Not a friendly smile, more of a grimace. Whatever it was, it showed far too many teeth, and I wondered if Callaghan was as lax about making dental appointments as he was about combing his hair, but the teeth were bright and straight. 'That's wonderful. One point for Boucher. Now for the second round.' He paused. 'Why are you in my living room?'

'Ted invited me.'

The front door flung open, admitting a painful blast of Boston winter, and Ted walked in. I think I wanted to kill him but I reminded myself why I was here. The subject of the evening was killing.

Or not killing.

'Hey, gorgeous,' Ted said, bending down to kiss me. 'Glad you could make it.'

Callaghan shut him up with a look. 'Okay, boys and girls, we're talking about prosecutorial discretion.'

I leaned close to Ted and whispered, 'I thought we were talking about the death penalty.'

'Are you an idiot?' Callaghan snapped.

It struck me. I was the only woman here. *Grow some balls, then, Justine.* 'No. Just first-year.'

Callaghan turned to Ted. 'Next time, Stuyvesant, you ask before extending an invitation to a One-L. Got it?' He didn't wait for an answer. 'Okay. Hardball question for Boucher. What's the number-one problem with prosecutorial discretion in death penalty matters? Extra points for an example that speaks to the point.'

I had no idea what he was talking about.

'Help her, Stuyvesant. Not too much. Give her the examples and see if she figures it out.' He raised both hands. 'Get it wrong—' The left hand made a sweeping gesture toward the door. 'Get it right, you can stay.' The right hand lifted a glass in the air. 'I might even offer you a drink later on.'

What a dilemma, I thought, but stayed quiet.

'Best examples I can think of,' Ted said, 'are New York's Robert Johnson and Philadelphia's Lynne Abraham, also known as The Deadliest DA. Not Johnson – just Abraham. They're diametrically opposed. Think *Men are from Mars and Women are from Venus* kind of opposed when it comes to utilization of the death penalty. Johnson even got himself superseded by the governor on the cop killing case back in '96.' He looked up at Callaghan like a dog who had just performed a trick.

'Okay. Good. Fine,' Callaghan said. 'Boucher, you're up.'

I didn't see what was so fine about it. I got two names and two cities and the title of a fucking self-help book from Ted. Not much to go on. Zero, actually. I looked around at the seven men seated in the living room. There were seven, after all. One of them was so bean-pole thin, I must have missed him when I arrived.

'Don't even think about bailing her out,' Callaghan said. 'What's it going to be, sweetheart? The door or the drink?' I swear he winked at me then. Under a lock of dark hair that shone with an oily gleam, his left eye closed and opened.

I chose the door.

Three weeks later, Ted convinced me to try again.

Callaghan lobbed me the same question. 'Boucher's in the batter box. So, Boucher, what's the number-one problem with prosecutorial discretion in death penalty matters? Want to try for strike two?'

I looked at my fingernails.

He began speaking, this time as if I weren't in the room. 'There's our other problem. First-years don't have the training for this kind of thing.' He glared at Ted again.

My first semester had been as hard as I thought it would be – if you multiplied what I'd expected and feared by a factor of ten thousand. By the end of the term, I was used to being belittled and humiliated. They could call it the Socratic Method, but that was like calling anorexia a healthy diet alternative. Classes were pure torture.

But they were fair. I could say that. They were fair.

The problem was – and I only figured this out while listening to Callaghan's wall clock tick off the seconds – I knew absolute dick about the law. I could quote torts cases and property cases and maybe even state the facts of a few of them if pressed, but I hadn't yet learned to think like a lawyer, to cut to the meat of someone else's argument, or to defend my own.

I stood, shrugged on my coat, and went to the door, expecting to hear Callaghan laughing behind me. All I heard was a disappointed sigh and words that sounded like 'She doesn't give herself enough credit.'

That night, I walked home, thinking of what Ted had told me when we first met, when I was sitting on the grass outside my first lecture hall, close to tears after being ripped apart in my first constitutional law class.

'It isn't always about what you know,' Ted said, taking a seat next to me. 'I mean, it's not Trivial Pursuit. More like chess. Maybe even not that complicated.'

I might have blubbed a few unintelligible words.

'Think of it like solving a problem where you already have the answer. Don't worry about the answer. It's there. Worry about the logic. Worry about the process. Work backwards if you have to. Work sideways. Tackle it upside down.'

I spent the next week either in class or at the law library. I scoured the Internet and read cases until the words on the page began blurring together. Then I tried again. Every batter gets three attempts, after all.

We were seated next to the fireplace, in the same chairs as before. Ted was on my right, and the skinny guy sat across from me. In the center of the circle, Callaghan started whistling the fucking *Jeopardy* jingle.

Okay, I thought. *Okay.* If I could find the answer, I could work out the logic.

We were here to talk about capital punishment. Callaghan was about as rabidly anti-execution as they come. Therefore . . .

Therefore, therefore, therefore. *Therefore fucking what, Justine?*

The whistling continued. He was on the third repeat. Maybe the fourth.

Therefore . . .

Ted's examples from the first meeting I attended were dia-metrically opposed. If the Philadelphia district attorney was known as The Deadliest DA, then the New York guy must be on Callaghan's side of the fence, so far over on that side that the governor had stepped in.

Work it through, Justine. Work it through.

Callaghan stopped whistling, turned to the bar to pour another drink, and eight pairs of eyes were on me.

I spoke, not daring to look up again until I was finished. 'Let's say we have two identical crimes – same circumstances, same evidence. Same judge and jury.' Out of the corner of my eye, Callaghan was turning around. Slowly.

'Everything is exactly the same. Except the prosecutors. One always seeks the death penalty – I mean she seeks it with Old Testament vengeance. The other never does. Therefore . . .'

Therefore . . .

'The fate of the defendant is entirely dependent on prosecuto-rial discretion. In Philadelphia, he gets the chair. In New York, he gets life.' There was a word for this. One word, one term that summed up everything, that was the answer to Callaghan's question. It was the one word I couldn't find in the cobwebs of my stupidly slow brain.

'The door or the drink, Boucher,' he said, raising the new glass. 'All you need to do is tell me the number-one problem with prosecutorial discretion in death penalty matters. Trust me, it's not that hard.'

I still didn't meet his eyes. I looked down at the frayed rug, the fringe that had unraveled in some places and stayed intact in others. If the chair I was sitting in had been placed a few inches to the right, the pattern would be different. If it sat two feet closer to the fireplace, the pattern would be different. If the chair didn't exist, the pattern would be different.

There was no pattern. The fraying was random, based on a decision to buy the chair or not, to position it closer to the fire, to move it right or left.

'Arbitrariness,' I said. And then I looked up.

Callaghan crossed over to me with a highball glass filled with caramel-colored liquid. I took it with both hands and drank greedily.

'Good job,' he said, and nodded. 'I knew you'd get there eventually.'

For the first time, I smiled back at him.

CHAPTER TWELVE

Only two pieces of mail drop through the letter slot today, meaning I don't have to face Matt the Angry Mailman. I slice them open with Ian's silver letter opener, shrug at the unsolicited credit card offers, and drop everything in the kitchen trash. But I don't let go of the knife.

If it hadn't been for Susan, I might have used this sharp blade of silver on myself the night Ian was killed. Believe me, I thought about it. And worse.

I thought about pills and razor blades. I imagined myself driving into town and walking into Bill's Gun Shop, picking out whatever looked heavy and harmful, even taking a course. Because some things you want to get right the first time.

They didn't use the telephone; they came to the door. I remember I said something like, 'Ian, you damn fool, you took the set without the house key on it again,' as I poured a second glass of wine for him and took it through the living room to the front door. I remember I was hungry, devilishly hungry for some reason, and I'd hoped Ian got plenty of tzatziki and fries to go with the gyros. I always liked to think the yogurt cut through the grease of everything else.

The doorbell rang again, and I fumbled with the lock. 'Idiot,' I said, smiling.

The two uniformed policemen didn't smile back.

'Mrs Justine – um – is it Boucher or—'

'What is it?' I said, squeezing my hand around the bowl of the wine glass so tightly it broke. I didn't notice the blood until later. I already knew what the men would say, in the same way you know a three-a.m. phone call isn't going to be your best friend asking for your carrot cake recipe or a colleague wondering where the latest budget report got filed. Some events, because of their timing or their completely out-of-this-world fucked-up-ness, need no further explanation. Ian was hurt, and hurt badly.

What wishful thinking on my part.

'Mrs Boucher? Can we come in?'

And so they did. I don't know how, but I managed to guide the younger officer to my bathroom and find bandages. He cleaned the wound on my hand while his older partner made coffee. There wasn't any Greek takeout, but I remember the house smelling of pinot noir.

That first week was a kind of hot and stifling cloud of hurt. I got through the days, made the calls for necessary arrangements with the help of Susan, got myself up in the morning, and fell into bed at night. But someone else was doing these things, some other woman was putting food I didn't want into my mouth and answering sympathy emails and reading trashy books with happier endings than real life could offer. Some foreign invader, a body snatcher, was opening my mail and paying my bills and, finally, returning to work.

After a week back on the job, I got handed the Milford case. The DA didn't want to give it to me, and I didn't want to take it. I didn't want to see the pictures from the medical examiner or read her reports. I didn't want to spend my days and nights reading about bite wounds in places no child, no person, should ever be bitten. But we were short-staffed, so as the saying goes, tag, you're it.

No, that's a lie. I did want the case, or that foreigner who had taken up home in my body wanted it. And she wanted it badly.

The torture and murder of Caleb Church was a prosecutor's dream. Clear evidence, a heinous crime, one suspect.

Sometimes I get philosophic, and I think about hypotheticals, extreme examples like: 'I'd never eat a fried tarantula,' and 'I could never hurt a dog,' and 'I'll never leave you.'

Once upon a time, I probably swore I would never buy a set of Star Wars china.

We love to throw around the word 'never'.

The fact is, a starving man will eat a spider – deep-fried or not. A father will shoot a rabid dog if that dog approaches his child. Couples will break their marriage vows for reasons far less serious than starvation and rabies, sometimes for no good reason at all. And guilty, overworked mothers will buy crappy made-in-China Star Wars dishes from Amazon.

Never say never.

For years, ever since my first day of law school, I said I would never send a human being to die. It didn't matter what the crime was, whether the victim was old or young or black or white. It didn't matter if the public carried signs reading 'Unjust Justine' or whether they screamed that I was soft on crime. It didn't matter if the evidence was bulletproof or if the defendant looked me in the eye and said, 'I did it, and I'd do it all over again.'

And then, one day, I did.

It was easy. All I did was paint the face of my husband's killer onto Jake Milford.

Oh, other bits and pieces of the case helped me along. If Milford's victim had been twenty-five instead of seven, I might have been satisfied with a life sentence. And if the boy hadn't been found with those marks on his wrists and ankles, those red and raw marks that had bitten into his flesh in the hours before he died, I might have seen to it that Jake Milford spent the next fifty or sixty years behind bars. If I hadn't seen the medical examiner's photos of the bite wounds, some so deep it seemed impossible a human had inflicted them; if those wounds had been limited to the boy's arms and legs and torso; if seven eyewitnesses hadn't picked out Milford from a lineup, each swearing they had seen him outside the boy's house an hour before the abduction; if they hadn't all spoken of the blue uniform with the Texaco star and the embroidered 'Jake' on the left breast. If Jake Milford hadn't shrugged during his preliminary and quietly said, 'Yeah, I guess I can't say where I was that day.'

If all of those things had been different, I might have acted differently.

Or not.

When seven-year-old Caleb Church's body was found discarded on the northern bank of the James River, my husband had been dead for just over three weeks.

You could say I was feeling raw. You could say I overreached in my discretion as a prosecutor, that I took personal pain and transferred it, passing that pain down the line, convinced I could rid myself of it.

But you could also say I understood that the delicate glass veil between the hypothetical 'never-would' and the very real 'but I'm in this now' had shattered. Whether families felt closure wasn't a statistic anymore, it wasn't a number or a percentage or a significant p-value in some criminologist's journal article. Closure was the empty look in Mrs Church's eyes, the lines creasing Mr Church's face, the repeated lies they told Caleb's younger sister each time she asked when her brother was coming home because there's no right way to tell a five-year-old that her brother was tied and beaten and killed and thrown like so much garbage into the muddy waters of the Mighty James.

When Ian asked that I would never seek revenge for him in that most permanent, irremediable way, I honored the request. I guess we'd made some kind of promise there during those meetings in Boston, some unbreakable vow that he and I sealed in front of a dying fire over the last drink of the night. Or maybe we sealed it much later on when he finally mustered the courage to take me to bed.

In any case, I didn't keep that promise. I broke it when I sent Jake Milford to death row.

I broke it when I closed the door on my own morals and let arbitrariness in.

CHAPTER THIRTEEN

B ack in Boston, winter had given way to a bright, blossoms-filled spring by the time I learned I was in love with Ian Callaghan.

On an April evening, in the same plush living room, nine of us hashed through the problems of arbitrariness, moved on to the Supremes' definition of 'cruel and unusual', and volleyed around anecdotes on the topics of closure, remedies for wrongful incarceration – $80,000 per year in Texas, zero in Arkansas. Then we moved on to that perennial favorite called 'the botched execution', which Callaghan referred to as the ultimate fuck-up, assigning readings with the stern warning that we review them on empty stomachs.

It was eleven o'clock when the evening took a surprising turn.

Callaghan brought up the Patterson case.

We all knew the facts – or at least the history. Gary Lee Patterson had been charged and found guilty of arson and murder. Forensic evidence indicated he had set his house on fire with his three daughters inside.

The oldest was two; the twins were one.

'It's the kind of case that could turn your most rabid anti-death penalty activist into an executioner,' Callaghan said. 'Three little girls, helpless, choking on smoke, being burned alive in their cribs. Witnesses said Patterson sat outside on his lawn while the fire spread. Psychologists interpreted his Iron Maiden and Led Zeppelin posters as signs of a sociopathic disposition.' He stopped here and looked around the room.

The skinny guy, the one I had missed when I first came in, laughed. He had a deep laugh and a resonant voice that didn't match the rest of him. 'Robert Plant's a genius, man. Guess that makes me a sociopath.'

Callaghan smiled. 'Four years later, Gary Lee Patterson was executed. Three years after that—'

'The original evidence of arson was contested and found to be flawed,' I finished for him. 'I believe one of the experts called it "junk science".'

'Junk science,' Callaghan repeated. He poured another round of drinks and passed them out. Beer for Ted and the rest of the guys, Scotch for Callaghan and me. The skinny man was drinking Manhattans. 'Junk science. A man died because of bad science. What do you say about that, people?'

We didn't have much to say.

'Fact,' Callaghan said, again taking his place in the center of the circle. 'Initial investigations found char patterns in multiple locations in Patterson's home. Fact: a jailhouse informant testified that Patterson confessed to torching his three children to cover up signs of abuse. Fact: the prosecutor said Patterson's tattoos indicated a history of violent behavior. At the time of the trial, these so-called facts were indisputable. They were absolutes.'

He paused and looked down at the floor. 'I'll tell you something. There's only one absolute. There's only one thing in this world that is indisputable.'

I knew what he was going to say.

'Death. Death is indisputable.'

'Death and taxes,' Ted said. 'Which is why I plan to make a shitload of money in a private firm once I graduate.'

Callaghan whirled around, stepped toward Ted, and leaned in until they were nose to nose. 'In-fucking-correct, Stuyvesant. Taxes change. Taxes are increased and decreased at the whim of legislators. Taxes are imposed and taxes are repealed and taxes are refunded. Taxes are not absolute, and if you want to compare a goddamned 1040 long form to a death sentence, you know where the door is.'

Ted looked as if he might shit himself. I was vaguely aware of my spine pressing hard into the back of the chair, hard enough to hurt. At the same time, part of me was drawn to the man as he spat fury.

Because Callaghan was right. You could correct a tax error. It's harder to restart the heart of a dead man. When Ted turned to me for support, I found I didn't have any to give.

'Okay,' Callaghan said, 'now for the final round where the prizes double.' We all stared at him with expectation.

'I asked you here tonight for one reason.' He looked at me then, and I realized he was different. A haircut, maybe. A closer-than-usual shave. A shirt that had been ironed and starched. All minor details that went unnoticed by the men in the room, but not by me. 'Here's the question on the table.'

So far, I sensed a logical sequence to the meetings. Callaghan had started with the academic questions of arbitrariness, but now he was going for the throat, moving from the theoretical to the practical and from the broad to the personal. It was genius. It was the reason I had come to law school.

He cleared his throat. 'How do you remedy the irremediable?'

No one spoke for a long time. We looked at one another, not wanting to be the first, not wanting to get it wrong. Ted mouthed an apology to me. Something like, 'Sorry I dragged you into this.'

I wasn't sorry. After my first two strike-outs, I'd come to love these meetings. Callaghan's Death and Drinks parties, they were sometimes called, and few students, let alone us lowly One-Ls, were ever graced with an invitation. I looked over at Ted, who might have originally dragged me here to make an impression. Now, he was out of his league, and I think he knew it.

The room dripped with old money. Or new money. But I got more of an old-money vibe. The furnishings weren't the latest neutral-modern Crate-and-Barrel fodder; they were old and shabby, rough around the edges. Like Callaghan himself, the rugs and tables were frayed and scuffed. Inside, though, inside they were solid. They were made of stuff that mattered.

I'd come to realize that I was, too. I was on ground zero of something that would finally wipe out capital punishment in the western world, going farther than Amnesty International had gone in all its years of work. I looked up at Callaghan as the men around me spoke. Each time one of them mentioned money, the man in the center of the room shook his head and made a buzz-you're-wrong sound.

He turned to me. 'Well? Anything to offer?'

I took a deep breath. 'You can't. You can't undo the undoable and you can't make it right. Doesn't matter how much money you throw at the surviving family members.'

'And so?'

I didn't speak at first.

'Think, Boucher,' he said, and all eyes were on me.

'Stop it at the source,' I said slowly.

'How?'

'Fix it so no prosecutor will ever ask for the ultimate punishment.'

He seemed intrigued, but he kept pressing. 'How?'

What I said next was something I'd been thinking about for months but never articulated to another human soul. It was an insane thought, way over the top in its boldness. 'Take the concept of certainty to its theoretical limit,' I said. Before Callaghan could ask how again, I finished the thought aloud. 'Leave prosecutorial discretion as it is, but with a caveat. If these prosecutors are so sure that they're willing to stake a life on it, why not make it their own life?'

The thing about the Socratic method – and maybe I only figured this out when I saw the look on Callaghan's face after I'd stopped talking – is that the person playing Socrates already knows the answer. Always. Callaghan knew what he wanted to hear, and he had teased it out of us. Or out of me – the rest of the room looked as if I had just suggested that we kill all humans with red hair, or something equally as heinous. Ted, whose hand had been resting on my thigh for several minutes, gulped audibly and withdrew his hand.

The skinny guy was the first to speak up, although he took a while getting himself together. 'Can't do it. You'd end up with a snake eating its own tail. Prosecutor asks for death, execution is carried out, new evidence surfaces, prosecutor gets zapped. But then the cycle starts all over again. Who's on the line if additional new evidence comes in? And who's on the line after that?' He shook his head. 'Nope. Can't work.'

Callaghan said nothing, only looked squarely at me.

'But you'd never get that far,' I said. 'The idea isn't to start a chain of quid-pro-quo executions. The idea is to change the system so no one ever asks for death. That's it.'

'Boucher,' Callaghan finally said. 'Our Manhattan-swigging friend is right. You don't battle death penalties with more death penalties.'

'Then a grass-roots campaign to make the public think about executions in a new way,' I offered. 'But big roots. Massive. Teams of people at every courthouse and every district attorney's office asking the same question of every prosecutor. Naming, shaming, blaming, whatever it takes. Convince reporters to shout out "How sure are you?" on courthouse steps across the country. Call out the prosecutors who ask for death in every single case that crosses their desks. Amplify any mistakes they've made. And – most important – shift the focus from the average guilty prisoner on death row to the innocent prisoner on death row. I mean, it's a spin that hasn't been exploited, right?'

There was some rumbling in the room, a few 'uh-huhs' and 'maybes' and, finally, thankfully, Callaghan called it a night. 'If you're still in, we need research in two weeks. Meet for coffee, talk it over, and figure out who's going to focus on what. Think grass-roots, legislation, constitutionality, politics. Let's see what we all come up with. Also, start thinking bribery and high treason if you have to. I have a feeling money is going to be necessary. Boatloads of it.'

'Um,' the skinny guy said carefully. 'Bribery? Really?'

'It's a joke, Phil. Grow a sense of humor.'

Ted was the first to get up. He went to the coat rack near the door, taking my parka down, holding it out to me, waiting like an eager puppy.

'Boucher,' Callaghan whispered to me when I passed him. 'You turn into a pumpkin at midnight?'

A few months ago, I would have dropped my eyes, stared at my shoes, or shot a desperate plea for help in Ted's direction. But that was before. It was before I realized I liked the pipe tobacco cloud that hung over Callaghan and followed him around like a shadow. It was before I realized he didn't look like Snape the potions master but like Alan Rickman without all that Snape makeup – handsome. It was before I realized he wasn't a sexist or a bully or a crackpot, only a man with a single mission and the kind of integrity that would see things to the end. A man made of solid stuff, like his furniture.

'I used to,' I said. 'Now I'm more of a prickly pear kind of a girl.'

He smiled. 'I tried one of those once. A little spiky around the edges, but the fruit inside is sweet. Good for breakfast.'

Holy shit. He was flirting with me. Blatantly. Not that I hadn't asked for it.

'Stuyvesant, thanks for another good meeting. I'll drive Boucher home. If, that is, she wants to hang around.'

Ted's face drew into a frown. Callaghan waved to the rest of the departing crowd as they went down the steps toward the street, splitting into pairs that walked off in various directions. I was in a Wonderland world right then, tempted by the drink and the diffident but kind of sexy Callaghan who had picked up his pipe and was puffing at it like Alice's caterpillar. Ted, standing there with my coat held out, began looking more and more like the hapless dormouse.

I did what a lot of women would have done. I compromised.

'Actually, Ted,' I said, taking my coat and hanging it back on the tree. 'I have a couple of questions for Ian that I never got the chance to raise before we broke up tonight.' *Excellent choice of words there, Justine.* 'I can hop the bus and I'll see you at your place in an hour or so.'

'The last #12 stops here in thirty minutes.' It came out like a pathetic whine. Ted was less worried about whether I'd catch the last bus and more concerned about limiting the window of opportunity for any kind of extracurricular high jinks.

'Fifteen minutes, then,' I said, kissed him, and watched as he started down the sidewalk.

Callaghan closed the door and faced me, one hand on the wood frame, the other holding his pipe. It was the closest I'd been to him, and I couldn't decide if I welcomed this new intimacy or not. Maybe he read my mind, because he turned abruptly away and started walking towards the bar. 'Are you sweating your exams, Boucher?' he called over his shoulder.

'Kind of,' I said.

'Want to review anything?'

'With you?' He was third-year, nearly finished. He was editor of the law review – a position my grades and class ranking would never be good enough for. He was intelligent and wealthy and absolutely intimidating. I could only think of one reason why he wanted to 'review' first-year Criminal Law, Torts, and Civil Procedure.

'I'm usually right about things, you know.' Callaghan still had his back to me.

I reached for my coat.

'Take Civil Procedure, for instance,' he said. 'Specifically, disclosure.'

'What about it?' My left hand held my coat; my right was on the doorknob, twisting it.

He turned around, but stayed in place far across the room,

98

swirling the glass of Scotch. 'Well, let's start with relevant information in my control. Must I disclose said information to you?'

'Are we talking Federal or State Procedure?'

'Oh, let's start with local jurisdiction.'

'Okay. Here in Massachusetts, I think we'd have to start with limitations on—'

'More local than that,' he said, not meeting my eyes.

My God, this was a weird way to flirt, especially from twenty feet away. I realized something then. Ian Callaghan was a softie. All the bullying and badgering and *Jeopardy*-jingle-whistling was an act.

'How local?' He still hadn't moved from the bar, so I took a few steps forward, expecting him to do the same.

He didn't move, only looked around the room. 'Um. Very local.'

'I'm afraid I don't know the Civil Procedure rules on this level,' I said. 'Never came up in class.' Five more steps.

'I don't either.' Callaghan dragged on his pipe, waiting. 'Maybe that brilliant legal mind of yours can make some up.'

'Don't make fun of me.'

'I'm not. I meant what I said, and I'm usually right about things.'

'Okay.' Five more steps. Still a safe distance. 'Let's say you're not obligated to disclose whatever information you have, but I could maybe give you some assurance that if you chose to do so, I wouldn't hold that against you later on if it proved to be to your disadvantage.'

He nodded, dragged on his pipe, sipped his drink.

'Well?' I said. 'Are those reasonable terms?' An old grandfather clock near the stairs bonged out the quarter hour. Fifteen minutes until the last bus.

'Justine,' he started. It was the first time he'd ever used my name.

'Ian?'

'Full disclosure: I'm very much in love with you. Now go on and catch your bus.'

I did just that, walking slowly towards the bus stop, riding back to my rental in a daze, and staring up at the ceiling above my bed for at least an hour before sleep came. At some point, I realized I was in love with Ian Callaghan, too. After hours of talking about death, it felt good to think about something that made me feel alive.

Death Row Inmate #39384

Here's a problem I've been thinking on for a while now: folks watch too many of those prison movies and read too many of the same kind of novels. So they have a different idea of the way things work. You'd think someone in the business would get it right, but now we get to another problem. Getting it right means knowing shit you really don't want to know.

I don't believe in ghosts, so I don't think I'll be coming to visit Justine at night in the years ahead. If I did, I would only be her imagination at work, like the old man in the Christmas story thinks when his dead partner turns up. No part of me, of who I am, will really be there, trying to reach out. What I'm saying is, I can't tell whether the woman who put me where I am will ever understand the last few hours of my life, but I can tell you that whatever she sees in her mind ain't the truth.

I did have dinner tonight, a pretty decent one, I guess, mainly because I got to pick whatever I wanted from the monthly menu. Nothing like the barbecue Emily used to make, roasted for hours in the oven and falling apart as soon as you looked at it. The biscuits weren't hers, either. They were from a can. A person can tell these things.

They shaved me, my right leg and my head, just after supper. There I was, strapped down with the cook's barbecue and biscuits bubbling around in my stomach, and those attendants went to work. When they were done, I felt like a girl. Not that being a girl's bad, but it ain't who I am. Who I was.

Then came the wait.

This is what they don't tell you in the movies, what they don't write down in the Department of Correction's execution manuals. For one good reason: they can't. The wait is personal, an experience that only exists on the inside of a body. And I'll tell you a truth, those four hours last a long, long time. Long enough to write all these pages.

A man thinks about things, thinks about all the things. Thinks about his first kiss and his first ice cream cone. Thinks about his mother and his grandma and his little sister and his wife. Thinks about that one time he went to the opera and didn't like it so much, but goddamn, if he could go back and watch that plump soprano sing in a language he'll never understand, he'd do it. He'd go every night for the rest of his life.

He thinks about the lies he's told and the trades he's made, stupid decisions, rash and not so well thought out, but there's no going back once a thing is done. Not for love or money. Not for anything.

He thinks about the first time he got laid, which was nothing more or less than fucking. He thinks about his wedding night, which was brand new, some crazy-ass discovery of what making love meant. While he thinks, he holds himself, trying to believe his left hand is his wife, but left hands are never as good as women, and his own could never be the same as Emily.

I saw Emily this morning, bright and early. We got less time than we should have, but that's a story I might not have time to tell. My God, she was beautiful. Wore her pretty green dress, the one I bought her last Christmas. Okay, so I bought it at TJ Maxx, but all the guys say if you look real hard, you can find gold just about anywhere. Jake Junior sat on her lap while we talked. He slapped the glass a few times like he was trying to break his way into where I was, and that caused some ruckus with the screws who were watching us, but I told him to keep his hands to himself and talk quiet, just like in church. You know what? My boy didn't slap the glass any more after that.

'They got that law, you know,' Emily said. 'Something about wrongful execution and remedies.'

'Ain't no way to remedy this one, honey,' I said, letting her know with my eyes to let the subject alone. Our son was staring at me.

She leaned in then, as close as she dared without firing off a million alarms and shortening our already too-short visit. 'I know you didn't do it, Jacob. I know you didn't k—' she looked quickly at Jake Junior '—hurt that little boy. So you were somewhere, and maybe you were doing something you weren't supposed to be doing, but you gotta tell me, baby. You gotta tell me before it's too late.' She was crying now, her thin shoulders shaking inside that pretty green dress.

I guess I just shrugged, and that made her cry more. 'Let's talk about something nice.'

We did, and it got us through the hour, but when our hour was up, Emily leaned in again. 'There's still that law. And I'm gonna study up on it. And if I ever find something, it'll be that pretty prosecutor sitting here behind this glass. I just want you to know that, baby.'

I had one more visitor before they sealed me back inside to eat and get shaved and wait. My sister-in-law came. I didn't think she would; I didn't even think she qualified as immediate family, but there was Mary Ann on the other side of the glass, looking only slightly less rough than the last time I saw her.

She had just a few words for me. 'You did a bad thing, Jake.'

'Yeah. I guess so,' I said.

'And you can't take it back.' The way she said this made it sound like a question, but we both knew better.

'Nope.'

She stood up then, signaling to the guard in the corner that we were through, conversation over, nothing to talk about. She'd lost weight over the years. I remembered at the trial she had been more Emily's size, round in the hips, her cheeks as full as they had been when we were kids. Mary Ann wore the same blue dress today, but it hung on her bones, and her cheeks were hollows, like someone had carved out pieces of her. When she turned back to me, I swear I saw a skull where Mary Ann's head should have been.

'I still love you, Jake,' she whispered.

'Yeah.'

After that, I had only two more visitors, a barber who

left me bald and a chaplain who looked like he'd rather be anywhere else. I guess he thought God's forgiveness didn't really go as far as people like me.

But I'm wrong. There's a third visitor this afternoon. He'll stay with me for six hours. His name is Wait.

CHAPTER FOURTEEN

As soon as Susan leaves with the boys for their Saturday sleepover, I call Daniel.

'Hey, beautiful,' he says. It's always the first thing he says and, most of the time, it makes me feel good. At least it makes me feel less bad.

'How about dinner and a movie?' I say.

'Depends. Are we talking veggie nuggets and *Shrek*, or sockeye salmon and *The Shining*?'

I can't help but laugh. Daniel has patiently watched *Shrek* from beginning to end about a hundred times in the year since we started dating. 'Not *Shrek*.'

'You know I'd come over anyway.'

'I know.'

After I rummage through the fridge and recite a list of everything I'm out of, I head back to shower. Under the hot water, I think of how good Daniel is with Jonathan and how much I both love and hate seeing them together. I want my boy to have a man in his life, a good man and a father figure. But I want that person to be Ian. It isn't only wanting my husband back, it's wanting everything that's happened since he died to vanish, for the slate to be wiped clean.

Because if Ian hadn't died, I wouldn't have fallen apart. If I hadn't fallen apart, I wouldn't have sent Jake Milford to die. And if Jake Milford hadn't died, there would have been no letter from his wife, no threatening 'piece of paper'. I spend three hours up in the office rehashing my meeting with Emily, and at five, there's a knock at the back door. Daniel has never used the front entry, not even the first time he came for dinner ten months ago. It's another of his habits I have a love-hate relationship with. I love the intimacy; I hate the reminder of what it's like to have a man about the house.

My best efforts at makeup have apparently failed because the first words out of Daniel's mouth when he sees me are: 'Jesus. What happened to you?'

I sweated this moment all afternoon. As many times as I swore I would put Emily's letter out of my mind, I spent the same amount of time rehearsing what I would tell Daniel. If I kept quiet about the letter, we'd settle down to one of his gourmet meals and a movie, followed by sex. My perfect Saturday. If I told him everything, I could kiss that fantasy goodbye.

Oh, hell, who am I kidding? Not telling him means the dinner will have no taste, the movie will be patches of color on a big screen, and the evening will end with me in tears.

'I have something to tell you. And it's going to require wine, so I hope you brought reinforcements,' I say, leading him into the kitchen and storing away enough groceries to feed the state of Virginia. There's a plastic bag that isn't from Safeway on top. 'What did you get?'

'Tofu barbecue. The state's finest. I figured we could spend the prep time doing other things.' He comes behind me and wraps me in a bear hug. I think I wince.

Barbecue. Of course Daniel had brought barbecue. I have no way of knowing what Jake Milford ate at his last meal, but it stings all the same.

I've never told Daniel about my time in Vita. Ian knew, of course. It's hard to keep that kind of a secret from the man who co-founded a grass-roots legislative revolution with you. And most of the country knew when the scandal over Jake Milford's trial hit the news and Vita kicked my ass to the curb. But people have short memories. The headlines featuring me were replaced by headlines about wars and viruses and school shootings. I stopped going by Boucher and took Ian's last name, and the district attorney's office gave me low-profile cases until recently. Eventually, I faded from the newspapers, and people like Daniel who spent most of their lives overseas, never knew that I permanently severed ties with the red suits and the activism once Ian died.

I turn away from Daniel and stare out the window for what seems like ages. In true April fashion, we've gone from sunshine to rain again.

'Hmm. Drizzle. Picturesque,' Daniel says from behind me, and I jump as soon as he speaks. He spins me around to face him and wipes away the first of the tears I've been trying to stifle since I met with Emily.

'Okay, Jussie. Okay. Let's go sit down, have a drink, and talk.' Daniel steers me toward the sofa, puts on some low and lyric-free music, and comes back with two glasses of wine. 'What's up?' he says.

'I got a letter from Jake Milford's widow yesterday.'

His eyes widen, but he doesn't say anything.

'She wanted to meet me.'

'And? Tell me you didn't, Jussie.'

Something in his voice, a trace of disappointment, maybe, tells me to lie, if only to save the argument for another day. 'No. Of course not. But all I've been able to think about is what if I was wrong? What if – oh, God, Daniel – what if—' I can't seem to choke out the words. *What if I sent an innocent man to die?*

'It's all right,' he says, and one hand rubs circles on my back. 'It's all right. Look, I know I never have to ask the tough questions. I put people in prisons that are more like five-star hotels that happen to have bars on the windows. But I know the Milford case. I saw the evidence. Anybody in your position would have wanted to see the end of that bastard. I would have. For God's sake, the Church kid was—' He looks away and covers his face. 'You know.'

I think I choke out an agreement.

His words shock me. 'I thought all you Brits considered Americans to be backwards and barbaric.'

'Not when we're talking about children.'

'So you think I should have gone the other way with Charlotte Thorne?'

'Not at all. There's no perfect answer, Jussie. We can talk about kids like Caleb Church and some people say, "All right. Little kid, hard evidence, send the murderer to the chair." Part of me can understand that thinking, the raw emotion involved when the victim is a child; part of me can never understand it. But then we get to a teenage victim, and the emotion isn't quite as raw, but that teenager is still someone's kid. What about a grown woman? Or someone's husband?' He strokes my hair. 'Sorry. I didn't mean to open a wound.'

'It's okay.' It isn't, and it never will be, but I say it all the same.

Daniel continues. 'So we can talk all day and all night about whether electrocuting some bastard is right or wrong, and we'll never get to the perfect answer.'

'Then there's the other question,' I say. 'Is it undoable if you get it wrong?'

'You'll go crazy if you keep on asking that.' He pulls himself up sharply. 'Hey! Remember those Vita people? Isn't that the line they used? "How can we undo the undoable?"'

'That's what we said.'

'What?'

'I was one of the Vita people,' I tell him. 'You could say I was the original Vita person.'

The pictures of me from Vita's early days aren't on my phone or my laptop. Those were the days before all this digital insanity, and those tiny cylinders called film weren't exactly free. You had to be judicious about photos. If it was a drunken college party, you took one. Maybe. If the event was important enough to be memorialized, you took a couple.

I've still ended up with over a hundred photos in the scrapbook I take from a high shelf and give to Daniel. That's how many events there were.

We flip through the first few pages from my law school days. Me. Ian. Ted Stuyvesant – before Ted bailed on the activist front and decided he could make better money elsewhere. Ian again. I want to linger on the shots of him the way I do when I'm alone, tracing his face with my index finger, imagining what his hair felt like, how his cheek could go from baby-smooth to rough in the span of a day. But that's not why I brought the album out this evening.

Daniel turns the page and points to a close-up of me standing at a podium. 'You haven't changed much,' he says, and glances from the photograph to me and back. 'Too bad I was in London instead of up at Hahvahd Yahd learning to not pronounce my Rs.'

'You already don't pronounce your Rs, honey. You would have fit right in.' I smile at him despite not feeling much like smiling. Daniel Hughes will never be Ian Callaghan, but he has some great qualities. Enough for me to have fallen in love.

'So this was really you?' He's looking at a different shot now, one that shows me from head to toe, from a blond ponytail tied low at the back of my neck all the way to a pair of low-heeled fake leather pumps I got at Payless. In between, there's my red suit. 'I never saw your name on the Vita site's About page,' he says.

'You looked?'

'A few of the other lawyers were talking about them one night, so I thought I'd check it out. Interesting group.'

'My name's not there anymore. Hasn't been for years. Besides, I would have been listed under Boucher. I go by Callaghan now.'

He leans back. 'Aha. So the shepherd went astray and the flock shunned her.' He closes the album. 'Just as well. From what I've heard, Vita's a bunch of radical ideologues, and radical ideologues always eat their own.'

'No, Daniel. They were right. The idea behind Vita was to respect life, not to ask for an eye for an eye. But there's a spin-off group that wants more than that. They want blood.' I tell him about the woman in the red suit. 'I think she's part of the spin-off. Vita was radical, sure. As in radical anti-death penalty. Not so radical it would turn around and push for the execution of a prosecutor. Kind of defeats the point of being anti-death penalty, if you know what I mean.'

'But Vita worked on the Remedies Act draft, didn't they?'

'We,' I remind him. 'And yes, we did. But only to make sure

certain other parties didn't let the act go too far, cover too much ground. Originally, there were a few activists and politicians who wanted it worded so that anyone involved could be on the hook – especially after Toby Barrett's little show during his sentencing. They wanted the buck to be passed to prosecutor, DA, Assistant DA, judge, everyone. When we reached the point where we knew the Act had enough votes, we did what we could. We limited remedies for wrongful execution to only one person – the prosecutor. People like me.'

'Hell of a compromise.'

I put the scrapbook away, turn the music up, and try to remember this is supposed to be a date night, not a law school seminar. Eventually, Daniel's arm goes back to its place over my shoulder.

'I'm glad you told me,' he says. 'Must have been tough for you to lose all that.'

'It was.'

The months after the Jake Milford trial were more than tough. They were pure hell. Ian was gone, early pregnancy left me weak and sick, my name was plastered on every newspaper in the country. I left the house only for work and grocery shopping, never to socialize. Susan became my sole friend, helping to run errands when I couldn't face showing myself in public. It was a miracle I met Daniel, and more of a miracle I was able to hold on to him once I summoned the courage to tell him about Milford.

'Daniel,' I say, 'I don't think I'm up for—'

He doesn't let me finish, only kisses the top of my head and holds me closer.

Death Row Inmate #39384

I said at the beginning that I had a story to tell. Some of the story is mine, and some of it ain't.

For six years, more than that if you add in the part before the trial and the part during the trial, I've thought about Caleb Church. He lived with his parents and his sister – a cutie-pie if there ever was one, and a girl that made Emily and me want to get down to business and make another baby as soon as we'd put some more money away. It was tough, with the mortgage and all the kid expenses and stuff, but I had a plan. I'd be lead mechanic in another year, and that meant a raise, but it also meant management experience and more benefits. Five classes a year, all paid for, at the community college if I wanted to go. And I did. I figured five classes every year would get me a degree in business administration by the time I was twenty-eight. And then, as Emily liked to say, I could write my ticket.

Caleb always had a big wave for me when I walked home from work. If I wasn't in a hurry, I'd toss a few balls with him on the front lawn of the Church place. I liked Caleb.

I noticed the way he smiled, even noticed the way his overbite made him look a little goofy. I noticed the way he called out, 'Mister Jake!' when I passed, even if I didn't have time to stop that day.

What I also noticed was that Caleb always seemed to be outside, alone.

His momma made an appearance every now and then, usually with a dust rag in her hand or an apron tied around her waist. Busy, busy, busy, that woman. Sometimes she'd come out with a glass of lemonade that she made herself, and she would talk about how her husband got home late from work and didn't have time to play catch with Caleb. Then she would duck back inside and return to her cleaning.

I saw Caleb the morning of the day he died.

It was a bright June day, the kind of day that makes you feel warm all over, that makes you want to skip work or school and just lie down in the grass. I remember that day. I remember that last chance I had to smell the color of green.

We tossed a ball back and forth for five minutes, as long as I could spare. My last toss went high, too high for a seven-year-old, and Caleb backed up without looking. Before I knew it, he was flat on his back in Mrs Church's azalea hedge, wailing like a son of a gun. I ran over, got him sat up, and checked for bruises. There was a small rip in his blue-and-white checked shirt where a branch had snagged him, and a bright drop of blood behind his left ear. I wiped at it with a clean hanky Emily had tucked into my pocket on my way out the door. Then I called for Mrs Church.

She had words for me, and not one of them was kind.

The way things turned out, I never made it to work. There

was a phone call, see, from a number I knew well. I had one of those candy bar phones, nothing special. I think maybe it had a parachute game on it. Real low-tech. But I carried it with me in case Emily might call before I got off work asking me to bring her something from the store. Usually, it was me that called her, asking if she needed anything. What with Jake Junior on the way and Em's part-time job at the library, I tried to help out as much as I could.

So. The phone call. I can't say who it was because life is complicated. I've learned that saying things isn't always the best route. People get ideas. Sometimes, my little brother gets ideas in his head, and when he does, trust me, you want to be on the other side of the state when that happens. You want to be invisible.

Now that it's nearly over, there's a part of the story that might or might not come out. That ain't up to me. But I can tell you the same thing I'll tell those people watching through the glass tonight when they strap me in the chair.

I've done a lot of shit in my life, told some lies and hurt some people. Same as everyone else, I guess.

But I didn't kill that little boy named Caleb.

CHAPTER FIFTEEN

In my final year at Harvard, I suggested to Ian that it was time to start making some waves. I went to Filene's Basement and bought the sassiest suit I could find, bright red and form-fitting. There were a pair of pumps on deep discount that matched it perfectly, so I bought those too. I never thought people would adopt it as a uniform after that; all I wanted to do was stand out. And a girl in a red dress always stands out. Think of *Schindler's List*.

'Listen to me!' I said from my makeshift soapbox in the corner of Harvard Yard. A few of the original group stood in the front. The skinny kid I met at Ian's first Death and Drinks party – I'd later found out his name was Phil Potts – had taken the morning off from his job at the Boston district attorney's office to be there. He and the others cheered me on with hoots and 'hear, hears' and plenty of thumbs up. Ted hadn't come, even though he was also working locally at a Boston firm. He dropped out of the drinks parties not long after I dropped him. I don't think his decision had anything to do with me. Ted simply wasn't interested in working his ass off for free.

'We have a problem in this country,' I said. Students and faculty started to join the crowd, maybe out of interest, maybe as a way to justify skipping class or arriving late to the boredom of another department meeting. I didn't care. I wanted people. Warm bodies on a cold February morning.

The thing about crowds is this: they're magnetic. They turn humans into sheep. If a woman stops along the street to look into the window of a jeweler's, the odds are two other people will stop. The two turn into four and the four into eight. There could be absolutely nothing in the display; the first woman had perhaps stopped to check her makeup or peer inside to catch the eye of a friend who worked there. But the crowd grows all the same. Like it was doing today.

Only what I had on offer wasn't 'nothing'. I had words to say, and those words were strong ones.

'And we need a solution,' I said into the microphone. 'We need an insurance policy against wrongful execution.'

Now there were two hundred faces staring up at me where only moments before there had been a dozen. I couldn't see the pavement anymore, couldn't pick out individual features. William and the others were lost in a sea of bodies. Even Ian, tall and unmistakable with his long hair and beatnik vibe, had disappeared in the throngs.

More important than the numbers was the fact that they were listening.

They were listening to me.

I had memorized dozens of relevant cases, the names of thirty wrongfully convicted men and women, but these people weren't here for a law seminar. They were here because they agreed with me.

'Can we undo the undoable?' I shouted. 'Can we bring the dead back to life?'

'No!' came a battle cry of voices.

'Can we prevent the undoable?'

'Yes!' Louder now. Deafening. It was five hundred voices and one voice, both impossibly reaching my ears at the same instant.

'Then we need to dig up every case of wrongful execution in this country. Every single one. I don't care how far back in time. We have to talk to the families, the spouses, the grown kids. We have to show America how many lives are destroyed when the system gets it wrong.' I think I kept speaking, but I could no longer hear myself over the roar of the crowd. It was deafening.

I had been self-conscious about the red suit when I took it off the hanger in Ian's bedroom that morning and zipped myself into it. I guess I was still all too aware of how I stuck out on that platform, a shock of brightness against the leafless trees and the washed-out, almost colorless brick of the buildings behind me. But a crazy thing happened. People started fishing around in backpacks and pockets. They pulled out anything they could find that was red – even remotely red. They waved red-spined case books and pink scarves.

The next time I spoke in the Yard, one month later, there were at least a thousand people. They had seen the fliers. They had heard me on the local radio stations. They had been dragged along by their friends. And they were all wearing Harvard Crimson.

Ian took me out to dinner after my second rally. He had called ahead and spoken to the chef without letting me in on the plan, and it was only when I had sat through five courses that everything clicked into place. The roasted red pepper bisque, the beet salad, the extremely rare chateaubriand, the raspberry sorbet, and the poached pears in wine (red, naturally) were all part of his surprise. I think I loved him more that night than I ever had loved anyone, and when we were finally home and away from the microphones and the crowds and the questions, we did all the things lovers do.

I wondered at the time if I would ever see sex as a perfunctory act. I didn't think I would. Not with Ian.

It took another ten years of speeches and a few hundred red-eye flights back and forth across the country. I traveled to Texas and Florida and Missouri, giving back-to-back talks on little sleep, working my cases on airplane tray tables, checking into one Motel 6 after another until they all seemed to blend together. Toward the end, Ian left Harvard, and we finally settled down in Virginia, where I had spent my first year out of law school clerking. It was the O'Dell case that brought me back here, although Joseph O'Dell was long dead, like the other eight men I had been researching. The difference here was that O'Dell had a unique supporter, a woman who had married him six hours before the time of his execution at Greensville Correctional Center.

The press coverage went viral. Wives and mothers of dead men came from everywhere, filing appeals for reexamination of evidence, sending me tear-stained letters of thanks, asking if I could get the word out about their cases. At one point, the Vita website crashed from an uptick in traffic and stayed down for three days.

That was when I knew we had won, when I learned that thousands of voices all singing the same tune could make anything happen.

I remember the day the last three states – Texas, Florida, and Virginia – finally threw in the towel and abolished the death penalty. It was a victory as unexpected as a national election upset, all thanks to an army of loudmouths that kept on getting louder, hundreds of feet pounding the pavement, Vita volunteers throwing one example after another of wrongful execution in the face of every voter who would listen. It was glorious.

But thanks to Toby Barrett and the passing of the Remedies Act, the glory was also temporary.

CHAPTER SIXTEEN

'I saw one of those red suits once,' Daniel says. He's chopping cabbage for coleslaw while I sit across the kitchen island and watch what looks like expert knife work. 'I was in Jacksonville, Florida for a few months working a fraud case. Intimidating.'

'They were,' I say. 'A paper document is one thing. A constant visual reminder of the stakes is another.' It was true. In the first two years after the Remedies Act passed, Vita had a few dozen volunteers in every state. We showed up at courthouses, at prosecutors' offices, anywhere we could be seen. 'Most of the time, we didn't even have to talk. Being there was enough.'

Except for that one time. That time, not even talking was enough.

'No kidding,' he says. 'They scared the shit out of me. And I do the boring stuff.'

I steal another piece of sliced cabbage. It desperately needs the dressing Daniel has started to make. 'Bank fraud is sexy.' We both know I don't believe this.

Daniel gives me a look and tops up my wine glass. 'Flattery will get you free drinks. Anyway, it's okay. Sometimes boring is safe.' He must see my face grow longer because the next thing he says is, 'Stop worrying. Milford was guilty. I would have signed off on him going to the death house for what he did.'

'I know.'

'Not like the Bantam case in Florida,' he says. 'The evidence in that one was always a bit iffy. If my name were Adrian Kopinsky, I'm not sure I'd sleep well, but then again, she's always been a hardcore bitch.'

I pick up my glass and set it down again without drinking. 'You knew Kopinsky? You never told me that.' Adrian Kopinsky is a more rabid death penalty advocate than the Philadelphia district attorney Ian used as an example in the first meeting I attended at his home.

'I had the misfortune,' he says. 'When I was young, dumb, and full of – you know. Well, thirty-eight or so, but I was a late bloomer.' He winces and actually gives a little shudder, like he's trying to shake off the memory.

'Ah-ha. You *knew* her,' I say. 'Wow.'

'In the biblical sense, my dear.' Daniel leans over the counter and kisses me. 'I like you inordinately better.'

'What was she like?' *I know exactly what Kopinsky was like,* I think.

Now Daniel refills his own glass. 'We're going to need more alcohol.' He sighs and starts looking for a bowl that might hold the small mountain of shredded cabbage on the cutting board. 'You know what she said when one of the Vita women came in before Bantam's arraignment?'

Before I can answer, he laughs. 'Well, I can only tell you what Adrian told me. She walked up to the woman and told her she'd rather ride the fucking lightning than see a guy like Donald Bantam take another breath. The Vita woman didn't so much as blink. Seriously. She stood there, looking up at five-feet-eight inches of red-haired bitch and said, "Ms Kopinsky, you just

126

might get your wish. I hope you reconsider." Then there were a few choice words, and it all ended with Adrian laughing and getting Miss Red Suit booted out of the office. I broke up with Adrian that night. I just couldn't, you know? I mean, the Bantam case was bad. Worse than I've ever seen, and worse than what Milford did.' He closes his eyes for a moment before continuing. 'But the evidence, Justine. The evidence never convinced me one hundred percent. And the Vita woman was right. Adrian should have reconsidered.'

The facts of the Bantam case come back to me in vivid detail. Although it happened years ago, and it happened in Florida, I remember the damage to the victim made the entire *Saw* series look like a children's bedtime story. And I remember that, despite my pleading that day in her office, Adrian Kopinsky went ahead and asked for death. She was the first prosecutor to do so after the Remedies Act passed. I was the next.

As I hunt for a salad bowl, I decide to tell him the truth. 'That was me, Daniel. The one who tried to talk Kopinsky out of it.'

'Wow. You really did get around.' There's more pride than accusation in his voice. 'Shame I didn't meet you back then.'

'I was married,' I say.

'I know.' He takes me in his arms. 'I'm just glad I met you at all.'

'Me too, Daniel. Me too. By the way, did they execute Bantam? I stopped following the case after . . . I mean, I just stopped following it.' . . . *after Ian died.* There's no reason to keep bringing my late husband into the conversation. He seems to be here enough, whether I like it or not. And whether Daniel likes it or not.

'Couple of years ago. And there's been some talk about botched blood samples.'

'Oh, shit,' I say. And my legs suddenly fail to hold me up.

Daniel catches me before I hit the kitchen floor. 'Stop it, Justine. You're not the same as Adrian. You've got a good heart, and a good mind, and you did what you thought was right. If you can't go back and you can't take it back, let's keep moving forward. Okay?'

I nod. Or I think I nod. Truth is, I'm lost in my own thoughts.

'You had more witnesses. You had blood samples.' Daniel pauses, still supporting most of my weight. 'Good samples. You had a man without an alibi who knew the victim and who pleaded guilty. And the little boy's family was on your side, Jussie.' He pulls me into a tight hug. 'Come on. Let's eat some barbecue, get drunk, and see what happens next.'

What happens next is I drain two glasses of chardonnay in rapid succession while Daniel heats up the barbecue and tosses the slaw with dressing. What happens after that is his phone rings. I catch the first three digits and don't recognize the area code.

Daniel's brow wrinkles when he sees the number. 'I should take this. It's an old mate of mine from Florida and he's just been diagnosed with prostate cancer. Poor bastard. Fifty-five and he's got fucking cancer.' He picks up and taps. 'Hey, Curt. How are things?'

I hear a laugh through the phone but can't make out the rest of the conversation, so I watch Daniel's face change. The furrow deepens, his eyes widen, and by the time he ends the call, he looks twenty years older. Good old cancer at work, doing what it does best, spreading fear and grief as far as possible.

'Bad news about your friend?' I say.

Daniel shakes his head. 'No. Curt's fine. Treatment's going well and he's back at work putting the insurance fraudsters of Florida behind bars.'

'So why do you look like someone died?'

'He didn't call about the cancer,' Daniel says, tilting his glass up and downing it in two swallows. 'He called about the Bantam case.'

I try to speak and find my throat has seized up. The best I can manage is a choky gulp.

'Actually, Curt called about a new case. They found a woman with gunshot injuries in her—' he stops, fills his glass with water from the tap, and downs it in one long swallow. 'With identical injuries.' He stops again and splashes water over his face. 'Jesus. It's bad, Jussie.'

I don't say a thing.

'They've got the man downtown, all fixed up with a court-appointed. Know what the public defender says?'

I still don't speak, only shake my head.

'His client did it. He did the job. And he did the other job. The one they put Bantam away for. Says his client is all ready to plead to both murders in exchange for a reduced sentence.' Daniel actually laughs now. 'A reduced sentence. From what? From a million fucking consecutive life sentences? Jesus.'

Suddenly I don't want any more wine. It's like all my taste buds have gone numb. 'Are they sure?'

Daniel looks as if he might keel over. 'I don't know. Yet. They're running fast-turnaround DNA tests and the entire staff is in the office today, along with a pack of people in red suits. Actually, two packs. And they're screaming at one another. Curt says one side calls themselves Vita and the other say they're working with the – what's it called – the Oversight Committee for Something or other.'

'The Oversight Committee for Prosecutorial Responsibility,' I say. 'We have one here in Virginia, too.'

'Did they come for you after the Milford trial?'

'No. Only Vita did.' I can see myself, sitting in my cramped office, two women looking down at me from the other side of my desk. The one-way conversation began with pleading and ended with what Daniel would call 'a few choice words' before I booted them out. 'I wish I'd listened to them. But I don't think I was capable of listening to anything after – I mean, back then.'

'Christ, Jussie.' He covers his eyes with one hand. With the other, he grips my arm. 'Kopinsky's going batshit, saying it's ridiculous. A hoax. But Curt doesn't buy it. He says she's frightened out of her wits.'

'Maybe you should call her,' I say, not really wanting him to. 'I mean, you two had something once.'

'Later. Let's have dinner.'

I don't bother setting the table. We sit at the kitchen island, picking our way through the meal in silence, then tune in to a rom-com on Netflix. Neither one of us laughs, and not much happens next.

CHAPTER SEVENTEEN

I wake before the light starts seeping into my room. 'Wake' isn't the right word. To wake, you need to have slept, and I don't think my body has done that. Next to me, Daniel snores softly, one arm across my chest, the other curled around his head like a protective shield. From the state of the sheets, I know he hasn't slept well either.

But he's asleep now, and I seize the opportunity.

My phone is in the kitchen where I left it last night. When I pick it up, the screen flashes three missed calls and a new voicemail from a number I don't know. It's only now I realize I've picked up Daniel's phone by mistake. Goddamn Otterbox cases. They all look the same. The area code is Florida, so it might be Daniel's friend. Or it might not. It might be Adrian Kopinksy.

I wake up my own phone and tap the numbers. Adrian – if the woman is Adrian – doesn't sound like a bitch when she answers. Her voice is thick with what might be a few decades of a two-pack-a-day habit.

'Daniel? Oh, Christ, Danny. I'm in the shit.'

Danny? My thumb hovers over the red End button as a clicking noise cuts her off. Then she starts again.

'Danny? Look, I'm sorry it's so early. But I need to talk to someone. Nobody at the office wants to be seen with me. The DA told me to go home and not come back. Like, at all. Not come back at all. What the fuck am I going to do?'

I don't press End. 'Hello? Is this Adrian?' I say.

'Who the hell is this?' So. The bitch is back. But only for a moment. 'Is Danny there? Are you his—'

'No. I mean, yes. He's here but he's asleep. I'm not his wife or anything.' *I'm just in the same place as he is at zero dark-thirty on a Sunday morning.*

'I see.' She pauses. 'Yes, this is Adrian Kopinsky. I'm sorry I called so many times early on a Sunday.'

'It's all right. I was already up. Sounds like you slept about as badly as I did.' I take a deep breath. 'I'm Justine Callaghan.'

There's a crash in my ear, then a long pause and the squeak of something being dragged, maybe a chair on a hardwood floor. After a few seconds, Adrian comes back on the line.

'Sorry. I dropped my phone. Are you *that* Justine Callaghan? As in Justine Boucher Callaghan? The one who came to my office after – you know – after Bantam?'

'Just Callaghan.' I don't tell her I wish I were anybody else right now.

'Oh, thank God,' Adrian says. It comes out like a sigh, and when the click of a lighter comes through, I almost tell her not to smoke another one but rethink it. We all have our own ways of coping. 'Listen, can we talk? I know I was a shit that day, but I need to talk to you.' She inhales, sharply, and for a second I actually find myself craving a cigarette.

Instead, I make coffee.

'Justine, are you still there?'

'Look, if this is about the new evidence in the Bantam case,

I don't know what to say,' I tell her while spooning heaping measures of coffee into the machine.

'But you're with Vita. You know people.'

'Not anymore. Not for seven years. Did you miss the headlines?' I don't tell her about the last time I ran into a Vita member, one of the original crowd who I'd mentored. It isn't because I don't want Adrian to know, only because I'd prefer not to relive being spat on and shouted at in the cereal aisle of my local Safeway.

The coffee machine starts to sputter, and I pour out a cup with a shaking hand while Adrian talks.

'I've been reading the papers. Not print – I can't even leave my fucking house because of the reporters outside. I've been reading them online. The story broke late last night. They're calling for my head, Justine.' She's crying now. The woman Daniel referred to as a bitch sounds unhinged. Then the bitch comes back. 'You started this. You have to be able to do something.'

I want to explain to her that it was never supposed to get to this point. I want to tell her Vita only wanted to abolish capital punishment in every state, and it wasn't our fault the whole thing backfired because of a few rotten apples like Toby Barrett who shocked some states into reinstating executions. I want to tell her there was no way to stop the Remedies Act from going through, so we did the best we could. We limited its power. I want to tell her all these things, but I have a feeling Adrian is way past listening.

She pulls herself together. 'What about the circularity issue? I mean, if I go—' she pauses, blows her nose, and recollects herself '—if they execute me, whose head is that on? Who's the insurance policy against that if they're wrong?'

'There's no circularity issue. You know that, right?' It's a hard pill to force down, but it's true. We worded the Remedies Act so the buck had to stop somewhere, and it stops with the prosecutor. 'I'm so sorry.'

'Yeah. Sure you are. How about you go sit in the chair instead of me? You sorry enough to do that?'

My coffee goes down wrong and burns my throat. 'I thought Florida was a lethal injection state.'

'We were. Until eight years ago. Did *you* miss the headlines?'

'No. I just forgot. Sorry.' Of course Florida had outlawed lethal injection. Like the rest of the fifty states, it had suffered from appalling statistics on botched executions. There were stories of kinked tubes, collapsed veins, dosage mix-ups, unpredicted chemical reactions, technician ineptitude. Everything I've heard about what happens when this so-called humane method goes wrong makes the electric chair sound good.

Unless you're one of the men or women scheduled to sit in it.

The chair has its own stories. As do the gas chamber and the firing squad and the gallows. We kept on inventing a new and improved method, and we kept on finding a way to screw it up.

Adrian is still talking to me. Or at me. She's gone from lethal injection being legislated out of fashion, to how the new evidence in the Bantam case is probably nothing, and ends up unloading all her fear and hate onto me. A mountain of it.

'You think it wasn't supposed to go this way, right? So what was I supposed to do with Donald Bantam when his prints showed up all over the weapon and his semen was in the chick's cooch and we had evidence – good evidence – that he'd been playing the stalking game for six months? And the victim was pregnant. Pregnant. As in blessed is the fruit of thy freaking womb pregnant. Tell me, Justine. What was I supposed to do?' She doesn't wait for an answer. 'I guess I don't need to ask, do I?'

Adrian has gone almost hysterical, the pitch of her voice rising to a new high. 'You asked for death a few years back. Oh, yeah. I remember the Milford case. Everyone in the country does. All I can tell you is you better pray hard.'

'I think this call is over,' I say. But I'm still shaking. I can hear it in my voice.

'You're what? Forty-something? There's no statute of limitations on the Remedies Act, Justine, just like you wanted it. So enjoy the next half of your life waiting to see if some new evidence crawls out of the muck.'

She laughs again and ends the call at the same time Daniel walks into the kitchen in his bathrobe.

'Bad night?' he says.

'Bad everything. Three guesses who that was.' I go to fix him coffee and manage to drop the mug on the floor. It doesn't break; it splinters.

'The Milford woman?' he says and steers me over to a chair. Lately, it seems Daniel is constantly cleaning up one or another of my messes. And I don't expect a broken coffee mug will be the worst of them.

'No. The Kopinsky woman.'

His eyes widen.

'Look, I picked up your phone by mistake, I saw it was a Florida number, and I thought it was your friend. So I called it in case he needed to talk to you. You're right. She's a bitch.' As if I wouldn't be riding the bitch train with a Remedies Act case hanging over my head and every reporter in Jacksonville setting up camp outside my front door. 'You should call her. I think she's in trouble.'

Understatement of the decade.

Daniel leaves me for a few minutes to make his call. In the kitchen, with a fresh cup of coffee I no longer want, I think about what Adrian told me. No more lethal injection in Florida. Only Old Sparky. But even the electric chair has its quirks.

I know what can happen. Because I've witnessed death gone wrong twice in my life.

CHAPTER EIGHTEEN

Shortly after I graduated and took up my clerking job in Richmond, Ian drove south from Cambridge. We then continued further south to Emporia, Virginia, to witness the first of three executions we would attend in our lifetimes. The town was sleepy, being the second smallest in the Commonwealth, and with the unexpected chill on this early autumn night, you could almost call it comatose. Dead. I remember Ian held my hand most of the way, except for when a sudden drop in the speed limit or a particularly nasty curve in the road forced him to downshift.

'You sure you want to do this?' he asked again as we approached the State Police Headquarters. There were already a half-dozen people milling about and talking. A few drank steaming cups of coffee; a few smoked.

I didn't want to do what we were about to do. I was twenty-five and had never been inside an emergency room, let alone watched a human being die. My knowledge – and there was plenty of knowledge – was purely academic. By the time I had finished my last round of exams, I had an encyclopedia's worth of names and dates in my head. I could tell you which states used which methods and recite the preparation procedures for hangings, asphyxiations, shootings, and electrocutions. I knew the last twenty-four hours of a death row inmate's life down to the minute.

But in those last seconds before I exited Ian's car, I realized I didn't know anything.

There was a quick round of hand-shaking when we entered the State Police building. A tall and grave man named Jeffries took our identification, matched it to the list, and told us he was the liaison for the Department of Corrections. He would be with us every step of the way. At the time, I wondered if he might end up actually carrying me those last few steps toward the waiting prison van because my legs had gone to jelly.

Ian held my hand for the ten-minute drive from Emporia to the prison in Jarratt as well. We had left Richmond after an early dinner, driving down on an interstate lined with trees turning their colors. The sun had been shining then, and I found it hard to concentrate on anything but life. Now it was full dark, not even a sliver of moon to cut through the blackness, and this part of the state was never known for its light pollution. No one spoke along the way.

The execution of Tim Sully was scheduled for eleven o'clock, but we arrived well before that. Jeffries ushered the twelve of us – six reporters, four men I assumed were volunteer witnesses, and us – into a small building a stone's throw beyond the main prison gate. I was the only woman in our little band of onlookers.

'Okay, people,' Jeffries said. He was serious, but not in an intimidating way. Jeffries had the demeanor of a no-nonsense schoolteacher. We sat down in rigid, uncomfortable chairs, which only added to my psychological discomfort, and Jeffries began his briefing. 'This will take an hour, more or less. I'll ask you to keep your question until the end if that's okay with y'all.'

The only question on my mind was whether I could run back to the van and wait for this nightmare to be over. I looked at Ian helplessly. Not because I wanted help, only because I knew I had to do this, and nothing could help talk me out of it.

'One of the questions people always ask is whether the chair in the death chamber is the original,' Jeffries said. 'I can confirm that it is the same oak, built right here in 1908 by the inmates. The wiring, however, has been updated since that time.' It sounded like a bad joke, but we only nodded at the deadpan steadiness of Jeffries' voice.

'The first man to die in the Virginia electric chair,' Jeffries went on, 'was Henry Smith, also known as Oscar Perry. He was convicted of raping a seventy-five-year-old white woman in Portsmouth. Two weeks later, Winston Green sat in this same chair.'

I knew about Smith and Green. I knew about all of them. Smith might have been guilty. Green, whose crime was that he had allegedly touched a twelve-year-old white girl, was a victim of shitty Jim Crow-era presumptions that if you were black, you were probably guilty. And if mistakes were made and it turned out you weren't, well, you were black, and nobody gave a rat's ass. There was no DNA evidence, no fingerprints, no defense lawyer. And Green was mentally disabled.

'Only one female has ever been electrocuted in the Commonwealth,' Jeffries was saying.

By now, I had tuned him out. I was already thinking of Virginia Christian, a sixteen-year-old house servant on the wrong side of the race fence. The girl fought back when her employer threw a spittoon at her during an argument. The jury deliberated for twenty-three minutes. No one seemed to care the employer had a record of physically abusing the girl.

Of course, for people like Smith and Green and Christian, the electric chair was almost a kindness. The alternative was a lynch mob in a time when lynch mobs had a license to kill. The whole thing made me sick.

I whispered to Ian, 'You have any idea how many cases like Christian's weren't even counted as wrongful executions?'

'Lots?' he said.

'Hundreds.'

Now Jeffries had moved on to the chair itself, to the act. We listened as he ran off numbers, as he described the exact placement of the restraints and the recipe for mixing a saline solution for the sponges that would be secured to the prisoner's head and leg. A few reporters sitting in the front seats wiped their brows as if the room's temperature weren't an uncomfortable sixty degrees. Their faces had gone the color of paper.

'We'll take a short break now,' Jeffries said. 'If anyone needs to use the facilities, you'll find them out in the hall to your right.'

I stood, told Ian I'd be back in a few minutes, and went to the room marked 'Ladies' where I vomited up my dinner. Probably my lunch as well.

In hindsight, it had been the right thing to do.

A woman in uniform with a name tag that only said 'Birch' caught me as I came out. She said, 'Come with me, please,' and escorted me to a closet-sized room smaller than the toilet I had just used. The rest of the men, including Ian, were herded to another, larger space. I supposed women constituted a minority in the execution-witnessing population.

'Phone, pens, keys, any medications you're carrying,' Birch said brusquely after she closed the door behind her.

I handed over my purse and told her to keep it, but this wasn't enough. For ten minutes, I got a pat-down so thorough it was almost a massage. Then Birch started with my hair and did it all again, running her hands along the straps of my bra, the waistband of my jeans, and every seam in every piece of clothing I was wearing.

When it was all done, she said, 'You're good,' with the same clipped voice.

'Thanks,' I said.

When she saw I had passed the test, Birch changed her attitude. 'Ever been to one of these?'

I shook my head.

'It ain't pretty. Fact, it's about a hundred miles south of ugly. You sit down in the back of the booth, and if things get too rough, close your eyes and sing yourself a song. I'd tell you to remember to breathe, but nature'll take care of that for you. You'll probably wish it didn't.' She gave me a pat on the arm meant to be friendly. It still felt like a frisk.

I guessed some habits are strong, even when we don't want them to be.

Back in the hall, I waited for the men to finish. Ian came out first, and we stood side by side, keeping quiet. I don't think either one of us knew what to say. The reporters were the same. Birch came over to us and started passing out sharpened pencils and notepads to anyone with a press pass.

At ten-thirty, we headed back to the van with Jeffries. It drove us through the inner perimeter and gave me a look at the bleakness of the grounds. Briefly, I wondered what it must be like to have this shithole as your last view.

On the short ride to the death chamber, housed in a low and flat structure known as 'Hellville' to the inmates, my thoughts turned to Tim Sully. And to the young schoolteacher he had attacked and left to die. Hellville sounded like the right place for him.

Still, I asked myself if I could ever be sure enough of anything to kill another human.

'You can back out if you want, Jussie,' Ian said as we stepped down from the van for the second time tonight. 'No one's going to think any less of you.'

'I'll think less of me,' I said.

He smiled and let it go. Ian knew this was necessary. Fastballs in the form of questions had already started flinging themselves at me during talks. They mainly came from the pro-death side, and I dodged them, but once in a while, some eager undergrad would squeeze through the crowd and ask me, wide-eyed, if I'd ever seen an execution. With the audio setups, those questions meant my answers reached everyone in the venue. Whether I wanted them to or not.

Jeffries held the door to Hellville open as we walked through. His lips moved as if he were taking a head count, making sure none of us wandered off toward the other buildings. I wanted to tell him he needn't worry.

And then we were inside.

What I saw first upon entering the viewing room wasn't the polished oak chair or the wires or the leather restraints. I saw the clock on the wall, marching along the minutes that remained until midnight. I fixed myself on its larger hand as Jeffries told us we could take a seat if we liked. I was watching the last minutes of a man's life tick by.

Ian gave me a look, but I only shook my head. I felt lost in a different body, and all I could think about was what I would do and how I would act if these minutes were my last. Would I be able to walk from my single cell to the room where I would die? Would I burst into tears? Would I stare at the floor or look toward the one-way mirrored glass of the executioner's booth, silently cursing the invisible man or woman on the other side? For the ten long minutes we waited in this room, I tried to put myself in Tim Sully's shoes. And I found out a thing: I couldn't. I would live and die without ever knowing what it was like to be him in the last moments of his life.

Not that we had anything in common, Sully and I. When the guards walked him into the room, the first thing I noticed was the jailhouse ink covering every visible patch of skin on his body. Ugly green-black letters and symbols made his knuckles seem as if they had been broken multiple times. His head, shaved, was a scabby mess of sores, and his limbs hadn't seen the sun for years. They weren't white, exactly, more the color of rancid butter. Yellowish and sickly, with the tell-tale tracks of decades of drug use. His left leg was bare and also shaved. He stared into the glass at us with blank, oily eyes that were the eyes of a lifeless toy.

The preparations were quick and practiced, and even here, Sully took on the role of a doll. Arm up. Arm on the chair. Strap on the arm. Four men repeated the process with the other arm before moving to Sully's bleached leg, adjusting more straps, placing saline-soaked sponges and electrodes on the targets of his skin. I thought I might go mad if the process took any longer.

And there was the hum. The constant, monotonous drone of the current that would release itself into Tim Sully's body.

I squeezed Ian's hand and swallowed, finding myself out of spit, as one of the attendants placed a second sponge and a gruesome-looking helmet on the head of the man in the chair.

143

A black hood went on over this, but I couldn't unsee the contraption. Or that final look from the eyes of the condemned man.

It might have been now when I stopped looking at the clock. The execution chamber was a mélange of gray and black, and my own eyes moved automatically to the only speck of color on the other side of the glass viewing window.

The red phone. The last resort.

Was Sully resigned? Or, like me, was he also willing it to ring?

I suppose I'll never know.

Just then, Jeffries was called out of the viewing room. When he returned, he wasn't alone. A middle-aged couple entered, both of their faces almost as pale as Tim Scully's bare left leg. From the faint lines on the woman's face, she might have been in her forties, but her eyes held the tired look of a woman old enough to be waiting for her own death. Jeffries introduced them as the parents of the victim, Mr and Mrs Sanderson.

The man took his seat, leaning toward his wife. 'I hope it goes wrong,' he whispered in a stage voice loud enough for the rest of us to hear as soon as Jeffries had walked back to secure the door. 'I hope the bastard burns like a piece of toast.'

I can't say I was hoping for the same, but I stayed quiet. The warden was asking if Sully had any final words.

A whisper of breath came through the speaker above us. Sully did have some final words. Two of them.

'I'm sorry,' Sully said.

At the same time – the same second – as Mr Sanderson stated that he was not a bit sorry, an earsplitting bang nearly knocked me out of my chair. Ian flinched but didn't jump back the way a few of the reporters did. In front of me, Mrs Sanderson screamed once before lowering her head. Her husband put one hand on her jaw and the other on the back of her neck, forcing her head up.

'Watch it,' he said. 'Watch them fry our baby's killer.'

Mrs Sanderson began to sob. Mr Sanderson released his hold on her neck and tapped his hand on her head. I suppose it was meant to be a reassuring pat, but it didn't look reassuring to me.

And then the second bang happened. The man in the oak chair, by now dead for some seconds, convulsed for another half minute before everything went quiet, and the blinds on the viewing window drew closed. The next words from the speaker were simply, 'The legal execution of Timothy Sully has taken place.'

And that was how Tim Sully died.

Looking back, what happened to him was a mercy compared to the second execution I would see.

CHAPTER NINETEEN

As soon as Daniel is through with his call, Susan appears at the back door with the boys in tow. Whatever magic she used on my son seems to have worked. He runs into the house, throws his arms around me, and then does the same to Daniel.

'We're getting new Star Wars plates!' Jonathan squeals.

I throw Susan a look and mouth, 'I'll pay you back,' while the boys are distracted by one of Daniel's always-ready card tricks.

'Don't bother,' Susan says. 'I called Amazon, told them I was you, and said the stuff arrived in pieces. They're sending out another set pronto.'

Thanks to a lie, the magical ability of Amazon to absorb its losses, and the postal service, Jonathan loves me again. I'll take the love whichever way I can. Jonathan has always been more than a son. He's a living piece of Ian.

'And,' Tommy says, 'we're going to the zoo! Want to come, Mr Daniel?'

Mr Daniel does.

'I can't make it,' I tell them, pouring Susan a cup of coffee and avoiding Daniel's eyes. Since I'm unable to figure out the optimal way to tell my current lover that I need to visit my dead husband, I decide on a fabrication. 'I have some errands to run. And there's a laundry mountain in Jonathan's room that some record-seeking climber might try to scale if I don't take care of it today.'

'Jussie,' Daniel says.

'Errands, honey. I said errands. And laundry.' Before he can say anything else, I ask Jonathan what he had for dinner last night. I already know Susan fixed them chicken nuggets and fries, but changing the subject gives my errand-running excuse a sense of finality.

'Nuggets. And fries with ketchup,' Jonathan says. 'And then we had a drawing contest.' He turns, bolts out the back door, and retrieves his backpack from Susan's car. 'I made this.'

I take the construction paper and pretend to study it carefully, sliding my glasses to the end of my nose, playing the erudite critic, as I always do when Jonathan brings me a sample of his art. 'This is good, kid.'

'You think so?'

'Better than a lot of the stuff in museums.' It is, actually. Jonathan's six-year-old fingers and a few crayons have done what art is supposed to do. They've made me feel better.

Daniel checks the drawing over my shoulder, one arm around my waist, the other resting on Jonathan's shoulders as if we were staring into a mirror image of the three of us. In the picture – and in life – we're smiling. We're not wearing lemon-yellow and black stripes, and we don't have antennae, but otherwise, it's pretty accurate.

'I think you should dress like this at your wedding,' Jonathan says.

'Really?' I say.

'I'll do it if you will,' Daniel says, squeezing me tighter. Then he whispers in my ear, 'I'm dead serious, by the way.'

And like that, the moment is over.

The boys want the zoo. Susan demands more caffeine, hands over her car keys, and asks if I can gas it up because she didn't have time this morning. Daniel kisses me and gathers up his phone and wallet.

When they pull out of the driveway in Daniel's car, waving through the windows, I know I love these people more than anything. Maybe even as much as I loved Ian.

I don't mind driving Susan's civilian tank of a Volvo to Hollywood Cemetery. The car acts as a shroud, providing a layer of disguise, and these days, pretending I'm someone else makes me feel safe. The radio doesn't work – I don't think it has in years – so I hum to myself as the road takes me through town and toward the banks of the James River.

Ian and I hadn't exactly made burial plans for either of us. It's not something you do in your forties. We went as far as stating that we both favored cremation, but Ian had quietly made that video of himself, left it on his computer for me to find, and I knew from it that he wanted to be in a place with trees. In my shattered state of mind after his death, I couldn't do much more than search Google for cemeteries in Richmond. Hollywood came up first, I verified it had a bunch of big-ass trees, and that was that. Funny how things that seem complicated end up being so straightforward. I don't think I realized until later that the remains of twenty-eight Confederate generals were buried beneath the sprawling grounds. But hey, a grieving girl can be forgiven.

The woman in the gatehouse waves me on, expecting I'll take the Volvo through the cemetery roads. It spans 135 acres, and the walk to the small chapel where Ian now lives is nearly a mile.

'I can do with some fresh air,' I tell her, then back up and pull into one of a few parking spaces, waving again as I pass the gatehouse for the second time.

'You take care, honey,' she says, her voice full of Southern charm and sympathy. I almost want to ask her what it's like to watch hundreds of people, all of them grieving, pass her by every day. But all I say is, 'Thanks. You too,' and walk on.

A family of three is ahead of me. Father, mother, and a boy who looks four or five. We're all walking at that uncomfortable pace where the people up front feel like they're being chased, and the person behind isn't going quite fast enough to pass comfortably. I decide to slow down, but I can still hear every word they say.

'I miss Grandma,' the boy says. His father nods. His mother, from the glassy-eyed look, misses Grandma more.

'She's in a good place,' the woman says.

'Where?'

'Heaven.'

I can tell she doesn't believe this.

'Are you gonna go to heaven, Dad?' the boy asks.

This elicits a soft, appropriate-for-a-cemetery chuckle from the father. 'Only if I'm very, very good. And not for a long time.'

The family turns right at the next junction.

I want to run after them, kneel in front of the little boy, and tell him to make every day count. Because it might, as his father said, be a long time. It also might be tonight, or tomorrow, or next week. It might happen when Dad goes for Greek takeout, calling a cheery 'Back in a jiffy!' as he closes the door behind him, the door that will be rapped on by two uniformed policemen in about an hour's time.

I continue straight along the trail, thinking I should have gone to the goddamned zoo.

The interior of Palmer Chapel is quiet and cold, well suited to a place of death. And Ian's niche, marked only with his name and two dates, is low on the wall. I curl up next to it, tracing the engraved characters, letting heat transfer from me to the marble until my fingers go numb. At some point, a middle-aged couple walks in, whispers, and leaves. I'm alone again with Ian.

Are you gonna go to heaven, Dad? Not for a long time.

It's a question Jonathan was never able to ask his father, but I wonder what the answer might have been. Knowing Ian, I'd expect rolled eyes at the suggestion of an afterlife, or a sarcastic, 'Not if your mother has anything to say about it.'

We hadn't planned a family. Like many, maybe like the couple I saw on the trail, we danced around the issue. Were we parent material? Is the world too unkind a place? Can two people be a family, or does a family require something more? In the end, we decided to give it a go, figuring we had far too much love to keep it all to ourselves.

Getting pregnant is supposed to be easy. Look at the world population. It was anything but easy for us, and the more we tried and failed, the more we wanted it to work. Susan told us we needed to relax.

'Stop thinking about it so much, guys,' she said one night at dinner. 'And stop wanting it so badly. You'll see. The second you stop seeing sex as some desperate act, Jussie will find herself knocked up. Maybe with twins. Happens all the time.'

'Easy for you to say,' I told her.

Susan took my phone and deleted every ovulation app and pregnancy tracking app and *What to Expect When You're Expecting* app right there at the dinner table. 'I mean it, Sis.' Then she patted her stomach, which looked a little less taut than usual. 'Worked for me.'

So I relaxed. Mostly. I still had visions of a growing baby bump, of Ian in the delivery room wiping sweat from my forehead, of the look of absolute wonder on his face when his son or daughter announced their presence with a loud and lovely wail. I saw us in bed with a tiny part of us, not talking, not saying a word, only loving that little creature. I dreamed of soccer matches and lunch boxes, of graduations and engagements and weddings. I imagined Ian and I would grow old and look into each other's eyes and say, 'Best thing we ever did.'

I didn't imagine I would be here in this crypt, saying to a husband made of ashes, 'What we've missed, Ian. What we've missed.'

When the pain of being here becomes too much for me, I run my fingers over Ian's plaque, feeling the engraved date that should have been forty, maybe fifty years into the future.

'I'm with someone now,' I tell him. 'Someone who's good for me and good for Jonathan.'

I think I hear Ian tell me it's all right, that the important thing is for me to move on and take care of our son.

'But what if Jake Milford was innocent?' I say. 'How do I take care of our son then?'

I wait a long time, but Ian doesn't answer.

CHAPTER TWENTY

When Susan calls to tell me she and Daniel have taken the boys to Mr Taco for a post-zoo snack, the clock in her car blinks 4:30. I'm far outside the city, somewhere in the vineyard-dotted country between Richmond and Charlottesville. Just driving. Keeping my eyes on the double yellow line in the road as if it might lead me to a new place free of laws and crimes and prisons. My own private Oz or Shangri-la.

It doesn't. Once I make a U-turn in the drive of a small farm, the double yellow line leads me back home.

But back home looks like a murder scene.

I leave the road and head up my driveway, nearly swerving Susan's clunker into a row of boxwood.

The bay window in front yawns open like a shark's mouth with teeth of jagged glass. My front door, which used to be white, is a mess of red spray paint inviting me [*you cunt*] to perform certain auto-sexual acts [*go fuck yourself*]. The car I didn't drive today slouches on four flat tires, its windows smashed. Pieces of Mercedes-Benz litter the driveway: a steering wheel, a battery, two visors. The makeup mirror of one visor seems to wink at me salaciously, inviting me forward.

No, thanks.

I throw the car into reverse and back down the drive. This time, I swerve into the boxwoods and Susan's car stalls. If I had it in me to curse Ian, I'd curse him for moving us out here into the middle of nowhere. Right now, I want to be in a McMansion, the type with two feet between it and the houses on either side that looks directly into the backyard of its architectural twin. It's ironic how privacy and safety can be mutually exclusive.

My first call is to Daniel, telling him not to come back to my place with Susan and the boys. It's hurried, my voice cracks, and I hang up before he can ask any questions. My second call is to the police. This one is interrupted by a series of badly typed text messages from Daniel and Susan. *U Ok?* and *WTF* and *Call me NOW* flash across my phone at regular intervals while I get bounced from one party to another until, ten minutes later, I'm talking to someone who actually has the authority to act. I'm told to stay in my vehicle, drive to the nearest public place – the dispatcher suggests a space near the entrance of Sam's Club – and wait. She takes my name and a description of Susan's car before hanging up.

I reverse, I drive, and I drag a clump of extirpated boxwood three miles before pulling into the crowded lot of the super-supermarket and parking illegally in one of the handicapped spaces.

Then I wait forty-five minutes.

Daniel is on fire when I call him back. I can't tell if he's angry with me or only frightened out of his wits. Apparently, this kind of vandalism doesn't happen in the cute little shire he comes from.

'They did what? Jussie, tell me you're okay,' he says.

'They broke my house,' I say. 'And my car.'

'Bloody hell. Where are you now?'

'In the dubious safety of a Sam's Club parking lot. Waiting for the police.'

'I'm on my way.'

As he says this, two cruisers turn off the main road and crawl toward me. I lower the window and put a hand out. 'No, don't,' I say. 'Can you and Susan hang on to the boys for a while? I'll try to be out of here as soon as I can.' I say this knowing the questioning and inspection of my house will take at least two hours. With luck. Without any luck – and it seems to be running low these days – I'll be tied up until tonight.

Daniel says he'll take the kids back to his place and fix them up with snacks and a movie. Before he ends the call, I can hear Susan going absolute batshit, wanting to know what's going on, when I'll be free, and what I'm doing for dinner. She's a pain in the ass of a sister-in-law, but she cares. Right now, that's enough.

The first cruiser pulls up alongside Susan's Volvo, and the uniformed young woman behind the wheel asks me her first question. 'Do you realize you're in a handicapped space?'

Why, yes. Yes, I do. 'You said "by the entrance". The only spaces near the entrance are handicapped. Where exactly did you want me to park?' Already I can see the next few hours of my life will require some serious self-editing.

The officer's name is Winsley, a young woman I haven't ever come across through work. She directs me to an empty area at the far end of the lot, and the two cruisers follow. Winsley gets out first, motions to the other car to stay put, and opens the driver's side door of the Volvo. 'You're Justine Callaghan? Or is it Boucher?' She pops a piece of chewing gum into her mouth and starts working on it with a fervor that looks like it might hurt.

'Officially Callaghan. I don't go by Boucher anymore.'

She notes this on a pad and frowns as if I'm making her life difficult. 'Address?'

I give it to her, but Winsley continues to stare at her notepad. 'You said "Callaghan", right?' I nod. 'I've heard about you. Nice move on the Charlotte Thorne case. That woman is a monster. You one of those soft lefties who thinks the American taxpayers should cover a lifetime's worth of room and board for people like her?'

Winsley's partner chimes in and drawls, 'Looks like one of 'em to me.'

I'd like to ask what a soft leftie is supposed to look like, but my better instincts tell me to shut the hell up.

'Okay,' Winsley says to the other car. 'You check out the house. Ms Callaghan and I will meet you there in—' she looks at her watch '—half an hour tops.' Then, turning to me as the second cruiser pulls away: 'Where were you when the vandalism occurred?'

I don't see how my whereabouts matter, but I tell her I went to the cemetery. 'Then I went for a drive. At about eleven-thirty this morning.'

'Why?'

'Why? I don't know. Take in the spring air? See the horse farms? Is there a particular answer you're looking for?'

She scribbles another note and cracks her gum. 'Mm-hm. And when did you arrive home?'

'Five. Five-thirty, maybe.'

'You went for a drive for six hours.' It isn't a question, but Winsley's voice has an element of wonder in it. 'Did you stop for lunch?'

'Is that relevant?' I say. At the same time, I realize playing the prosecutor with a cop will not win me any points. Her face, already hard, has turned stony. 'I mean, I didn't. I just drove.'

'Mm-hm.' She points to the Volvo. 'You said your car was damaged. Is this a second vehicle?'

I tell her it belongs to my sister-in-law.

'And where is she?'

'At the zoo with her son and mine. And another friend,' I say, not liking the third-degree interrogation, as if I'm the one worth investigating.

'I see. So we have a beautiful spring day, your sister-in-law takes your son to the zoo, and you don't go.' Winsley makes another note. 'Interesting. Tell me, what made you skip a Sunday outing and go driving alone? Because, see, that doesn't make a lot of sense to me. Not when a hot-shot prosecutor like you probably doesn't get much time with her kid. I'd think you'd want to spend the day with him. But you went for a six-hour drive alone.' More scribbling. More gum-chewing. 'Where exactly did you drive?'

I am so not liking the tone of her questions. 'Toward Charlottesville.'

She responds with another monosyllabic grunt. 'Charlottesville's an hour away. Seems to me that if you drove six hours, you could have made it to West Virginia. Maybe gotten across the state line into Pennsylvania. Unless you stopped somewhere, but you said you didn't.'

The radio in her cruiser crackles, and a voice comes through. 'Broken window, some nasty red graffiti on the front door, and a wrecked Mercedes. No sign of entry or further damage. Over.'

'Got it,' Winsley's partner says. 'We'll be there soon. Over and out.'

Then she rechecks her notes and turns to me. 'Can you help

me out here? Because I'm confused. You didn't go to the zoo, you drove for six hours, you didn't stop anywhere, and you made it all the way to somewhere between your home and a city that's an easy hour from here.' For the first time since she got out of her cruiser, Winsley smiles.

She knows she's winning.

It's a feeling I'm not accustomed to, being on this side of the question-and-answer playing field. Under Ian's sweatshirt, my skin starts to prickle. 'I said I didn't stop for lunch. Not that I didn't stop.' This is the truth. After leaving Hollywood Cemetery, I made it halfway to Charlottesville. I never made it much farther than that. At one point, my hands shook so badly I was forced to pull over. If I didn't, I'd end up tumbling the car off the road, and even Volvos have their limits. So instead of driving, I sat staring at a herd of cows until their shadows grew long and the farmer finally rounded them up and into his barn.

'I asked, "Where did you stop?"' Winsley says.

'I don't know. A farm. A vineyard maybe.'

'Ah. Lots of those places out in the country. Maybe you took a tour? Signed up for a tasting?' She fishes around in her cop utility belt and draws out a small plastic case that looks like an ancient cell phone with a tube sticking out of its side. 'Could you do me a small favor and blow into this?'

'You're kidding.'

'Not at all.' Chew. Crack. Pop. The gum is driving me batshit.

I blow a zero into the breathalyzer, and Winsley pouts like a kid who just dropped her ice cream cone.

'Okie-dokie. You passed. I'd give you a lollipop but I'm fresh out.' She puts the breathalyzer back in her belt. Right next to her sidearm. 'Did you see anyone while you were out today? Anyone at all?' The notebook is out again.

'No,' I lie.

'Here's what I'm thinking. Maybe you did that job to your own house, Ms Callaghan.'

'What the fuck?' The words come out before I can stop them.

'No need to take that tone with me. We're all trying to help you here. It's a little hard for me to believe you, though. A crazy story about wanting to drive but not really driving. You didn't stop anywhere. You didn't go to a restaurant or see anyone.' She looks down at my shoes, the shiny Bally loafers. 'Doesn't look like you went for a walk in the country. Not with those fancy guys.' Then her attention turns to my clothes, and she points at a spot on the cuff of my sweatshirt. 'Plus, you got some red paint on you.'

'It's old. This is – was – one of my husband's work shirts.'

'Uh-huh.' Winsley touches the material with the end of her pen. 'Much as I don't like to say it, Ms Callaghan, I'm having a difficult time understanding how you spent your day.'

I'm having a difficult time understanding how you spent your day.

All at once, I feel sick. The words bring it on. They were the same words I used when Jake Milford sat on the witness stand six years ago.

Death Row Inmate #39384

Someone told me once there were over a billion people staying in hotels every night in the United States. That's one-eighth of the population of the whole world. Kind of crazy when you think of it that way.

With all that checking in and checking out, and room service ordering and sleeping, and working and fucking, it's no wonder none of the staff came forward. Not that I wanted them to, but I thought at least one person would have seen my picture in the newspaper and gone, 'Oh, man! That dude was here on the day they say he killed a kid.' Then that one person would have run to the phone and called the police and told the whole story, and I wouldn't be where I am now.

I'd be home with Emily and Jake Junior, watching the tube, eating popcorn, drinking root beer.

I'd be saved.

The problem is this: if they recognized me, they would have recognized her. And now we're talking major shitstorm. For both of us.

Before I spill the beans, I need to talk about the accident, about the first time I traded one life for another life and the first time I understood what regret really means.

It was early February, colder than a witch's tit after a short vacation from winter, and me and my brothers decided to go play down by the lake. Momma called us her three little stooges, sort of a mashup between the pig story and the crazy guys on that old show. I didn't know what a stooge was, but that was all right. I loved my momma, and if she wanted to go around calling me a little stooge, then it couldn't be such a bad thing.

Whatever we were, we were different.

Benny was the oldest, two years older than me, but I was in the third grade by that winter and had caught up to him. Kris had gone from preschool to real school in the fall, and he was doing a pretty good job of catching up, too, because we both took after our dad, wherever the hell he was these days. Benny was more like Momma, thin and small, but with a heart of gold.

'Don't you boys go on that ice,' Momma called as we headed out the door, bundled against the wind with marbles in our pockets that rattled like the chatter of teeth when we walked. 'And you watch out for your little brother.' That one was meant for me. Benny might be older, but he was afraid of Kris more than I was.

The lake had a glaze on it like sugar icing, all white and shiny, catching the sun so it looked more like a frozen carpet than a lake. I took one of my marbles from my pocket and flung it out about ten feet, just to see it bounce and roll before coming to a stop.

Kris said, 'That's no good. I got a rock.' And he threw the

rock as far as he could. It hit the ice with a sharp crack, but it stayed there on top of that icing sugar blanket. 'I'm goin' out. You coming, B-b-b-benny?'

And this was another thing. Kris wasn't only big for his age, he was mean. By seven years old, my little brother had gotten sent home from school twice. You name a schoolyard crime, and Kris had done it. Kicking, biting, punching. I guess he took after our dad in more than just size.

Benny stood there on the bank, shivering even in what we all called turbo-winter clothes. He shook his head. Benny never much liked speaking when Kris was around, and he never much liked being in Kris's company when I wasn't there to protect him.

'F-f-f-fraidy cat,' Kris called, and stepped out onto the ice blanket. 'See, nothing to be scared of. I'm gonna go skating.'

Skating, for us, was mainly sliding around on our boots. Poor man's skating.

Benny called back. 'Y-y-you sh-sh-sh-shouldn't.' He stopped there.

'Come on, Kris Kringle,' I said. 'Ma's gonna pitch a fit if you fall in.'

'Aw, bullshit,' my younger brother said. And he slide-skated further out. 'See? Easy-peasy Japanesy!'

I noticed something then. I said the lake looked like it was coated with a sugary glaze, but it wasn't all that way. More like a blind man had slapped on icing in patches so that some parts were solid white and some you could see the dark of the cake showing through. I called out again, but Kris was far out into the middle now, sliding backwards, waving his elbows in a funky chicken kind of a move.

The dark patch was just behind him.

I ran down to the side of the lake, not watching my feet. Sure enough, I fell, but worse than that, my left leg didn't land on ground when I scrambled back up. I stood there, looking first at Benny, then at Kris, and my leg was cold. I'll tell you something, cold isn't the opposite of hot; cold is the same as hot. It burns.

Before I knew it, Benny was running. He flew past me and started screaming at the top of his lungs. No stutter, only clear and clipped words: Stop. Don't. Thin ice.

And then everything started happening.

I pulled my soaking leg, now numb, from the freezing water. Kris laughed. Benny shouted and flung himself forward. There was a cracking sound, like fabric being torn, as the ice that wasn't really ice swallowed up my two brothers. I raced toward them, slipping and falling, crying tears I hadn't cried since I was a baby.

Both Kris and Benny were flailing now. The laughing and shouting stopped, replaced by wordless gurgles. I watched as their hands either slipped off the patches of semi-solid ice they grabbed or came away with a thin slab of frozen water. I screamed for them both, but the lake was a mile from nowhere. That's why we came here. To do kid stuff in private.

Finally, Benny managed a word. 'Kris,' he said.

Stupidly, I thought about the *Titanic*. I thought about how the men stayed behind and let the women and children board the lifeboats. Well, some of the men, I guess. Some were cowards and probably scrambled to save their own skins. I thought if we were in a *Titanic* movie right now, Benny would be the one saving the women and the children. Kris would be the coward.

And me? I'd be the lifeboat.

I slid onto my belly and stretched out, the way they always say to do in the Boy Scouts. Not that we were scouts, but there were kids in school whose parents had enough money for the uniforms and stuff. It had something to do with making your weight spread around so that there was no single point on the ice that took the whole load. Inch by inch, I crab-crawled forward, trying not to disturb what was fast becoming thinner ice as I went. I held out both of my arms, one toward Benny and one toward Kris.

Kris grabbed for both of them.

He was heavy. Not fat, just goddamned big for his age. Like one of those little terrier dogs that's all muscle, and his soaked snow gear didn't help. It was a time pulling him out of the water. It was so much time that when I had him on safe ground, Benny had stopped thrashing and gone under.

I saved my younger brother's life on a cold February morning at the lake. I think if I've ever committed a crime, that was it.

So the story about where I was when Caleb Church got killed is tricky.

CHAPTER TWENTY-ONE

Officer Winsley spent another hour and a half dicking around with me back at my house before she drove off. Now, I'm on the road to Daniel's, squinting at headlights as they approach in the oncoming lanes. I've only just realized that my calorie consumption for the day hovers somewhere around fifty.

I don't think Winsley believed I had vandalized my own property – you'd have to be living under a rock not to have noticed the Justine-hate that's been in the news this weekend. But the more she quizzed me, the more apparent it was that she was enjoying herself. She kept up with the questions and the confused looks, and at the end of it all I was too tired to get bitchy with the woman. I called my handyman and asked him to board up the front window and repaint the door. Then I put in the claim with my auto insurance company for the damage to the Mercedes, and packed two suitcases full of clothes for Jonathan and me. When these minor tasks were out of the way, I headed out of the Village and toward Daniel's house in the Fan District, a lively part of downtown Richmond that makes my neighborhood look like a retirement community.

The clock in the Volvo glows nine when I finally pull into a street space and kill the engine. Still, I wait a full ten minutes before getting out and starting up the flagstone walk to the old Victorian's front door. I need a happy face, but I can't seem to find one. I wonder if I'll ever find one again.

I should have left the city after Ian died. I could have packed up, driven across the country, and settled in a new place. Arizona, maybe. Somewhere with sun so strong and warm you can't help but go through your days smiling. I called a few realtors, even started that frenzied pre-move exercise of running around the house with a Hefty bag and decluttering. In the end, I couldn't leave. I couldn't sign the listing agreement in the same way I couldn't clean up Ian's office and turn it into my own.

My more serious mistake was not leaving after the Milford case.

What a crock of shit. The mistake had nothing to do with staying or leaving.

Daniel must have heard my car door closing because he's already in the doorway when I reach it. Behind him, Susan makes one of her worried faces, her eyes and mouth in the shape of three perfect Os.

'I'm all right,' I say, calming her. 'Peter's boarding up the damage to the house tonight and the insurance company has already come for the car. No one got in.'

'Bloody hell,' Daniel says and takes the suitcases. The house smells of tomatoes, garlic, and pungent basil – typical Daniel food. I think I've fallen in love with him all over again. 'I put the boys in the guest room upstairs. They're zonked out. Susan's going to stay on the sleeper sofa in the telly room.'

'Susan's not going to make it to the telly room if she doesn't go there right the hell now,' my sister-in-law says. 'Sure you're okay?'

'Absolutely.' I hug her, tighter than usual, and she comes back with the same.

'No one deserves this, Justine.' I'm expecting her to add something typically Susan-like, along the lines of 'Except for you,' but she doesn't. She only holds on tight and strokes my hair with a gentle hand.

I do deserve this, I think. I very much do.

Once she heads upstairs, Daniel takes me into his arms. 'Food first, then I want to hear everything. Absolutely everything.' The way he's looking at me, I know he isn't talking about my house.

If it's possible to eat without tasting a single bite, I've achieved that. The pasta looks and smells wonderful, but when it goes down, I know it's nothing more than fuel. After I've emptied a bowl barely enough to satisfy a cat, Daniel clears the dinner plates and pours me a solid two fingers of whiskey.

'Drink this. Not all at once,' he says, and sits me down on the sofa. 'And tell me about your day.'

'I went to see Ian this morning. At the cemetery.'

'I know. You forget you're talking to one of England's premier hunters of international banking fraudsters. And I do that on a lot less evidence than a pair of puffy eyes. Beautiful as they may be.' He lets go of my hand and waggles his fingers at me. 'The Great Daniel knows all!' Then he turns serious again. 'So what prompted that?'

'You'll be angry.'

His eyes shift towards the coffee table, where Jonathan's drawing of the happy bumblebee family lies among a scattering of legal notepads and financial statements. It's been embellished since I saw it this morning. Now Mama Bee sports a lacy veil and a bouquet of daisies. Papa Bee has a top hat, jauntily cocked

169

to one side. Daniel lifts his hand away from mine. 'It was what I said about getting married, wasn't it? Stupid of me.'

I laugh for the first time in what seems like years and lean into him. 'I'm the one who was stupid. For going to meet Emily Milford the other day. I'm sorry, darling. I didn't want to get into it last night. And then, after the news about Adrian, I didn't want to get into it at all. It's the last lie I'll ever tell you.'

It won't be, but it sounds like the right thing to say.

'I'll call it delayed truth-telling if you promise not to meet her again,' he says, drawing me closer. 'So, did she rip into you in person?'

I shake my head and lean further into the space between Daniel's arm and chest, close enough to hear his heartbeat. 'I wish she had. Oh, Daniel, I wish she had.'

'Go on, then.'

I've always been a strong woman, not the kind to fold, but when you're tucked inside the safe place of flesh and love and genuine concern, things have a way of coming out. Whether you want them to or not.

'Emily Milford says she found something,' I say. My eyes close, and I go on, partly out loud, partly in my mind. I'm floating somewhere between then and now, between Ian being alive and Ian being dead, between grieving wife and soon-to-be mother. It's confusing, this state of being. But I try. I need to gather my thoughts first.

I wanted to die, I think.

Most people don't know what it's like to be married one minute and widowed the next. It can happen with a phone call or a knock on the door. It can happen like the snap of a finger. There's shock and there's pain and there's disbelief. And, speaking of belief, forget about those Kübler-Ross stages. Denial, anger, acceptance, whatever. They come in jumbles; they weave in and out of one another. There's no progression, only recursion and confusion. In the morning, I could say, 'I'll go on. I'll survive this.' In the late morning, I'd tell a different lie, maybe more truth than lie, when I said, 'I don't want to live without him.' Grief isn't a journey from one point to another. It's a goddamned labyrinth without a thread to lead you toward the exit.

There was no take-back, I think.

When Ian left me I was pregnant by barely a breath. My little boy might have been the size of a dust mote, maybe smaller than that. I had no symptoms, no hints, nothing to make me think I was anything but on my own. I believed Ian, and every trace of him, was gone.

But Susan had been right all along. The moment I stopped stressing about whether I'd get pregnant, I did. It was a week after I signed off on Jake Milford's case that I found out.

And a week was seven days too late.

I pour all of this out in one long and twisting tale. Daniel listens without speaking, and when I have nothing more to say, he envelops me in his arms. We sit in absolute silence, listening to the quiet sway of the hall clock's pendulum. I tell him about Emily, about her finding something, about her uncertainty. I tell him about the ghosts who visit me at night, about the first gruesome electrocution I witnessed, about the second – which was more than I could bear. I tell him every detail of my past and every fear that haunts me in the present.

Including the fear that he'll want nothing more to do with me after this evening.

I'm wrong.

Daniel doesn't ask questions and doesn't try to soothe me with words. We stay like this, folded into one another, for a long time. When his phone rings, he moves to silence it without answering, but I see the area code on the screen and recognize it as a Florida number.

'You should answer it,' I say. It's not that I want to break the spell between us, but I've got Adrian Kopinsky on my mind. I need to know what's going on. I need to be a part of it.

As soon as I think the words, I regret them. There are two ways to be a part of what's going on with Adrian.

'Curt?' Daniel says. His voice is a little sleepy, thicker than normal.

I wait, listening to his half of the conversation.

'I see,' he says. 'Oh, Christ. I see. Does she have representation?'

Curt's voice is barely audible.

'I see. And yeah, I know she can be a bitch,' Daniel says. 'But this isn't right. How sure are they about the bloke they have in custody?'

What Curt says sounds like 'dead sure'.

'What is it?' I mouth.

Daniel holds a hand up. Curt's talking fast now, and I can't make out the words anymore.

'Timeline?' Daniel says. There's more muddled sound. 'I see.'

I leave Daniel on the sofa, run to the downstairs hall bathroom, and throw up my meager dinner.

CHAPTER TWENTY-TWO

The second execution Ian and I attended was a lethal injection, a method touted as painless and humane when it was first introduced. We were both ten years older than when we had witnessed the first killing. We were also happily married, if unhappily up to our ears in work and house debt. We drove down from Richmond, handed over our identification at the State Police Headquarters, and boarded a prison van to Jarratt. I wondered at the time if it was the same van.

Once again, twelve of us were on board. Eight reporters and two other volunteers besides Ian and myself. Once again, Jeffries was our chaperone for the evening. He filled us in as to what we would see while we sat in hard folding chairs. As before, he was pleasant in a serious kind of way. He reminded me of an undertaker, all smiles masking a gruesome job.

'This will be quick, folks,' Jeffries said. 'To be completely honest, there won't be much for you to see.' He looked at the reporters as if apologizing for the lack of exciting visuals. 'But that is the point. Lethal injection is the most sensible option, and I'm quite confident it will render all other forms of execution obsolete.' He went on to describe the process.

'The condemned will enter the death chamber already secured

to a gurney,' Jeffries said. 'Once the condemned is in place, two intravenous tubes are inserted, one into each arm, and a saline drip begins.'

One of the reporters, the only other woman in our group, raised her hand.

'I'll take all your questions afterward,' Jeffries told her. 'Let's get through this and see if some of them are answered, okay?'

The reporter nodded.

'Three drugs will be introduced when the warden signals the execution may be carried out.' He looked at each of us in turn as he spoke. 'Now, this is important. Some of you may have come here thinking that it's just one shot and one chemical. It isn't. The lethal drug without a previously administered anesthetic and muscle relaxant would be anything but humane. And, despite certain views to the contrary, we are not barbarians here. We are carrying out justice according to the law.'

Some law, I wanted to say, but kept my mouth shut. At least this evening's death would be gentler than the one I watched a year ago.

'States vary in their protocols.' Jeffries slid the cover off of a whiteboard on the wall we were facing and began to write. 'We're in Virginia, so I'll only talk about Virginia. And—' he looked at the female reporter in the front row '—I'll only answer questions about Virginia. Here, we use a three-drug protocol.'

He began to write, starting with the number one, which he circled. 'Sodium thiopental,' he wrote next to the number. 'A common barbiturate often used during surgery, although in this type of situation a much stronger dose is utilized. There are a few states using midazolam, which Virginia ceased utilizing after unforeseen reactions occurred in other states. Sodium thiopental, in the doses we use, effects unconsciousness in about thirty seconds.'

I remembered the unforeseen reactions. I remembered reading about what were called some of the worst botches the states had ever had. The midazolam, administered first, was supposed to render the recipient unconscious and relieve any pain associated with the following drugs in the cocktail.

It didn't.

In one case, the prisoner experienced temporary unconsciousness only to begin seizing moments later. Bucking, actually, according to the internal reports. In another, the midazolam failed to relieve pain. I didn't like to think about lethal doses of potassium chloride running through my veins, burning me alive from the inside.

Jeffries wrote a number two on the whiteboard and circled it. 'After flushing the lines with a saline solution, the second drug is administered. Here, we use a muscle relaxant, also commonly employed in surgery.' He wrote 'pancuronium bromide' next to the number and 'Pavulon' in parentheses. 'Again, lethal injection involves much higher doses, with a goal to paralyzing the lungs and diaphragm.'

A few hands went up. Jeffries made them go back down with a gesture of his own hands. 'I know what you're thinking. We still need the third drug.' He wrote a three on the board with 'potassium chloride' next to it. 'The simple answer is this: we want certainty. Certainty of death. After another saline flush, this last agent induces cardiac arrest. And then we're sure. Now, if I can move on to what you will see.'

It was that word again. Certainty. I felt blood rush to my head and could hear my own heartbeat in my ears, a steady and torturous pulse. Ian squeezed my hand, but this only made the pulse worse.

'You will witness the placement of the intravenous lines,'

Jeffries said. 'Other than that, there isn't much to see. Everything that happens once the drugs begin to flow into the condemned's system happens internally. This will be a quiet execution. A gentle, but sure, death. Very much like assisted suicide.'

In spite of Jeffries' calm voice and reassurance, I knew differently. This was nothing like assisted suicide, not in its philosophy and not in its protocol. Assisted suicide requires free will. And only one lethal dose of barbiturates is required. As far as I could see, the only thing right about Jeffries' claim was that both were irreversible.

After a rigorous pat-down and another van ride through the prison grounds, we were in the viewing room with the death chamber on the other side of a large glass window. We sat, and we waited. A few of the press exchanged notes on drugs and dosages. Otherwise, we were mostly silent.

At eleven-thirty, Robert Bellamy was wheeled in. He was strapped to a gurney, four black bands running horizontally across his rail-thin body. The cuffs, apparently cinched to their limit, still seemed to float around his ankles and wrists. On his arms, the track marks of a lifetime of intravenous drug use stood out like three-dimensional tattoos, same as Sully. He moved his head from one side to the other, left, then right, then left. It lolled there, almost lifelessly, and he stared at the window of the viewing room with eyes that had glazed over. Already, Bellamy looked dead.

Jeffries told us the entire procedure, from the insertion of the lines to the pronouncement of death, would take approximately thirty minutes.

It wasn't true.

We all watched in silence as the technicians moved around Robert Bellamy's immobilized body, tapping the pale skin on his wrists and the inside joints of his elbows, looking for plump veins. We watched them circle around again, turning limbs, searching for any part of the shrunken and shriveled man that would allow a catheter. We listened when they leaned towards one another, whispering. At some point – I couldn't say when – a new individual entered the room. He was clad in green scrubs and wore a pair of surgical gloves on his hands. A cart rolled in, and the latest arrival chose a shiny piece of steel from the array of tools laid out on top of it. I heard the words 'can't stick it' and 'cutdown' and 'saphenous' and, from behind me, one of the reporters gasped.

Another – the woman with the questions – said something like, 'Oh, no. Tell me they're not doing a venous cutdown.' I don't think she was speaking to anyone but herself.

I turned to Ian, but he only shook his head.

We only needed to wait a few moments to find out.

Bellamy lay on the gurney, his arms straining against the straps as the doctor cut. A drape over his left thigh turned dark red with blood, and Bellamy's fists clenched hard enough for the knuckles to turn a bluish-white under the overhead lamps.

'I can't,' the woman reporter said. 'I can't do this.' It was all she managed to say before she fell forward and collapsed on the tile floor at my feet. At the same time, Bellamy groaned. Then the groans turned to whimpers.

I think he was crying.

This was in earlier days, before the state began preparing its executions behind closed doors.

And still, it wasn't the worst I would see.

CHAPTER TWENTY-THREE

Daniel is no longer on the phone when I return from the downstairs bathroom. He's slumped against the back of the sofa, a glass of Scotch in his left hand nearing the tipping point, the iPhone in his right gone to a black screen, a nothingness. It matches his eyes that seem to be both looking at me and not looking at me.

'This is bad,' he says.

The blank gaze and the robotic shake of his head tell me it's beyond bad. I don't even need to ask about the rest of the phone call. Adrian Kopinsky is about to pay for her error, and the reality of her death has hit home. Hard.

Daniel starts to ramble. 'I could ignore it. Know what I mean? I could wake up every day, go to work, come home, make love to you, and all this shit would stay off in some kind of la-la-land. She'd be a girl I used to know, shagged a few times, got angry with, called it quits with. Part of the past. But it's different when that girl is going to die. I don't know how it's different, but it is. She wasn't all bad, you know? Adrian wasn't all bad.' His voice trails off, and he takes a long swallow of his drink before topping up the glass. 'Adrian,' he says again. Then he grasps my hand and pulls me gently onto the sofa.

Up until a month ago, maybe a week ago, I thought I could let Daniel go. I was sure I could return to the unattached single-parent life I had before we met. I told myself Daniel wasn't Ian and never would be; he was only a convenient replacement. Like most things, we only realize how desperately we cling to them when they're on the brink of leaving us.

Whatever happens, I need Daniel in my life now. I need him to stay the course with me. For the first time since meeting Emily, I'm fully aware that I could be the next Adrian Kopinsky, that I could be taken from my son.

That I could be gone in the blink of an eye and the throw of a switch.

'This sounds serious,' I say. And then a thought comes, a terrible and dark revelation. He's still in love with Adrian. That's what's eating at him. I seem to fall apart on the inside, and everything hurts – bones, skin, muscles. Everything. As if I'm dissolving. My eyelids fall, and I try to block the next words. If I don't see or hear what comes next, maybe it won't be real, like that tree falling down in the forest. All of a sudden, I don't want to be here.

'Hey, you,' Daniel says, taking my face in his hands. He runs his thumbs under my eyes and wipes the tears away. 'Hey now, love. What's all this?'

I pull away. 'Don't. Please don't.' Somehow, I make it to my feet. 'I'll go up and sleep in the boys' room. Jonathan and I can go to Susan's place first thing in the morning.'

'Are you daft?'

'What?'

'Yes. Exactly. What? As in, what's going on?' He reaches up and tries to take my hand again but I move too quickly, and he barely brushes the cuff of my sweatshirt.

I'm at the door in seconds, Susan's car keys clutched in one hand while I try to make sense of a deadbolt that doesn't want to turn. All I want is to be outside, in a car, driving anywhere. I want Daniel behind me, a shrinking silhouette in my rearview mirror.

Daniel has other ideas, and the same idea. He's already sprung from the living room and now presses himself into my back, drawing me against his body. He's whispering, but I don't understand the words. A blazing ball of panic has taken over deep in my chest. If I could run from it, I might be okay. But I can't. I'm trapped.

'Jussie,' he whispered into my ear. 'Jussie, love. I won't stop you from leaving. But I don't want you to go. I need you here, now. And I think you need me.' His breath is irregular and hitched, and I realize I'm not the only human in the room who is crying.

'I do. God, Daniel, I do.'

My hand drops from the lock, and Susan's keys fall to the floor with a tinny clinking sound. Daniel turns me toward him, and suddenly we're as attached as two people can be as we kiss and cry and stumble our way down the hall to his bedroom. I love this room, love the way the morning sun creeps through the blinds, how it wakes me gently, a moment at a time, teasing my consciousness into a new day. Tonight, I don't see the room at all. I don't feel the mattress under my body or the down pillow under my cheek. I seem to float somewhere above this bed, and Daniel floats with me, moving when I move, staying still when I stay still. We become two pieces of a puzzle, fitting into and around one another.

In these moments, Ian has always tried to interrupt, or I've allowed him to interrupt. I've let him visit, Ian in the same bloodstained shirt with the small hole in the front and the larger one in the back. There's often been a sliver of time when I thought

181

I wanted him to come between us. I think I see him now, but only briefly. Ian smiles, then turns, and then he is completely gone.

One other observation before I drown myself in Daniel.

He called me 'love' tonight. He's never called me 'love' before.

At midnight on this early April Sunday, everything changes.

CHAPTER TWENTY-FOUR

There's sex, and there's making love, and there's good, old-fashioned fucking. I don't think they've invented a name for what Daniel and I have done. Consuming, maybe. Burning from the inside out. We're gluttons tonight; we're involved in a painless kind of self-immolation. We break apart into pieces and reassemble as something new.

When it's over – and I don't believe it will ever really be over – both of us are too wired to sleep. We lie tangled in sheets, our limbs knotted together. By the time we pull ourselves apart, the clock on Daniel's nightstand is blinking a very early hour in vivid green. Three a.m. Longer than I've been up in a while. But we're not finished talking.

Daniel starts. 'Of course I'm worried about Adrian. I know what I said about her, but she has a human side. Few get to see it.' He rolls over. 'I'm sorry. I shouldn't be talking up my former sex life after what we just did.'

Now it's my turn to comfort him. 'I think that's normal. I mean, we all weave in and out of relationships. They begin and, one way or another, they end. But somewhere between the beginning and the end there's always love. Right? Unless you want to start filling me in on your escapades as a young man.'

He rolls back, laughing. 'You're only my third, Jussie.'

'Mine, too.'

'I'm worried about you, love,' he says. *Love.* The word makes me want to sing and cry at the same time. 'No. That isn't right. I'm terrified. What happened with Adrian happened fast. She's in custody and they're fast-tracking the hearing. The Oversight Committee moved quickly on this one. Who knows? Maybe that's their MO. Come in fast and go for the kill. And your old Vita cronies aren't exactly speaking out in her defense – probably because they can't stand her.' He covers his eyes with one arm and speaks to the ceiling. 'If anything happened to you—' He pauses, turns away from me again, and lets out a hopeless sigh. 'You'll think I'm crazy for saying it, but if anything happened, I don't think I could keep going. Not with what we're talking about.'

'Oh, Daniel. Nothing's happened.' *Yet,* I think.

I found a piece of paper.

Without warning, he gets out of bed, throws on a robe, and leaves. He's back in a minute with an iPad tucked under one arm and a legal pad in his other hand. The hint of a smile brightens his face, mischievous and boyish. Right now, Daniel looks like a ten-year-old about to get up to something.

'Just hang on,' he says, falling back against the pillow and opening a new browser window. I watch while he types in two words: *British Airways.*

'What are you doing?'

He keeps typing. 'Is your passport current?'

I nod.

'And Jonathan's?'

'Yes.'

'Thank God. How soon can you pack?'

The screen on his laptop shows a booking in progress. Three passengers, one way, from Dulles to Heathrow. The date is tomorrow.

I used to have conversations with Ian late at night. We talked about hypotheticals. What would you do if . . . ? Where would you go if . . . ? Most of them centered on inconceivable scenarios or situations we felt were long in our futures. What if one of us was diagnosed with dementia? What if we couldn't have a child? Where would we go if the dollar took a tailspin? A few were even silly: What would we munch on if they stopped making M&Ms? Where would we like to make love? That last one resulted in a few interesting experiments, some of which were repeated, some better left unmentioned.

We never talked about what we would do if we found ourselves in the kind of trouble that Emily Milford's piece of paper could create. It isn't what you would call a predictable scenario, like your husband going for Greek takeout and never coming home. Trying for two years to conceive and then finding yourself pregnant in the worst of times. Being dead sure of guilt only to have one short sentence unravel that certainty.

I found a piece of paper.

Now, here with Daniel as he taps away and enters names and credit card data, I realize I'm in a situation that never crossed my mind.

'I'll put the passport details in tomorrow,' Daniel says. 'After we go to your place and collect the stuff, okay?' Then he clicks *'Confirm'* without asking. 'Eight o'clock from Dulles. Direct flight. We'll sort everything else out once we land in London. And I'll talk to an old mate of mine. The way I'm thinking, they'll never succeed in extraditing you. The UK's been against the Remedies Act from the get-go.'

Suddenly I'm ice cold. 'What's the rush, Daniel?'

'They're executing Adrian on Tuesday. Curt says a bloke named Stuyvesant worked the case.'

I go colder. 'Stuyvesant?'

'Yeah. Ted Stuyvesant. He and his group work freelance for whichever state Oversight Committee wants them.'

'That's ridiculous. I knew Ted. He was only ever interested in money.'

Daniel types on his iPad and brings up a crowdfunding page. 'Five hundred thousand and counting,' he says as $500,035 turns into $500,680 in a matter of seconds.

CHAPTER TWENTY-FIVE

I alternate between shivering and sweating tonight while Daniel sleeps next to me. We didn't officially turn in until nearly four o'clock, and at the time, I thought I'd be able to sleep. I was wrong.

For several minutes, I feel like a clockwork toy wound too tight by an overzealous child. Then I lapse into a state of utter lethargy, my limbs unable to move, my batteries depleted to zero. It's a cycle, a vicious one, that repeats and repeats and won't allow rest either in body or mind.

So I decide not to let my mind rest. I decide to imagine things.

For instance: what was Emily Milford's sleep like on that first night after they transferred Jake to death row? Did she toss and turn like a colicky baby? Did she sweat feverishly while she visualized her husband in a cell? I suppose she did. I would have. Her mind must have wandered from one possibility to the next, denying Jake's culpability for a moment, then asking herself if she really had the devil for a bedmate. She would wonder if she should have known, if there had been clues all along – a little too much attention paid to Caleb Church, sudden changes of mood, a benign and fatherly smile that masked the killing jaws of a wolf. But then she would shift into a new phase, as quickly as a roadster with an oversensitive clutch. *Not Jake,* she would think. *Not my husband. Not the father of my child.* Because the utter ridiculousness of it all would be too much to bear. No one lives happily with another human for years without seeing him; no one can be that blind.

It's the debate that kills sleep, the constant fluctuation between two opposing evils. Either he did it, or he didn't. Both possible truths wreak their own havoc on the soul.

I didn't suffer that when Ian died. I suffered, of course, but I knew there was only one truth. In that terrible sureness, I was protected from the kind of doubt that must have destroyed a part of Emily Milford.

I imagine Emily on the last night, worn out from a day of grieving a man who, for the moment, still had a beating heart. Oh, the questions she must have asked herself, the numb waiting for a midnight telephone call, the bitter understanding that a system had finally filtered the wheat of facts from the chaff of fantasies. An indisputable product had been calculated, as sure and as unchangeable as the product of two times two. She must have only been able to conclude that justice was done, that her questions were at last answered.

I found a piece of paper.

Different questions run through my head now. They match the steady tick-tock of the grandfather clock in Daniel's hall as I creep past it.

Run or stay. Run or stay. Run or stay.

Upstairs, Tommy and Jonathan are tucked into sleeping bags. In the dim, gray light of dawn, I can make out their hands curled into loose fists, their thin arms casually flung across their faces as if to shield young eyes from the world. At six, there's little the world can do to them that they're able to understand. They have protectors in Susan and in me.

As I watch them sleep, the sleeping bags rising and falling with each shallow breath, I think parents must be like eyes. We each of us start with a pair. Some of us lose sight in one or the other before we're born; some later. I knew a girl with a glass eye in high school. You couldn't tell by looking at her that there was anything different. Maybe if you looked very closely, you realized something was off: the right pupil didn't dilate or contract. It didn't track you the same way the left, living eye, did. But who pays attention to such things? To the rest of us, Shirley had two good eyes.

To Shirley, the situation must have been quite the opposite. If a passing car shot a pebble in her direction, she might think, *Please, not the other one.* If crackling bacon in a hot frying pan spat grease on her face, she would worry more than the rest of us did. I wondered how many times a day her parents would caution her when she bicycled down the street or came a little too close to the family cat. I'm sure their warnings were incessant. After all, Shirley only had one good eye left.

Like my son only has one parent left.

Right now, running makes sense.

I leave their room and descend the stairs. It's brighter now, more straw gold than twilight gray. Daniel's home starts to come alive one piece at a time, and the tick of the pendulum clock is no longer my only focus. Old framed maps on the walls chart out a million different directions; family photographs taken at racecourses – Newcastle, Ascot, Epsom – feature smiling strangers who might become Jonathan's and my new extended family. With both my and Ian's parents already gone, the only family we have now is Susan.

In the kitchen, the coffee pot seems to wink at me. *Go on, then, darling. Start me up.* I'm tempted, but the coffee isn't pre-ground, and I don't want to risk waking up the household with the buzz of the electric grinder I find. So, tea then. Daniel, like all good Brits, devotes an entire cupboard to tea. I take two bags of Earl Grey, drop them into a mug, and add water from the tap. I wince. This is not quite the way Daniel makes tea. While the microwave does the heavy work, I sneak back into Daniel's room and find my handbag on the floor next to the dresser. Quietly, I slip out my phone.

An earsplitting bong in the hallway makes me jump. I mean, it's a chime that should be capable of waking the dead, but Daniel doesn't so much as stir when the clock bangs out its six-a.m. alert. And I was worried about a coffee grinder. From upstairs, there's a noise that sounds like a pair of wide-awake six-year-olds. They don't fit with my morning plan to make a phone call.

I head back up the stairs, past the maps and the family photos that tell my future, hoping Susan is still asleep. The weekend has mostly been about me, but it's brought back to life all the grief we both felt for Ian. I know how hard it was on her seven years ago. I check the television room at the back of the house first and find my sister-in-law in the same clothes she was wearing yesterday, still as a statue. She must have been out since the moment her head hit the spare pillow Daniel put down for her. On the ottoman, a pile of sheets remains folded and untouched. I close the door softly before backtracking toward the front where the guest room is.

'Mom, I'm hungry,' Jonathan says. He's sitting up, the sleeping bag bunched around his waist, rubbing his stomach. Next to him, Tommy does the same. Like twins.

'Daniel told me you each had two bowls of spaghetti for dinner,' I say. 'And bread. And ice cream. And popcorn. And Coke, which you're not supposed to have at dinner, but we'll let it slide this time.'

'Yeah, but we're hungry,' Tommy insists, and I find myself wishing I had the metabolism of a six-year-old. Or at least the appetite.

'Tell you what,' I say, kneeling down on the floor. 'If I get you a snack, will you promise to stay here for a little while longer? Then I'll make you pancakes for breakfast. Deal?'

Jonathan rolls his eyes. 'Mommy, you can't make pancakes.'

'Yes, I can. I always make pancakes. You like them, remember?'

'I mean you can't make pancakes today.'

'Why on earth not?'

He looks over at Tommy, who shakes his head sadly as if I've just asked the world's stupidest question. 'Because it's Monday.'

'Okay . . .'

'And on Monday there's school, and when we have school we have to rush around, and when we rush around we don't have time for pancakes.'

School. Christ on a pogo stick. I'd forgotten about school.

The boys are both staring at me, waiting.

'Very clever, Jonathan. Your dad would be proud of that fine legal brain of yours. But I have information you don't have.'

They exchange looks, sizing me up for the Stupidest Mom of the Year Award. At last, Tommy pipes up. 'You mean it's not Monday?'

'Okay. That's it. You two are worse than a couple of high-priced lawyers,' I say. 'It is Monday, and we're having pancakes. We're having pancakes because you're not going to school. And you're not going to school because I'm the Mom and I say you don't have to. Any questions?'

There are, as I expected, none. A few cheers, though, erupt from either side of me.

'But,' I say, 'one condition.' Jonathan and Tommy search my face eagerly for clues. It's rather satisfying knowing I have them hooked. 'You stay up here until that clock—' I point to the digital readout on the nightstand '—shows the number seven with two zeros after it. Think you can handle that?'

'You mean seven o'clock, Aunt Justine?' Tommy says.

'Exactly.' With a quick kiss for both of them and a ruffle of their identical strawberry-blond hair, I leave the room and go downstairs to make my phone call.

I'd much rather be mixing pancake batter.

CHAPTER TWENTY-SIX

Daniel's clock bangs out the half-hour. Six-thirty. It's early for retirees and the self-employed, nearly mid-morning for the average commuter or the parent of small children. Still, Emily's voice is flat and sluggish when she answers. Maybe it's always like that these days.

'Hello?'

'Mrs Milford?'

In the background, a small voice, not so different from Jonathan's, squeals. 'Is it Daddy? I wanna talk to Daddy!'

Emily sighs into the phone. 'Who is this?' Then she speaks to her son. 'No, Jake Junior, it isn't Daddy.'

These few seconds stretch out into an eternity. Emily hasn't told her boy what happened to his father. It seems ludicrous at first, until I start to think it through, to question how anyone could possibly tell a six-year-old child that on the same day he last saw his father, men strapped Daddy to a chair, soaked a sponge, and pulled a switch. That a doctor, whose purpose is to prolong life, stood by with his stethoscope, waiting for a human heart to stop. That Saturday morning visits would not happen anymore.

The answer is so clear: it's an impossible task.

I wonder what stories I would have made up if, instead of being a pea-sized embryo inside me, Jonathan had been a walking, talking small human when Ian was killed. Because I could have made up lies. I could have shielded Jonathan from the funereal rituals and told him sometimes daddies go away. It wouldn't be a total untruth – thousands of fathers walk out and never return. They don't have to be dead, just scumbags.

Or, if I want to entertain more extreme fantasies, what would I have said to Jonathan if his father died in a different way? 'Oh, honey, you see, some people decided that your daddy is too evil to live, so they made a really powerful toaster, put him inside it, and dialed up the setting to *burn*.' Or, in earlier times, before lethal injection was ruled unconstitutional: 'And so a doctor gave your dad a shot, and that shot had poison in it, and now your daddy is dead.'

No. I would have taken the same route Emily has. Avoid, avoid, avoid. Sooner or later, the lies would become easier. That's the way of lies, I think.

Emily comes back on the phone. 'Who is this?' She sounds as if she's aged overnight. More than that, she asks the question as if she doesn't care, as if she's doing nothing more than following one hundred years of telephone etiquette.

'Justine Callaghan,' I say. 'I mean, Justine Boucher.'

'Oh.'

Upstairs, the floor creaks. Susan's awake.

I get ready to spit it all out. 'I need to talk to you, Mrs Milford. About the—'

'Yeah. I know what it's about. So talk. I have to get Jake Junior to school and I have an appointment at nine.'

When Emily said she was meeting with a woman from the Oversight Committee next week, I didn't think it would be

Monday. I didn't think it would be so soon. On the other hand, wouldn't Wednesday come just as quickly? Or Friday? Or next month? I've often put myself in Jake Milford's shoes. He waited years, but they must have gone by in a blink. I remember my mother telling me when she turned seventy, not long before she died, that her life seemed to have only lasted an hour. An hour. Such an interminable amount of time on a rainy day, such an infinite span when waiting for that cute guy in your geometry class to ring, such an eternity to a woman panting and sweating on a delivery room bed. Time is supposed to be a constant but seldom is.

'I need to know what you found,' I say. 'Please.'

I found a piece of paper.

I hear the younger Jake ask for more cereal, and I wait, listening to the rattle of Cheerios or Rice Krispies being poured. Jake mumbles a 'thank you' around a mouthful of crunching cereal, and Emily says something to him that doesn't come through clearly before coming back to me.

'I told you I had to think about what I was gonna do with it,' she says. Then adds, 'That's why I have an appointment this morning. I gotta think this through.'

'Please, Emily,' I say. 'I need to know.'

'Yeah. And Jake Junior needs a father. My momma used to tell me something about wishing. She said, "Wish in one hand, tacky in the other. See which fills up first." Never did know what tacky meant when I was a kid, but me and my brothers figured it out later on. Anyway, that's what Momma said about wishes.' She pauses, munches on something that sounds like dry toast, and comes back with a question of her own. 'Let me ask you something. What do you think about abortion? You pro-life or pro-killing babies?'

On the surface, Emily's question is simple, binary. For decades, the average American – male or female – has been either pro-life or pro-choice. Every January 22, the black-and-white divide swarms around the United States Supreme Court like an oversized chess set, handmade signs identifying which color piece you are. No room for gray in that game.

For me, the question has never been simple. I can't tell another woman what to do with her own body, but I know what I would choose for myself. 'I'm pro-every woman gets to make her own choices, but I wouldn't have an abortion unless there was a medical reason,' I say, not knowing where this rabbit hole is leading. No. That's a lie. I know where – and how deep – it's going.

'So you think it's not okay to kill a baby, but it's okay to kill a man,' Emily says.

'I don't think—'

She doesn't let me finish. 'See, I don't get that kinda thinking. Because it ain't okay to kill anyone. Least, that's what my momma taught me to believe.'

'I don't think it's okay to kill a man. Or a woman,' I say. 'In case you haven't figured it out, I'm against the death penalty.'

'See, that's where I get confused. You say that, and then you fight tooth and nail to write some fancy words into a new law that sorta says the opposite. And then you send my husband to sit on death row for six years.'

I'm searching for a way to explain this. Maybe to Emily, maybe to myself. 'I—'

'I ain't finished yet. You want something from me today, and I want something from you. I want you to listen. I heard the news about that lawyer in Florida. Oh, yeah, Ms Boucher. I read the news, too. They say they're gonna execute her tomorrow because the new evidence ain't got no holes in it. Who has to sign *that* form, Ms Boucher? Whose fault is it if they're wrong again?'

Adrian Kopinsky, the subject of our morbid little chat this morning, had forgotten the Remedies Act has no authority beyond the original prosecutor, so it's no surprise Emily Milford doesn't know this. 'The buck stops with the lawyer who asked for the death penalty, Mrs Milford. That's in the Remedies Act.'

There's silence on the phone. I can't tell whether Emily has run out of words or whether she's processing what I've said. A chill runs through me as I ponder another possibility.

I found a piece of paper.

'I don't know about all that stuff,' she says at last. 'All I know is you're trying to save lives by taking lives.'

'That's not the way anyone wanted the system to work.'

'But it did work out that way,' Emily says. 'It did. And I guess my next question is: what are you gonna do about it?'

I want to tell her the same thing I told Adrian. That I'm powerless. That someone built a machine and now has no way of hitting the kill switch. Instead, I ask my question again. 'What did you find, Mrs Milford?'

The wait for her reply is endless. From the hall, Daniel's clock chimes seven. Susan appears at the foot of the stairs with the two boys in tow. Daniel, in a dark blue robe, smiles at me as he comes into the kitchen. I'm surrounded by witnesses as I wait.

'Ms Boucher, I found a hotel receipt in Jake's things. From down Bluefield. That's four and a half hours away from here, so when I tell you the date matches the day Caleb Church was killed, I guess you can figure out the rest on your own.'

I think I manage a whisper. 'Oh.'

'Look, I gotta go now. But I'll meet you at the park again. At noon. By then, I'll have made some calls.' There's a moment of silence, and then, 'I still haven't decided anything. Not yet.'

She hangs up, and I'm left with four smiling faces watching me.

Death Row Inmate #39384

So. The hotel. I figure this part of the story will get out sooner or later, and I guess I might as well talk about it.

It wasn't really a hotel, more of a motor inn, the kind of long, flat place with a row of doors and a parking space out front of each unit. The name of it was the Little Walker Motel. Not the Big Walker, on the north side of town, but its smaller, cheaper sister. The Big Walker had cable television and a diner attached. The Little Walker had a sign that permanently spelled V-N-C-Y because a few letters had either fallen off or been stolen. I don't right know if the lights on the N-O even worked. It was daytime when I arrived and still daytime when I left.

At noon on the day Caleb Church died — and from what I hear, noon was about two hours earlier than the last time his momma saw him — I pulled into the Little Walker's empty lot. Only one other car was parked there, one I recognized. I put my pickup truck seven spaces farther down. If anyone was looking, they would have seen the two vehicles, but I wasn't worried about anyone. I was worried about my little brother Kris. I'll be honest, I wasn't too worried; Kris and Mary Ann lived a town away in some shit-kicking place called Pounding Mill, and my brother would have had a time trolling around all the motels in southwest Virginia. I still parked as far away as I could get. Growing up with Kris, I knew the risk better than most folks.

This wasn't the first time he'd hit Mary Ann. But I wasn't prepared for what I'd see when I knocked on the door of number sixteen, all the way at the end of the row of rooms. Fact is, I probably didn't need to see. Hearing Mary Ann's voice as she lisped 'who ith it' told me most of what I needed to know about how badly he'd beat her up this time. Well, it told me something about how he'd messed up her face.

'It's Jake,' I said.

The door stayed closed, but I heard the squeak of bed-springs through it and the pad of feet as she walked over. 'Where wath the place you kithed me? When we were kidth?'

At first, I was taken by surprise. Then I realized why she was asking. 'Round back of Farmer Miller's farm. By the well,' I said. And I won't lie: I got a pain in my heart then, thinking of me being sixteen and Mary Ann being fourteen, remembering that pretty pink frock she wore to services on Sunday mornings. She looked like an angel in that dress, a little angel in pink and white gingham, like that old song by Roger Miller.

Now, most fellas my age would have been paying attention to some of Mary Ann's other features. Instead of the dress, they'd see how her body was starting to bloom, how one day she all of a sudden-like had a waist and hips and breasts. I won't lie and say I didn't notice how she was changing, how she wasn't a little moppet in pigtails anymore – after all, I was a guy high on hormones and short on options for handling them. Some things you just can't help. But what I noticed about Mary Ann was her smile. Always big as the sun and twice as warm. You could die in that smile, and you'd die a happy man.

But I'm getting away from things here. Or, maybe I'm not. I want to tell you the story about the motel, which is to say I want to tell you about the story that could have saved my life. To get to the motel, though, we gotta go all the way back to Miller's farm, to that day I kissed Mary Ann's mouth, and to all the rest of the shit that happened afterward, all the stuff that disconnected us and then ended up connecting us back up.

No. I never hurt Mary Ann, not in the physical way and not in the emotional way. Don't think that for even a second. I was raised better than that.

I suppose if I was raised better than that, then Kris should have been, too, but some things you can't blame on a mother. Some people, I think, are born bad. Like my little brother.

That icy day at the lake wasn't the worst of him, only the beginning of the worst. You could say it was like throwing more kindling on a fire that probably would have gone on smoldering anyway, and would have eventually erupted into flame even without help.

Benny, I'm pretty sure, was already dead when I dragged him out of the water. I remember yelling so loud I thought they'd hear me in the next county. But no one came for over a half-hour, and when Mr Miller and his wife did roll their old

International truck up to the side of the lake, I was still yelling. Partly from fear, and partly from anger, but I'd be lying if I told you that being soaked to the skin and freezing didn't have something to do with it. And all the while, as Mrs Miller put her best nursing skills to use and tried to breathe Benny back to life, Kris just sat there wailing like a baby, going on about how I told him and Benny the ice was hard enough to skate on.

None of it had an ounce of truth to it, but that didn't prevent Momma from giving me a thrashing with a sturdy wooden spoon when we finally got home from the hospital that evening. I didn't even cry while she held me down, one of her meaty arms pressing into my shoulder blades so that I was mashed into the kitchen table while her other arm – just as strong – swung back and down, raining pain on my behind. Kris sat on the step stool in the corner, hunched over, hands over his face, shoulders shaking in a weird kind of rhythm.

It looked as if he was crying, but I knew better.

After the funeral, things really weren't the same. As if they would be. But when I say they weren't the same, what I mean is, they were about as bad as they could get. Momma worried herself over my little brother like a cat over a kitten. She'd go grocery shopping on Wednesdays and come back with three paper sacks for me to empty and put in the icebox or in the cupboards.

'Here you go, Kris,' she would say. 'Momma bought you a treat.' And she'd dig into her skirt pocket and pull out a candy bar. Only the one.

When the television went on after supper, we always

watched what Kris wanted to watch. Even if it was something violent like that half-real, half-fake police show.

'I got a better idea,' I'd say, leafing through the newspaper listing. Didn't much matter what I suggested – Disney, Nickelodeon, *The Simpsons* – Momma's response was always the same, like a prayer you memorize to recite in church.

'You mind your business, Jacob. And if you can't mind your business, you do your math problems. Then you can take out the trash.'

So on and on we went like that, all the way into our teens.

When I asked Mary Ann to a high school dance, Momma shook her head. 'You? Lord no, Jacob. You think Mrs Munro is gonna let someone as irresponsible as you take her only daughter out?'

Which explains a few things. One, how I missed my chance with Mary Ann Munro. Two, how Kris ended up dating her. And three, why I found myself at the Little Walker Motel in Bluefield, Virginia, on that same day Caleb Church was killed.

I said before this wasn't the first time Kris had beat up on Mary Ann. The first time was on their wedding night when my little brother, high on a case or so of cheap supermarket champagne, got upset because she didn't turn the faucet in their hotel bathroom all the way off. Imagine hitting your new bride because of a water faucet. I don't know – I've always been unable to imagine that, even though I grew up with Kris. I figured all those bullfrogs he threw firecrackers at and little kids he pushed around was Kris getting his anger out, maybe because he spent so much time at home smiling at our momma with that sweet smile of his, making her feel like she was the Number-One Momma of all time.

I shoulda known better.

Of course, he sang the same old song every wife-beater sings. Next morning, he was sorry as hell, promised he'd never do it again, loved her more than life itself. He'd rather die a miserable death than hurt her.

Yeah, right.

Mostly, the beatings were the sort of thing that only needed a few days of Mary Ann staying home or, if she had to go out, covering up with that see-through costume all abused wives wear: scarf, sunglasses, a pound or so of concealer makeup. Long sleeves. He was smart, Kris. He never did enough damage to put her in the hospital. Just enough to keep her in line, as he would say.

I wonder if he ever knew that he was breaking two hearts and not one.

She opened the door and let me in, and I saw right away, even with the heavy curtains drawn and the lights out, what was wrong.

No. I can't even. I can't say all that was wrong with Mary Ann's sweet face. But I can say that the odds of her smile being what it once was were on a par with the odds of one of them toy poodles winning a greyhound race.

It took me about a minute to make the decision. I didn't call ahead or tell her what I had planned. I just bundled her shattered body into my truck and drove to the Women's Place in Roanoke. I'd known about it for a good while, told Mary Ann a million times to head there on her own. She didn't. She'd gotten to know Kris's old song by heart. The one that always started and ended with the same line: *It'll be different tomorrow, baby.*

Oh, they looked me over good when I knocked on the bright blue door of the Women's Place shelter. They checked the blood on me, and they counted up the wounds on the woman I was carrying. I was thinking at the time, *How many deadbeat husbands kick the shit out of their wives and then drive them to safety?* Not many, was my bet. Guys like Kris don't believe in getting the outside world involved.

Finally, it was Mary Ann who lisped through her broken teeth and told them I was just a friend, one of the good guys, she said. Only it came out like 'good guyth'. They had a doctor on call and whisked Mary Ann off to an examining room before showing me the door to the administrator's office. I stayed there until evening, watching the sun set outside the window and the city grow dark. I told them all the things they needed to know about Kris Milford.

But I never told them my name.

I had good reasons for staying silent on that one.

CHAPTER TWENTY-SEVEN

I burn the first four pancakes and have to scrape a mess of charred batter into the trash bin. The entire kitchen reeks of smoke now, bringing back one of my worst memories. I force it into the darkest corners of my mind as the griddle sizzles under a rush of cold water as Susan steps in to take over breakfast duties. She won't win any prizes for her cooking skills – Susan's idea of a square meal is boxed mashed potatoes and ground beef mixed with Hamburger Helper – but compared to me this morning, she's Julia-fucking-Child.

'Scram, you,' she says. 'I'll call you when it's ready.'

As if I could eat. Before I leave the kitchen, I fill her in on what Daniel has been up to. Susan's eyes widen, and she twists an invisible key on her lips when I tell her to keep it quiet.

'Of course,' she says, gathering the boys closer to watch the pancake action.

In Daniel's bedroom, while I'm pulling on my jeans and one of his shirts, he lobs one question after another my way. Who was that on the phone? What's wrong? Why won't you tell me? I feel like an amateur tennis player with an automatic ball chucker gone out of control.

'Just calling Jonathan in sick to school,' I lie. For the second time.

'He's not sick.'

'No. But I need to take him home to pack, and I don't want to wait until this afternoon.' I say this, hoping like hell Daniel will swallow it, that he'll think there's nothing unnatural about requiring a six-year-old's help in throwing clothes into a couple of suitcases. Because I need my son with me today for other reasons.

I know. It's a shitty trick, parading Jonathan in front of Emily Milford. It's cowardly. Low. Not a ploy I ever thought I would resort to. In taking him to town, I'll be using my own son to garner sympathy, not unlike one of those street beggars who line the sidewalks of foreign cities, displaying their filthy children to better their chances of making a euro or a forint or a rupee. I'll be the woman standing at stoplights with her sign advertising: *Three jobs, four kids, no money!*

I'll be Emily herself at the trial.

Oh, yes. Emily threw her own pity parties every time she waddled down the courtroom aisle, every time she rested a protective hand on her swollen belly, every time she struggled to sit down or stand up under the weight of a growing fetus. I noticed it, Judge Petrus noticed it, the press noticed it. But I don't think Emily had us in mind.

I think if the crime her husband had been accused of weren't so violent, or if Emily was more middle-class and less under-educated white trash, I would have attained something like pariah status during the Milford trial. How could I, a woman, be so cruel as to let the wheels of justice roll along their way while I knew those wheels would make an orphan out of a child who was yet to be born? But the question never came up. Not once did anyone call me out on the decision to ask for Jake

Milford's death. It was like they wanted it. After so many years of being denied justice, the public needed their pound of flesh.

On top of making a terrible, irreversible decision, I had support. Mountains of it.

'I said, "Do you want me to come with you?"' Daniel says as he pulls three shirts from their hangers and starts the complicated process of folding.

'No!' I say quickly. Only after the word comes out do I realize he's not talking about accompanying me to the park, but to my vandalized house.

He raises both hands in a gesture of surrender. 'All right, darling. All right. Just asking.'

Daniel's not the pouting type. As sensitive as he is in bed, he doesn't show much emotion during the day-to-day business of work and play – unless you count his latest out-of-character ranting over the Yankees' habit of executing their baddies. Maybe there is something to that British stiff upper lip after all. But now, as he smooths out the second shirt on the mattress, I see I've wounded him.

'Hey,' I say and come around to his side of the bed. 'I'm sorry I snapped. I think I got all of five minutes of real sleep last night.' I bury my head against his chest and breathe him in. It's part apology and part making sure he's unable to see the stress I know is readable on my face.

Later, while I'm driving into town toward the Broad Street park, I'll wonder if I should have told him everything. Now, though, in this quiet moment, I have too many unanswered questions. Emily has said she doesn't know what she'll decide, and the truth is that I don't know what I'll decide. I only know the decision needs to be mine, uninfluenced by this man I love.

Susan hollers from the kitchen. 'Pancakes ready, you two! Come and get 'em while they're still above room temperature. I can't promise they're good, but for the moment they're warm.'

I force a dry pancake down, leaving the syrup and the butter for everyone else to enjoy, then get Jonathan into his clothes. He's not himself any longer, not like he was earlier this morning, and helping him dress is more like clothing a rag doll than a living boy.

'Everything cool?' I say.

He shrugs, nods, holds out a wooden left arm for me to buckle his Mickey watch onto. A pang ripples through me. Ian and his Mickey Mouse wristwatch – how childish I thought it was at first, until I began to find it charming.

We're halfway out the front door when I remember I'm carless.

'Susan?' I say. Before I can ask for the keys to her wreck-on-wheels, she's got Tommy outside and is opening the back door of the Volvo for him. 'Oh – no – I can't let you chauffeur me all over town.'

'Why on earth not?'

There's no good answer to this question, so I make one up. 'Poor Tommy will be bored stiff.' Here I am again, blithely using a child as a shield. If I practice enough, I'll be able to rent myself out to the city's drug dealers before long. *For hire: Woman with small child available for night-time protection. Not even criminals shoot a kid!*

Daniel must see the panic on my face because he runs down the steps and proffers a set of keys on a ring with a blue police box dangling from it. A Tardis. Or a Tahdis. I'm never exactly sure because Daniel has that British habit of not pronouncing Rs unless they aren't there. It's another newness I'll have to get used to, along with separate hot and cold taps, televised humor I don't understand, and all those lexical oddities that Jonathan will pick up and I won't.

I'm not knocking England; it's a fine place full of fine people. But I'll always be a stranger in a strange land while I'm there, and always will last my lifetime. Which, I suppose, is the point of going. To have an always I can look forward to.

Jonathan's awfully quiet in the back seat as we drive. I sneak looks at him in the rearview mirror and wonder if I've unwittingly passed some of my nervousness on to him, if I've modeled stress instead of serenity through a wince or an unconscious curl of my lip. Who am I kidding? Of course I have.

'What's up, Jon-Jon?' I say, lightening the mood. The chirp in my voice is as fake as a cartoon character.

'Nothing.' The weight of this word is so much more than nothing. It hovers in the air with the potential energy of a lead brick teetering on unstable supports.

'Aw, come on. You can tell me. Did Tommy say something mean?'

'No.' Another leaden syllable.

I pull into the empty lot of a Mexican restaurant and stop the car. 'Okay. Let's talk,' I say, swiveling around to face him.

Jonathan's lower lip trembles. That lead brick is about to drop.

'Hang on a second.' I'm out of the front seat and into the back in about three seconds. 'There. That's better. Come on over here and give me a hug.' When he doesn't move, I follow my own instructions. The change in him from when he and Tommy woke up is remarkable: Jonathan sags against me like a broken toy. I can only think of one reason why.

Susan.

God bless her and goddamn her. She's got a big heart, but a bigger mouth. And no filter.

She doesn't mean harm. I know that much. Still, in my line of work, when you're looking at a dead body, the fine line between murder and manslaughter, between intent and accident, doesn't change the fact of death.

As soon as Jonathan stops sobbing, I lift his chin up with one hand and meet his eyes. They're Ian's more than they are mine. 'Did Aunt Susan say something to you?'

He nods weakly.

'And?'

'I promised Aunt Susan I wouldn't tattle.'

Terrific. 'That kind of promise doesn't count if you're telling your own mommy.' What the hell. It sounds good. At six years old, I'd probably have bought the lie.

'Really?'

'Cross my heart and hope to die,' I say, drawing an X over my left breast. 'But you don't have to tell me if you don't want to. It's just that I kind of have the idea that you do.'

Another nod. A little less weak.

I wait until he's ready.

'Aunt Susan said we were going away and I might not see her for a long time. Or Tommy,' he says with a sniffle. 'Is that true?'

'No. We're going on a plane trip, but that's all.'

He cocks his head to one side, reminding me of another of Ian's habits. 'How do I know you're telling me the truth?'

I point to my nose. 'You see this?'

Nod.

'Is it growing?'

Shake of the head.

'There you are, then.'

We stay in the back seat of Daniel's Range Rover for a few more minutes. Then I buckle him back in and go up front. A thought bubble flashes in my mind:

I'll kill her for this.

What a stupid thing to think. And how often we all think it.

CHAPTER TWENTY-EIGHT

I don't know whether it's fate or coincidence, but I park in the same spot I pulled into on Friday afternoon. For the past few days, life has been an infinitely looped video with no pause button.

Ian's smile on my six-year-old's face. Emily Milford wearing the identical cotton print dress she wore for our first meeting. The phrase *I found a piece of paper* repeating ad infinitum in my head. And, to top off the crow-flavored ice cream sundae that I'm forced to eat: the woman in the cherry-red suit standing alone by the far gate, speaking into her phone but keeping her eyes on Emily.

I was stupid to come here. Stupid.

'Let's go home, Jonathan,' I say with one foot on the ground and one still pressing on the brake.

I'm too late. He's already spotted the swings and the tottering, spring-mounted animals and is out of the car like a shot, urging me to come explore the rest of the playground.

'Come on, Mommy. Just for five minutes. Please?' The 'please' is drawn out into a plaintive whine.

'Five minutes. And then we have things to do.' I check my watch. Eleven fifty-five. Four short hours until we need to be on the road north toward Washington. I know I'll be with Emily for more than five minutes.

As we walk through the gates and into the sparsely populated park – it is a school day, after all – Jonathan stops gawking at the swing set and focuses his attention on Emily. She's sitting on the same bench, worrying the cotton material of her dress as she keeps watch over her own boy with a laser-like focus. And why wouldn't a woman like Emily be extra vigilant? Jake Junior is all she has left. A fifty percent loss makes us overprotective when it comes to what remains. I know from experience.

'You go ride one of the animals while I talk to my friend,' I say to my son. 'How about the panda?'

'Pandas are boring. I want the lion,' Jonathan says back, as if, here in downtown Richmond, pandas were as common as squirrels. He runs over to the herd of bouncing and tottering animals on sturdy springs, each with a pair of handles protruding from their ears. Before he can swing a leg over the lion, Emily's boy runs up, sticks out a hand in a very un-six-year-old-like way, and introduces himself.

'I'm Jake Milford. That's my ma over there on the bench. Wanna play on the merry-go-round with me? Ma says she's too busy and my dad's not around . It kinda stinks, cuz all the other dads always push their kids on the swings and stuff.'

'What happened to your dad?' Jonathan says innocently.

Jake's small shoulders move up, making a V around his head. Then they drop back down. 'He's in a big building with cages on the inside. Ma says it's like a time-out for grown-ups.'

Emily lets out a sigh as long as a Sunday, and my heart breaks at the words. In my mind, I hear all the explanations I would invent if the shoe were on the other foot.

Your daddy had to go away before you were born.
Your daddy sleeps in a different place.

No, your daddy isn't coming to live with us.

I never needed these lies, as it happened. And if I might have said them to the growing baby inside me, they fell on innocent ears too undeveloped to understand.

In every cloud, as they say.

The boys run off to spin themselves dizzy on the miniature carousel, and I move toward Emily. She isn't wringing the cotton of her dress; she's reading a small paperback. I'm ashamed of the feeling of surprise that washes over me, more ashamed when she snaps it shut. The cover doesn't display a half-naked hunk of a cowboy, but the simple title *One Hundred Love Sonnets*. Written by someone named Neruda.

I feel the shame reddening my face, its heat chiding me for passing judgment on this woman.

'You like poetry?' Emily asks.

'Not really,' I say, taking the spot next to her on the bench. 'I'm afraid I don't understand it. Too used to technical writing, I guess.'

'Yeah. Some of it's hard. I like the short ones, mostly. The stuff that's in plain language for plain people.' She looks down at the book, then up at the cloudless spring sky. 'There's one in here I really like. I read it every day. It's about going on after someone dies because if you don't, he'll see that you're all stuck in grief. He'll see that you aren't laughing or moving on, and if he sees that, he'll die all over again.'

'That sounds nice,' I say, memorizing the title of the book on her lap.

'I don't understand all of it, but I understand that part about not wanting to see the love of your life suffer. I've been tryin' real hard not to suffer, you know? I suppose you've been tryin', too.'

217

I look at her with a question in my eyes.

'Oh, I checked you out on the Internet when I was at the library. I work there a couple of days a week.' Sure enough, the book has the tell-tale sticker on its jacket. 'So I know all about your husband. You glad the guy who shot him is still alive?'

I nod.

'What if they hadn't banned the death penalty?' she says, looking at me hard with clear eyes that seem tired of crying. 'Would you be okay with things if the man who shot your man paid with his life?'

'I don't know.'

'You sure about that?'

The fact is, I'm not sure at all. I know I'd always said I was sure. I'd said it in Ian's Cambridge living room; I'd shouted it in Harvard Yard. I had collected at least a dozen examples of wrongful execution and followed up with the parents, siblings, and spouses. The amount of time I spent talking with the surviving families of murder victims about closure wasn't all that much, if I'm honest.

And isn't honesty what the law is about? That search for a crystal of truth in the mud of uncertainty?

I lean back against the hard iron of the park bench and close my eyes for a moment. I was the first survivor I'd really known, actually spent time with, talked to. Not that I proved to be an engaging conversationalist after Ian was killed, but we don't consciously carry on conversations with ourselves. They happen all on their own, whether we want them to or not.

Emily waits for me to answer, one eye on me now, one tracking the boys as they hop from merry-go-round to swings to slide. In the few minutes we've been at the park, Jonathan and Jake Junior have become friends. I don't expect the same instant camaraderie to happen between Emily and me.

Perhaps I'm wrong, though. She lays one of her hands on mine in a motherly gesture, stilling my own shaking hand. 'You know what I think? I think it's impossible to say what you would do until you're there. Like those women who insist they'll do natural childbirth, like they know exactly how they're gonna handle the pain. Yeah, you know what? If I had a nickel for every time I've heard about women screaming for the epidural while they're in labor, I could put Jake through college. Maybe even law school.' She sighs, not taking her hand off mine. 'No one ever knows what she'll do. Not until you're standing in the middle of it all.'

'What about you?' I try this on automatically, only realizing what I've asked after the words come out. I've just asked this woman if she wants a quid pro quo. If she wants the woman responsible to pay with her life.

Emily calls out to both boys to be careful of the rust on the swing set's chains because it will rub off on their clothes. She's a good mother, attentive without being helicopter-ish, concerned without living in constant fear. Everyone else I know would worry about tetanus. Emily just wants to lighten her laundry load. I find myself liking her more and more.

'Now there's a good question,' she says. 'When that judge read out Jake's sentence, I felt like something inside me was on fire. Not a small fire, either, more like one of those brush fires you see on farms, piled so high it burns for days.' She shivers. 'And it seemed like I would keep on burning for days on end. That's how angry I was. One night, I put Jake to bed and went on the Internet. I looked up how to murder someone and not get caught. You know they have sites that tell you that shit? Lots of 'em. Anyway, I must have been a little crazy, because I know I could never kill anyone. But back then, I thought the only way I could put the fire inside me out would be to throw an ocean of water on it, and I thought you could be that water. All I needed to do was find you and shoot you dead.' She laughs now, a high, girlish giggle. 'That's how crazy I was.'

'I guess I'm glad you changed your mind,' I say, feigning a casual lightness I don't feel. The pressure of her hand on mine seems to strengthen.

Emily's laughter dies down. 'Never had to change it. I knew as soon as I started looking around the web that I couldn't pull the trigger. And I knew even if I could, I'm not smart enough to get away with it. That would leave my boy an orphan. I don't know. Maybe I'm smarter than I think. Jake always said I was, but I never believed him.'

I believe her. I believe her all the way. Emily is young, poor, and uneducated, but she thinks harder than most people I knew at Harvard. Certainly more than Ted from Ian's weekly Death and Drinks salons during the law school years, good old Ted, who has the integrity of a wet Kleenex. It's possible the woman on the park bench with her hand on mine and her eyes sweeping a steady arc from me to the boys and back is more insightful than I am.

So much for an Ivy League education.

She checks her watch, then looks over toward the far end of the park where the woman dressed in red stands, now accompanied by a tall man with his back towards me. 'I talked to them this morning,' she says. 'Well, actually, they talked and I listened. Asked a ton of questions.'

The woman in red turns her head toward us as if she's heard. When her eyes meet mine, a thin smile spreads on her lips.

'I didn't tell them what I'm about to tell you,' Emily says.

A silent *But you still might* works its way up my throat and stays unspoken. The cotton of my jeans where my hand rests is damp with sweat.

'Remember how I said I begged Jake to spill the beans? Even if he was in a hotel room with some tootsie he met on the Internet?'

'Yeah.' I really don't want to hear the rest of this.

She laughs again, but not with her eyes. 'Well, I'd bet all the hair on my head that Jake was in a hotel room with another woman on the day Caleb Church was killed.'

I thought I had mentally prepared myself, but the words strike me like a wrecking ball. Nothing was real before this moment, not the found piece of paper, not Emily saying it was a hotel receipt. They were only phrases with a faint meaning, a possibility. Driving over here after Jonathan's meltdown, I explained them away. A wrong date, a misread name. Surely this scrap of evidence was nothing more than a mistake, Emily's own wishful thinking. There could be no viable alibi because an alibi would mean I was wrong. An alibi would make me the criminal.

Oh, Ian. What have I done?

There's an ocean of words flowing through my head, none of them the right one. My feet seem to want to move, but all my muscles have atrophied. I go limp, and a glimpse of Jake Junior, the boy I robbed of his father, floats into my peripheral vision. At this minute, I am the worst person I know.

'I don't understand,' is all I can manage.

'Yeah, well. I'm getting ahead of myself here.' After another stern, but not too stern, warning to the boys to try just a wee bit harder to keep their clothes clean, she swivels on the bench and hunches toward me. It's a little-girl pose, a secret-sharing attitude.

'See, Jake was a good man, but after he was born, God must have run out of goodness when it came to the Milford family. He's got a younger brother who's about the meanest piece of shit this side of hell.' She glances toward the boys as if to make sure they're both out of earshot. 'Wife-beater,' she whispers. 'Jake Junior doesn't even know he's got an uncle. *That's* how hard me and Jake worked to keep Kris away from us. He tried, though. Found our telephone number when we first got married and started calling all the time.'

I still don't understand, but Emily's urgent tone keeps me quiet.

'Then the calls stopped, as sudden as they started. We forgot about Kris and went on. We didn't know he got married himself until the phone rang one night.' She closes her eyes now, maybe to watch the movie play out in her memory. 'I picked it up, and there was this crying on the end of the line. Like a dog might cry if you kicked him upside the head for no reason and without no warning. The woman kept on asking for Jake. Kept on saying how sorry she was. I looked across the kitchen at my husband, and I thought the worst thing ever. We'd only been married a few years ourselves.' Emily pauses, fishes a tissue out of her purse, and blows her nose into it. 'I passed the phone to him and stood there, just seething. Then the anger kind of melted away and my heart sank.'

Without thinking much about it, I give Emily's hand a firm squeeze.

'Silly me. Jake only had to curse under his breath once and say his brother's name before I knew what was up. Then he kissed me and went into the spare room, the one we were fixing up in yellow and green for when that little ball of energy would come along.' She nods toward Jake Junior, who has progressed to teaching Jonathan how to not be a wimp and to go *even higher* on the rusty swing set. 'Kids. I don't like him playing so hard, but I gotta let him be a kid, take his falls, pick himself back up again. Jake would want it that way.'

Emily shrugs once, fiddles with the gold band on her left fourth, and continues her story. 'Anyway, that night when my husband came back out of the spare room, he was madder than a rabid dog. Didn't have to say a word; I just knew. Then he took me in his arms – he had big arms, Jake did. Working man's arms, but gentle when he wanted them to be. And he promised he would never lay a hand on me, no matter what. He said he'd rather die than hurt me. At first, I didn't know what he was talking about, but I'm not stupid. I put two and two together after I heard him yelling at Kris through the phone and telling him to leave Mary Ann alone. It was their wedding night, see. Kris and the woman he married.'

My blood goes cold.

'So that was the first time. There were others. Plenty of phone calls, but always to Jake's cell, never to the landline again. And then there was that last phone call, on the day Caleb Church died, and Jake got in his car and said he was going off to work. With all the fuss and the arrest and everything else, I'd almost forgotten about it. But you see, I sometimes go through Jake's things.' She takes out a phone, the old candy bar kind, cheap and scarred and looking like it had been dropped on a battlefield more than a few times. 'I got this after – you know.' She flinches even as she avoids the painful words. 'He put a password on it, but bless his soul, Jake was never one of those creative types. Took me one try. Month and date of our wedding. I called my own number with it this morning, just to hear that ringtone that I'd put on so I always knew when it was Jake calling me and not some robot from halfway around the world asking if I was having trouble with my Windows software. Do you think that's silly?'

'No,' I say. 'Not silly. Maybe a little masochistic, though.' I never thought about doing the same with Ian's phone, and I'm glad of it. We had our unique ringtones, too, and I think the sound of a few bars of 'Ode to Joy' blaring out of my iPhone might have sent me over whatever edge I've been teetering on.

'Yeah. I get that. So I started scrolling through the numbers and I found a whole passel of them with the same 276 area code. That's where Kris and his wife live, see. In some one-horse and two-trailer-park town called Pounding Mill. Jake always said it made sense his brother would pick a place with that kind of name.' She holds out the phone, and I squint at the numbers.

'Did you call it?'

'You bet I did,' Emily says. 'It's a store called Pop Shop in Tazewell. Makes sense, I guess. Battered wives are smart enough not to make calls from their home phones.'

I nod. I've seen spousal abuse cases before. You work in the DA's office long enough, you see just about everything.

'I didn't get very far, though. The woman who answered said she didn't know any Mary Ann Milford and told me not to call again.' Emily leans toward me. 'That's when I knew she was lying. Because I only asked for Mary Ann, not for Mary Ann Milford. You want to know what I think Jake was doing down in that hotel?'

I do and I don't.

Emily doesn't wait for my answer. 'I think he was trying to save that poor woman. They were sweethearts once, back when they were kids.' She wipes at her brow with the back of one arm.

'But I don't believe they were up to anything. Jake wasn't like that. I think he was just being Jake. A good man, sort of an everyday hero.'

I feel the shudder of her body next to mine, and I can't tell if Emily is laughing or crying.

'I hear they give heroes one hell of a funeral. At least they're supposed to,' she says.

Then the boys run over, proffering a pair of squiggling earthworms they've dug up from the soft earth around the spring-loaded pandas and lions and horses.

'You put those back where you found them, Jacob Benjamin Milford. Let 'em live their little worm lives in peace, you hear? It's what your daddy wants.'

Jake Junior nods. 'Okay, Momma.' And they run off again to bury their treasures, to put them back where they belong, to make a wrong right.

'Cute as buttons,' Emily says, sighing. 'Well, we better be off now.' She presses the receipt from Bluefield with her dead husband's signature just above the Little Walker Hotel's logo onto my lap. 'You keep this. Better yet, maybe destroy it. I don't want what I thought I wanted any longer. It's best we leave this all alone. Best for Mary Ann if her husband don't know Jake went down to interfere in their domestic squabbles. I'll tell you, I'd like to clear my husband's name, but I wouldn't put it past Kris to kill that poor wretch of woman, and I can't have no more killing in my life.' Then she calls to her boy, and he comes running back again, a smile on his face as if nothing in the world were wrong.

When I start to pull my hand from under Emily's, I realize I've been holding it all this time.

CHAPTER TWENTY-NINE

As Emily walks through the gate at the far end of the park and Jonathan rambles on about his new best friend, I'm unsure what to think. Our goodbyes were friendly but quick, over in a heartbeat. There were no requests to keep in touch, no drawn-out apologies or widow-bonding cryfests. Only a curt nod from Emily as she took her son's hand, and a final promise that her last letter to me was, in fact, the last one she would ever send.

I get up to go, urging Jonathan to dust off his jeans and T-shirt before he turns Daniel's car into a mud-bomb. He laughs, and I want to laugh with him. I really do. I should feel lighter than I have in days. Maybe in years. I'm safe, and my boy won't grow up parentless. But I've done nothing more than trade one sack of bricks for another, heavier burden.

Lost in these thoughts, I don't notice the woman walking toward us, not until she's standing next to me.

'Can I have a word, Ms Boucher?' she says, skipping over the usual social niceties of introductions and handshakes. We both know they aren't necessary. Her red suit does the work, like mine once did.

I remember those days well. It was all about intimidation.

'We don't have time,' I say and continue walking.

'Strange a little boy isn't in school today,' she says, more to Jonathan than to me, then checking the skies for – what – signs of snow?

'He's sick.'

'Really.' Not a question, not a hint of surprise, only one flat word hanging heavily in the air, waiting for other words to replace it.

'What do you want with me?'

She looks at me directly, her eyes steady, but doesn't answer.

When I trained my early Vita recruits, a dozen or so young idealists who likened both Ian and me to the second coming, I had a written script for their interactions with prosecutors, not so different from the play-by-play this woman gives me now.

First, use their name. Use it over and over again. It's a reminder you know who they are. Second, don't answer questions. You're the questioner; they're the questionee. Third, look at them. Look them straight in the eye and don't blink. Get close, be formal, stand tall. Essentially, I drew every tool I could from a handbook of bullying and psychological manipulation.

I was frighteningly good at it.

Now, I pull myself up to my full height. I smile. I refuse to let my eyelids fall, even for a millisecond. I allow the silence between us to draw out until it's taut as a tightrope because I know this woman has nothing on me, not after my talk with Emily.

Finally, she speaks. 'Ms Boucher, I'm one of the leads on the Milford case.'

I say nothing. It's another tactic. Let them talk as if their words don't matter.

'We're working with the Oversight Committee, who I'm sure you know are continuing to look into his execution. What did you and Mrs Milford have to say to each other? You seemed close. Friendly.' She leans her head to one side, waiting. When I don't answer, she continues. 'So I'm wondering, what could two women like you have to talk about? I can't see anything in common except for a couple of young sons, but they go to different schools, don't they?' She looks me up and down, taking in my shoes and purse. 'Don't imagine you were discussing fashion. Emily Milford strikes me as more of the Walmart sort, and I can't see that as your kind of place. What I can see – what I saw pretty darned clearly from where I was standing – was some paper exchanging hands and both of you looking at a phone as if it were the Hope diamond. Strange.'

I don't like where this is going.

'It's all a bit coincidental,' she says, tapping a finger to her lips as if in deep thought. 'That Mrs Milford suddenly makes a U-turn and doesn't want to talk to us anymore, especially as she seemed so eager after the execution. Can you think of any reason for her change of mind?'

I can imagine this woman is thinking about plenty of reasons, all of them green and crisp and wrapped up in bank envelopes. A photograph or a video swapped for a wad of cash. Silence for money.

Speaking of money, now the man from earlier is striding across the playground, a Starbucks cup in each hand, smiling broadly at me. Everything on him, from the red necktie to the perfectly tailored suit, to the ridiculously expensive-looking shoes polished to within an inch of their lives, screams one syllable: *Wealth*.

'I'd introduce you,' the woman says, taking one of the coffees. 'But I think you and Ted already know one another.'

'Hello, Justine,' Ted Stuyvesant says.

I force myself to nod.

To the woman, who might not be his wife, he says, 'Sorry, babe. After bouncing between here and Florida all weekend, I needed caffeine. Skinny latte okay with you?'

Jonathan tugs at my hand. 'Can we go now, Mommy?'

The woman leans down, hands on her knees, until she's at eye level with him. 'You're quite the little man,' she says. 'How come you're not in school today? Sore throat?'

Jonathan shakes his head. 'We have to go home and get ready. For a trip.' And then, a non-sequitur only a six-year-old could introduce. 'I like your outfit.'

'Thanks, sweetie. I like it, too. What kind of trip?'

Don't, Jonathan. Please don't.

'An airplane trip.'

Now her eyes meet mine, and a smile spreads across her lips, a clownish grin that makes me understand why people find clowns terrifying. 'I see. Well, I'll let you go, then. Ted and I have a mountain of paperwork waiting for us at the office.'

I send Jonathan to play on the spring-mounted lion, close enough for me to keep an eye on him, far enough so that he's out of earshot. 'What the hell happened to you, Ted?'

'What happened to me? Well, after you dumped me for that asshole in tweed, I started thinking. I started thinking about what he had that I didn't, and I figured it was money.'

'That's not fair, Ted.'

'Fair? Fair is not going on a date with one guy and ditching him for another. Bet you even slept with him on the first night. I mean, I don't want to call you out for whoring yourself around, but sometimes a spade is a spade and a whore is a whore.' He sets his coffee on a nearby bench, shoots his cuffs, and I get a glimpse of shiny silver on each wrist. Maybe platinum. I'm figuring platinum.

'We had a goal,' I tell him. 'You were on board with it once.'

He chuckles. 'I followed the money, honey. The champagne-and-social-justice crowd has plenty of it. See, Justine, there are people who don't like the death penalty. Then there are people who *really* don't like the death penalty. Those folks pay me to make sure the Remedies Act is enforced swiftly and without prejudice. Simple, really. And I have to say, they pay pretty god-damned well.' He checks his fingernails. They're manicured. Manicured, for Chrissake.

'Do you have any integrity at all, Ted?'

Once again, he laughs. 'That's an interesting question, coming from you.' He turns to the woman. 'Come on, Joanna. We're done here. For the time being.'

I wave Jonathan over and start walking towards the car. When we reach the edge of the park, Joanna or Joanne or whatever her name is, calls to me. 'If you know something, Ms Callaghan, you should come forward. Get it all out in the open. We'll give you the best deal we can, within the law.'

I call back without turning. 'Nothing to come forward with.'

'Maybe not. Maybe so. We're in the dark at the moment but we have resources. Think about that.'

Jonathan and I walk briskly to the car, sun on our backs, a storm cloud hanging over my head, dark and full of acid rain.

'Did you like her red outfit?' Jonathan says.

'Sure.' *I used to wear one exactly like it.*

'I liked it. A lot.'

I manage a weak smile as I tuck him into the car seat, and I realize if I know anything at all, it's this: with a half million dollars and counting, Ted Stuyvesant and his crowd certainly have resources. Maybe enough resources to persuade Emily to tell them what she knows – with or without the receipt. Enough resources to keep going, to never give up.

I'm not sure they should. I'm also not sure it matters. One way or another, what I did to Jake Milford is a thing I own, a possession I bought that isn't returnable or exchangeable, that will stay with me as long as I live.

Death Row Inmate #39384

I was home for all of two hours before they arrested me. Emily had made us supper — her mother's meatloaf recipe with succotash on the side. I miss those suppers. Guess I always will. We were still at the table, her asking me how my day went, and me lying through my teeth about an engine overhaul that kept a few of us guys late at work.

That's when the news came on.

Authorities say the body of a seven-year-old boy was found on the banks of the James River this afternoon . . . stay tuned for updates.

My wife's face, already pale from her being pregnant, went the color of paste. 'Oh my God,' she said. 'His poor, poor parents.'

We listened to details, what details there were.

'They ain't saying who it is, baby. They ain't talking any details,' Emily said. She's forgotten her dinner now and is fixed on the small television I'd set up in one corner of the kitchen so she could watch her favorite shows while she cooked. I never thought you could put a woman in a sealed-off room and expect her to be happy while she went about chopping vegetables and peeling potatoes. Or a man, for that matter. You gotta give cooks a window, a radio, a way to see they're still connected with the world. Sometimes I think that was the problem with my own ma – all toil, no fun.

'They ain't gonna,' I said. 'Little kid. Parents might not even know yet. Might only think he's gone missing, maybe got lost.'

I was right; the reporter on the screen didn't mention any names. She didn't have to. As she stared into the camera, her eyes shining some, another woman joined her. The second woman wore a uniform and held a clear plastic bag, the kind you see on those CSI shows. At first, I thought the light was playing tricks with me, that whatever was inside the baggie wasn't a piece of blue and white checked cloth, that it didn't in any way match up with what Caleb Church was wearing when I saw him early this morning.

Emily stood to start clearing our plates. Right then, watching her move toward the kitchen, her head bent a little and her hair falling over her eyes, I wanted to tell her everything. I even heard myself pouring it out, explaining what a lying piece of shit I'd been, telling her all the things I knew my brother had told his wife. *It'll never happen again, baby. I promise. Tomorrow will be different.* In my case, that promise would have been true, but the part that came before the promise wasn't something I wanted to say out loud. Not to my wife.

I'll tell you a secret: I'm a coward at heart. I might be a big man, plenty of muscle and nothing to laugh at in a street fight, but when it comes to Emily, I melt like chocolate on a radiator.

You see, there's more to the story, and some of the story

I haven't worked up the courage to tell takes place in the same motel room in Bluefield with Mary Ann. The scene and the day are different. A whole lot of stuff was different.

I opened my mouth, thinking, *This is it, Jake. You gotta tell it straight and tell it true.* And I probably would have done that if the phone on the kitchen wall didn't start ringing. Emily shook off her soapy hands in the sink, gave them a quick pat on her apron, and picked up the receiver. If she looked pale before, I don't know what the right word for her was now – it was almost as if she'd gone transparent, like she wasn't all there. I watched her eyes, still glassy, as they widened into circles and held me in focus. She didn't say anything after 'Hello,' only stood there with the wet patches on her apron and a dazed expression on her face. Then she dropped the phone, or, I should say, the phone seemed to float through her fingers like they'd lost their grip on just about everything in the material world.

I picked it up and heard a woman's voice. She didn't sound like a woman, and she sure as shit didn't sound like Mrs Church from down the street. She didn't sound human at all. Except for a few ugly words, I couldn't pick out the whole message. Something about hoping the bastard got what he deserved. Then, nothing. Only the dead silence of an ended call.

If I'd had a shred of sense in me, I would have followed Emily as she bolted across the dining room and up the stairs. I would have wrapped myself around her, dried her tears, and made love like I'd never made love before. I would have done all those things because if I'd been thinking clear, I would have known it would be the last chance I had to be with her that way. What I did was stand in the kitchen, staring at the plates smeared with meatloaf and hot sauce, listening to my wife's sobs come tumbling down the staircase.

I don't know how long it took them to ring our doorbell, and everything after that is a little blurry. Words like 'you have the right to' and 'could be held against you' still echo in my head. Also, they used my full name, and when someone uses your full name, whether it's your mother or your teacher or a guy with a badge, let me tell you a truth: when they do that, you know you're in deep shit.

Come morning, they didn't waste any time getting me a public defender. He was a short man with red hair, a pimple on his forehead, and looked as if he might have graduated from law school the week before. Maybe not so long ago as that. My first thought was that I was being represented by the legal equivalent of Doogie Howser.

'Mr Milford, I'm Martin Kelleher, and I'm afraid you are in some serious trouble here.' He said this quickly as he sat across from me in the same small, gray room where I'd spent most of the night listening to my life change, one repeated accusation at a time. He didn't shake my hand. I noted that right away. In fact, Kelleher refused to touch the table between us, as if some of my wrongdoing might rub off on him. The way it went was, he asked questions, and I answered them best I could. Or he talked, and I listened. When he told me to agree with something, I agreed.

'You will plead not guilty at your arraignment.'

'Okay.'

'You may change your plea at a later date.'

'Okay.'

Agreeing with the man didn't seem to get me into his good

236

graces; I could tell by looking at him, at the narrowed eyes and the curled lip – body language, they call it. To Kelleher, I was like some dangerous animal he was supposed to be helping out, but all the time we talked, anyone with a working pair of eyes and a lick of common sense could see he hated the job he'd signed up for.

I guess that's what they call irony.

'Mr Milford,' he said, 'can you account for your whereabouts on—' he checked a sheet in his file folder, even though the day in question was only yesterday '—between eight a.m. and five p.m. on Tuesday the twelfth of June?'

I didn't answer straight away, much like I didn't answer the hundred and one times they'd asked me the same question last night. 'Afraid I can't at this time,' I said.

But man, I wanted to. I wanted to show them my phone with the call from Mary Ann and the receipt from the motel. I wanted to explain all about the Woman's Place in Roanoke. I wanted to tell them I was a hero, not a murderer.

I wanted to. And I didn't. I knew my brother too well, and I knew I had to talk to Mary Ann first.

Kelleher's face drooped with disappointment before it changed to a different kind of expression, some strange mix of fear and hate. I thought about asking him why he did this job, why he bothered going to law school if he was the kind of man who had already made up his mind about me.

I didn't say that, either. I just stayed quiet with my cuffed hands in my lap, trying not to pick at my fingernails.

'You aren't making this easy for me,' Kelleher said.

'I'm not the one who studied up on the law,' I told him.

He sighed, scratched out a few notes on his legal pad, and

stood up, signaling to the cop on the other side of the door. 'I'll see you at ten tomorrow morning,' he said as he walked out. He didn't say another word, and he didn't look back. I figured if my own lawyer hated me that much, the other side would think I was the devil reborn.

Sleep should have come easy that afternoon, but it didn't. I lay on a hard bunk in a cell, listening to my own heartbeat tick off the seconds, playing a childish game of will I or won't I.

I was frightened for Mary Ann.

See, my brother Kris wasn't stupid. He'd been smart enough to graduate high school, even though making it through meant threatening Willie Stokes with daily beatings if the kid didn't get Kris a homework assignment in time for him to copy it in his own hand. Same thing with the jobs. Kris wasn't the best man on a construction crew, far from it. Most days, he didn't bother to get to the site on time, and when he did, he screwed up six ways from Sunday on the simplest tasks. But he always persuaded one of the other guys to clock in for him or cover his mistakes. Kris had a good head on him when it came to the art of persuasion.

I was frightened he might not only track Mary Ann down, but that he'd persuade her to come back home with him. And I was frightened of a whole lot more than that.

The thing of it is, Emily wasn't the only woman in my life who was pregnant when I was arrested for the murder of Caleb Church.

CHAPTER THIRTY

Daniel calls as I'm pulling out of the parking space near the playground, wanting to know if I'm ready to head to my house, collect our passports, and start the drive up to Dulles airport.

'Why don't you get the passports? From the travel binder in the upstairs office. Lowest shelf on the left. I'll come straight to your place and we can head from there.' This third lie in three days slides out so easily, I barely notice.

We can still make it in time to check in for the overnight flight. An easy ride up I-95 means we don't need to leave for another six hours, but I'm starting to wonder how easy that ride will be knowing what I know now. And if Emily's word is as good as I believe, running isn't necessary. After all, I'm the one holding the evidence. The hotel receipt from Bluefield is safe in my purse, folded into a neat square. A few seconds with a match or a Bic lighter, and I can turn it into ashes, make it disappear, deconstruct a something into a nothing.

But.

Jake wasn't like that. I think he was just being Jake. A good man, sort of an everyday hero.

That's the 'but', and I'll never be able to make it disappear.

From the back seat, Jonathan announces, 'Jake Junior says his daddy doesn't live with them anymore. He has to stay in some different place all the time. How come?'

If I had an ounce of character, or if Jonathan were older, I could tell him the truth. I could tell him I'm the reason that little boy's daddy won't ever come home. As it is, I shrug and answer him in the lamest way possible, hoping he doesn't hear my voice falter. 'Sometimes dads have to go away.'

'Like Tommy's dad?'

'Yes. Like Tommy's dad.'

The analogy is as flimsy as a house of cards in a high wind. My sister-in-law's husband ran out on her in search of a newer model; Emily's husband didn't have a choice.

'Can Jake Junior get a new dad?'

'Maybe.'

'Where do kids go to get a new one?' Jonathan asks this as if there were a shop full of waiting men, all clamoring to father a kid who isn't theirs. Daddies-R-Us, maybe. Wal-Daddy. FAO Daddy. I imagine rows and rows of men – short, tall, athletic, intellectual. There would be the aisle with bedtime story readers, the one with signs like *Loves to play catch!* and *How about we go fishing?*, another full of men with tags hanging from them proclaiming *I'll never leave your mom for a twenty-something floozie* or *Of course I won't become addicted to opioids and die on you, kid* – all of them screaming *Pick me! Pick me!* I can see salespeople hovering as customers peruse the wares, promising guaranteed satisfaction and free, no-questions-asked returns. And the prices? No problem – all those single men would pick up the tab.

If only life worked like that. It would be every single mother's dream come true.

My thoughts turn to Daniel. I didn't find him in a shop, but at a café in downtown Richmond that Susan dragged me to last year. He didn't come with a lifetime guarantee, only with an air of honesty and a kind smile for Jonathan once I had worked up the courage to spill the beans and introduce them. I know I lucked out, and I know Daniel will help me raise my son. I know he'll never complain, not even in those terrible teenage years that are bound to tax the patience of the most phlegmatic of men. But I know something else, too. I know Daniel, no matter how much he tries or how much he wants to be, will never be Jonathan's father. There will always be that hard line in the sand, the one that spells out *I'm the substitute, not the real thing.* Thinking of it makes me want to cry, not for me or for Jonathan, but for Jake Junior. I've taken away something I can't replace. I've done a thing that is undoable.

'Mom? Earth to Mom!' Jonathan says.

'Yeah, sweetie. I'm right here.'

'Can we get ice cream?' He's pointing at a corner store on the other side of the stop light. A triple-decker cone with its Neapolitan mix of vanilla, chocolate, and strawberry does precisely the job the sign painter intended. It tempts like a siren to a lost sailor.

'At ten in the morning?' What the hell. 'Sure.' I pull into the small, three-space lot between the ice cream store and the neighboring dry cleaners, park, and begin unbuckling Jonathan from his car seat. It's a task I've been able to perform blindfolded for six years, even if the seats have changed sizes and the buckles switched configurations. Through the rear window, my eye catches a poster fixed to the window of the dry cleaning place.

You can help a domestic abuse survivor. Donate to Safe Harbor now!

There's a web address and a phone number at the bottom of the poster, but I don't want either of them. I already know who I need to call. Today.

Jonathan asks for chocolate in a wafer cone, and the girl in the ice cream store holds it under the soft-serve machine for an extra couple of seconds, topping it up to an impossible peak. 'Here you go, little man,' she says. Then, to me: 'Another one of those school holidays?'

I nod.

'Wish I had the day off. It's nice outside.'

I nod again. The truth is, I hadn't really noticed, but it gives me an idea. As soon as we're in the car and Jonathan has licked his cone down to a manageable hill of chocolate, I offer to take him back to the playground, holding his ice cream as I drive the two blocks. Once again, we do the unbuckling boogaloo, Jonathan holds my hand as we cross the street, and then he's busy asking each member of the spring-mounted menagerie if it would like some ice cream.

Seated on the same bench where I talked to Emily only a half-hour ago, I pull out my phone and find the number of the Pop Shop in Tazewell, Virginia. A woman answers the call, her voice thick with the South's drawn-out vowels. I ask for Mary Ann Milford.

There's a long and pregnant pause, and I know this woman recognizes the name.

'It's important I talk to her,' I say before she answers in the negative.

'You callin' about collection on the car again? 'Cause if you are, I ain't got nothing to say.'

I assure her I'm not in the repo business, that only scum would find job satisfaction in taking away honest folks' property, and then add what I hope makes me sound trustworthy. 'We met at a, you know, a shelter a while back. Mary Ann told me if I ever needed her, I could call you.'

'You in trouble, honey?'

'I guess you could say that.'

She pauses again, but this time there's a sigh instead of silence. I'm getting through. I feel like shit about lying, but I'm getting through. 'The last time we talked,' I say, 'we said we'd help each other out if we could.'

A chuckle. *Mary Ann* help *you?* Christ on a racehorse. That girl can't even help herself. As far as helping her, only thing with a chance in hell of doing that is a Mack truck running over that shit-kicking husband of hers.'

'Can I just talk to her?'

'Hang on,' the woman says. There's a clatter that makes me think she's dropped the phone, a customer in the background asking if he can get five singles in change back, and the hiss of what sounds like a deep fryer. Then, another voice comes on the line, small and mouse-like, barely audible over the background noise.

'Who's this?'

'A friend,' I say.

'I don't got no friends. Not anymore. And I don't know you. I'd recognize your voice if I did. I'm good at voices, see. I could have been one of those book readers, like for books on tape. Although I guess they don't use tape anymore.'

It's time for another lie, one that hurts as I hear myself speak words that are light-years from the truth. 'I was a friend of Jake's,' I say.

'Uh-huh.'

'Listen. Do you think I could come down to see you? We could meet at a coffee shop in Bluefield, maybe. Or wherever you like.'

'That's funny.'

'What is?'

'Me meeting you in Bluefield. Or me meeting anyone, anywhere.'

'I need to know something, Mary Ann. I need to know if Jake Milford was with you on the twelfth of June seven years ago.'

'How do I know you ain't a friend of my husband's?'

I almost laugh, imagining Kris Milford and me being friends. 'I'm not.'

'Well, I tell you what. You take your fancy city-girl talk and put it where the sun don't shine. 'Cause I don't believe you, honey.'

Jonathan leaps off the bouncy lion and starts running toward me at the same time my phone rings. Daniel again. One way or another, this phone conversation needs to end.

'I'm Justine Boucher, Mrs Milford. I was the prosecutor in Jake's trial. You can look that up, if you want.'

'Maybe I will and maybe I won't.' She pauses and tells a customer she'll be right with him. 'What do you want, Ms Boucher?'

I tell her the truth. I tell her I want to set things right.

'I'll be at work all day. Until six. You come down here, and if you are who you say you are, I might talk to you.'

Before I can say I'll be there, the line goes silent.

CHAPTER THIRTY-ONE

The next time Daniel calls, he sounds less like himself and more like Churchill on the warpath. 'Where the bloody hell are you, Jussie?'

'On my way,' I say, which is sort of true if I leave out the part about where I'm on my way to.

'I've got the passports. And I pulled out some winter clothes from the attic for you and Jonathan because everything in your bedroom wardrobes screams summer in Richmond. Hate to tell you, but we only get two weeks of summer in England, and everyone's inside watching Wimbledon. It's why we're so pale.' At least there's a hint of the old Daniel in this, but I don't know what he'll turn into when I drop Jonathan off and show him my taillights.

The day has become unusually warm for mid-April, and I turn on the air conditioning, accidentally hitting the radio on-button with the back of my hand. The AC gives off that funny chemical-burn smell as it starts up. The radio static fills the car, and I have to chase away another memory as we drive through the city to Daniel's. Before I know it, the memory is chasing me down. It catches up, wraps itself around me, and I'm not in the past anymore, but in the present. Inside the memory.

It's no longer April in Richmond, but a year after the botched lethal injection, and I'm back in the Greensville Correctional Center. Ian and I are riding in another van towards that low and flat structure called Hellville along with a pair of lawyers, a half-dozen reporters, and the parents of the victim – still begging for clemency. We climb out of the van, tugging our coats tighter to combat the winter wind that whips at us in this flat part of Virginia. Jeffries, still in his role of prison liaison, quickly shuttles us inside, invites us to arrange ourselves on hard plastic chairs in the viewing room, and instructs us to wait.

Most of it happens in the same way as the first electrocution I witnessed. The prisoner is walked into the room, head shaved, left leg bare as a newborn's skin. The well-rehearsed placement of straps and sponges and electrodes takes only moments, but my mind measures the moments as if they are years. Once the preparations are complete, the only sounds are the hum of electrical current, the soft scratch of pencil on paper as the reporters make notes, the sharp intake of breath from the victim's mother, who hasn't stopped sniffling since we arrived.

'Do you have anything you want to say?' the warden asks after an interminable pause.

'I am innocent.'

I know this case inside and out. I know the man in the chair is not right in the head. I know the jury's verdict was not unanimous. I know very few people who want this execution to proceed. I also know that once the machine is set in motion, it's nearly impossible to shut it down.

The woman behind me stops sniffling and begins to sob; her husband does his best to quiet her. Then there's silence again, a short time where everything seems to hang in the air around us. I will the phone on the wall to ring. Although I'm not a praying person, I'm praying now, hoping someone has listened to the churches and the families, to the Pope and his archbishops, to anyone who can put a stop to this. Because the man in the chair isn't right in the head. And if there's anything worse than killing, it's killing a person who isn't right in the head.

This silence is interrupted by a bang, which I'm ready for.

I'm not at all ready for the foot-high crown of fire shooting from the almost-dead man's skull. I'm not ready for the blanket of smoke that fills the execution chamber. I'm not ready for the sick stench of burning hair and skin and tissue filtering into the viewing room. And I'm not ready to watch as the electricity is cut off and the man in the chair struggles for breath as the blinds close.

Someone yells, 'Sponge! Who checked the goddamned sponge?'

There are a thousand things that can go wrong with any process, and electrocution is no different. A misplaced or unsecured electrode, an improper jack connection, a flaw in the current. In this case, a sponge is the problem – a simple sponge that should have been natural but was switched at the last minute for a synthetic alternative.

Jeffries herds us out of the viewing room. Half of us, including myself, are doubled over, hands clenched around our stomachs, trying to hold back what wants to come out. The second we're outside, I'm the first to vomit. I'm not the last.

In the car now, I shut off the air conditioning and the radio, and roll down all four windows. A rush of spring air floods the vehicle and blows back my hair. I let it wash over me all the way to Daniel's house, as if it has the power to wipe the slate of my memory clean.

It doesn't.

CHAPTER THIRTY-TWO

I'm a lawyer, not a psychologist, but my day's work is less about statutes and procedure than about why people act in ways that, on the surface, make no sense at all.

I drive the four and a half hours to Bluefield without music because everything on satellite radio seems to be a love song today, and I've got the idea I lost whatever love I had in my life when I left Daniel on the front porch of his house. He stood there, one arm on Jonathan's shoulder, not waving, his face a blank, expressionless mask. Except for the disappointment – that was painted on in broad and colorful strokes. Four suitcases lay piled next to him, destined to return inside and be unpacked. The long drive and the rush to get to Mary Ann before she left work meant I had no time to explain in full, only to make half-hearted promises that I'd be back late tonight and would call from the road.

He didn't seem to care.

If my mind were clear, I would spend the drive wondering about Daniel, playing through various scenarios and explanations in my head. He does care, but doesn't want to show it. He's worried about me, but knows I need room. He's over me, but he'll wait until tonight to say so – front porches and small children are shitty venues and audiences for the final act of a romantic tragedy.

As it is, I'm not thinking of Daniel. I'm thinking of Jake Milford. I'm thinking of a primitive instinct called survival.

When my mother was dying, I asked how long she thought she could go on before deciding on a permanent exit. The bone cancer had begun eating its way into her, and morphine only went so far in easing the pain. Still, she looked at me with watery eyes and shook her head. It wasn't that she feared the moment of death, but the nothingness that came after that moment filled her with dread. So she hung on, each day and each week bringing a new brand of misery, until the disease took all the fight out of her and she no longer had a choice.

On the seat next to me, my phone vibrates, and I let the car's Bluetooth system answer. It's Daniel. Suddenly, I want to talk to him more than anything.

'Hiya,' he says.

No 'Hiya, Jussie' or 'Hiya, babe' or 'Hiya, love' – only that one word with an empty hole after it. As soon as I realize I'm shaking, I pull onto the gravel shoulder. 'Hey.'

'How about explaining this to me. Pretend I'm a six-year-old and not very bright.'

'I don't know if I can. Not yet, Daniel.'

'See any red suits lately? I need to know.'

I tell him about the conversation with Emily, and then about the unpleasantness with Ted at the park. I tell him I've got the hotel receipt from Bluefield.

'Destroy it,' he says.

I know he's protecting me, protecting himself, protecting the two of us together, but I can't agree until I know the rest of the story, and maybe not even then. Instead of a direct answer, I change the subject – sort of. 'I was thinking about my mother when she was dying. She refused to let go. I mean, Daniel, that cancer had its teeth in her bones, and she still wanted to make it through one more day.'

'That's what humans do, Jussie. We hang on to the bitter end, even when hanging on hurts,' he says.

We make small talk, dancing around the subject of where I'm going and why. Daniel makes a final attempt at mining for details, and I make another promise to tell him everything on the drive back to Richmond tonight.

'I love you, Jussie,' he says. 'More than anything. But you can't keep me in the dark on this. Between Adrian's – you know – tomorrow and your taking off all the time, I don't think I can cope. I'm sorry, but I have to say that. Bye, Jussie.'

'I love you, too,' I say to a dead line. He's already ended the call, and the goodbye had a ring of finality to it that I don't care for. I don't care for it at all.

After five minutes of working that Breathe app on my watch – which, by the way, doesn't do a goddamned thing to calm me down – I put the car into gear and ease into the slow lane, thinking that Daniel's right, that we do hang on until the bitter end.

So I have to ask myself why anyone would choose death, particularly the kind of barbaric death I've witnessed in execution chambers. I have to ask why, if Jake Milford was innocent, he made a choice so antithetical to the human condition. All he needed to do was produce a piece of paper.

I found a piece of paper.

The question – *Why?* – looms before me like the endless rolling hills of Southwest Virginia. To make sense of what Jake Milford did, or what he didn't do, I need to ask a different question. I need to know what trumps the will to survive.

Pain, I think, must be one of those trump cards. It didn't work for my mother in her last days, but her own fear trumped the trump, rather like the queen of spades taking the trick in a game of Hearts. Still, I can imagine the kind of pain that would blot out everything else, a pain so fierce and piercing that it becomes an opaque curtain whose only exit is death. Without the morphine, my mother might have decided differently.

As far as I could tell, Jake Milford wasn't in physical pain, but my conversation with Emily this morning makes me wonder. He had a childhood sweetheart, the sweetheart grew up to be a battered wife, and who wouldn't worry his head off over that dumpster fire of a situation? Who wouldn't want to hide his innocence if the proof of innocence meant more pain for someone he loved? Sure, the police-and-shelter solution seems like a better one, but only if you're ignorant of the dismal success rate when it comes to protecting women. My guess is Jake wasn't ignorant.

In the end, I believe Jake Milford was trying to escape pain through death. Another person's pain, but still.

Maybe, in the end, the trump card in the game of life and death is always pain. It simply comes in different shapes to all of us.

CHAPTER THIRTY-THREE

The Pop Shop's cute name matches its grimy exterior in the same way 'puppy' is the right thing to call a diseased jackal. It's dismal, this salt-box of a building with a green roof that saw its last coat of paint when I was still teething. An ice machine hums on one side of the double doors; a Coke machine stands at the other side, a hand-scrawled sign proclaiming it's out of service. The lettering on the sign looks like it's seen a winter or two.

So this is where the rural poor work and shop and fill up their trucks with gas, I think, and feel as if I should know places like this, know more about them than Washington and Richmond and New York. This is where Mary Ann Milford spends her days, and – if her home life is even half as shitty as Emily described – she's probably happy to be here.

I pull up alongside a vacant pump and fill the tank with high-test gasoline. The clock in the car tells me I've made good time down from Richmond, just under four and a half hours. When the pump clicks off, I go inside to pay, leaving the car where it is. I'm deep in Virginia gun country, and the last thing I need is the owner thinking I'm doing a runner.

The Pop Shop is one of those cash-only places, low-tech and low-brow, with a sign reading *Do not ask for credit unless you like being disappointed* on the greasy glass door. I fish for a few tens from my wallet without taking it from my purse because something tells me this isn't the time to flash Gucci leather around. It's the time to blend in. Luckily, I grew up in rural Virginia, and putting a little extra drawl in my speech won't come off as fake.

Right away, I know which of the people in the shop is Mary Ann. There are only two women, one who saw sixty pass by at least a few years back, and one who is younger than I am. She's leaning her chin on one bandaged wrist at the cashier's stand, staring off into space as if a television might be playing on the far wall. Something about her stare doesn't seem right when I approach her.

'Pump number three,' I say, offering four ten-dollar bills. I add a can of Coke from the cold case next to the counter. 'And this.'

'Thirty-seven fifty-five,' she says.

'Are you Mary Ann?'

'Yeah. You the lawyer?'

'Yeah.'

She gives me my change, counting it out coin by coin and adding two singles. 'Let's go around back.' Then, to the older woman: 'Janice? Take over for a few minutes?'

'Sure, honey,' Janice says, replacing her at the counter. 'You holler to Pete if you need anything.' The woman eyes me as she says this, and Pete looks over from where he's restocking soup cans in one of the aisles. The thirty-eight on his hip reminds me I'm not only in gun country, I'm in open-carry country. Then again, it's not as if I'm unfamiliar with the sight. I do live in Richmond, after all. And Richmond is a far cry from San Francisco or London when it comes to firearms.

Mary Ann asks me to follow her back through the store and leads me out the rear exit. The back of the Pop Shop is a barren plot of land, occupied only by an industrial garbage container and a pickup truck with one flat tire. Across the street, there's a brick house. *Some view for the owners of that one,* I think.

'I only got a few minutes,' Mary Ann says, lighting a cigarette. 'Folks'll be coming home from work soon and we get a rush sometimes.' She offers me the half-empty pack. 'Want one?'

I take a cigarette and cup my hands around it as she lights it for me. I haven't smoked since my college days, but this is another blending-in moment, and I intend to take full advantage. My cough gives the game away, though.

'You're a little rusty,' she says.

'I quit twenty years back. Still miss it, though.'

'I should quit. But I only have one or two a day to calm my nerves.' She looks around and lowers her voice. 'Kris don't like it much, so I got a bottle of mouthwash over by the cash register. And gum. And some hand lotion.'

I nod toward her bandaged wrist. 'I imagine Kris doesn't like a lot of things.'

'You could say that, I guess.' She's still quiet, still peeking around as if her husband might be listening.

'You're safe with me, you know?' I say.

Mary Ann takes in a deep breath, lifts her chin slightly, and then, as if even this is too much, looks down at the asphalt again. Her next words kill something inside me. 'It's funny you said you wanted to meet me. See, I don't meet people, honey. Kris drives me to work in the morning and picks me up at five sharp. Calls the Pop Shop every hour or so to check I'm still here making the money that pays our rent and utility bills while he stays home with our boy. My son should be in first grade now, but my husband delayed it. Said the boy was better off at home for another year. Know what I think? I think he wanted to put off having to take our son to school and go fetch him back. Interferes with his luxurious sports and beer lifestyle, if you know what I mean.'

I imagine what this woman's day must be like, how it starts off with her rising at dawn to make breakfast, careful to keep the cooking sounds to a minimum. How, still tired from the day before, she puts in another in a long series of shifts at a job that pays – what? – ten an hour? How she stays put and waits for the phone calls, how she gets picked up and driven home only to face laundry and more cooking and *Get me another beer, woman.* How she crawls into bed, wanting nothing but sleep, and knowing if he wants something else, she'd better oblige. All these images of a woman trapped, a slave to her own husband, flash through my mind. I want to weep at the sight of them.

Instead, I steady my voice. 'But you stay with him.'

She takes a long drag on her smoke and blows it out slowly in a series of rings. 'I got my reasons. Actually, I got one reason. Blond, blue-eyed, and six years old. If it weren't for Caleb, I'd be back at that women's place in Roanoke on the first bus out of here. Only stayed for a few days, but it was a good place to be. Nice people. Some who had it better than I did, some who had it worse. But still nice people, I guess.'

'How come you left?' *And how come your son's name is Caleb, of all things?*

This time she raises her head to meet my eyes; there are tears running down her cheeks.

'I didn't leave,' is all she says.

As tempted as I am to put a hand on her arm, I reconsider. This woman is a china doll on the verge of cracking. 'Then what happened?'

'I went outside, around back, to have a smoke. They don't allow smoking in the house, see. By the time I knew what was happening, Kris had me in his truck and we were on our way back home.' She stiffens, drags on her cigarette again, and looks straight at me. 'You're looking at my eye, aren't you?' she says. 'Well, go on and take a look. It's glass in there.'

'I can't hardly tell,' I say. Something about being around her makes my speech sound natural. Funny thing, dialects. We move in and out of them, conforming without even realizing what we're doing. 'How'd it happen?'

'How do you think?'

So much of our conversation is unspoken, but we follow one another along, filling in the blanks. We're both women, and we've both seen something of the world. 'Police?'

Mary Ann laughs, tossing the butt down onto the gravel and grinding it with the heel of one loafer. 'Tried that. More than a few times. Kris is a good liar.'

'Too many men are.'

'It isn't just that.' Mary Ann shivers, even though the day is warm and bright. 'He told me if he so much as smells a cop, he'll hurt my boy. And when Kris says "hurt", he ain't talking about no love tap.' Now she laughs again, a nervous, jittery laugh. 'Anyway, you could say he was unhappy with the situation.' She puts one hand to her belly and the other to her right eye. 'Really unhappy. Punched me blind and told me if I didn't go along with his story and tell the doctors I fell onto the corner of the kitchen table, he'd wait until the baby was born and then I could watch what would happen. I spent a month wiping pus and ooze out of one eye and wiping tears from the other.'

I finally reach out to her, but Mary Ann flinches. I get it – she's hand-shy like a dog who's learned that hands are only good for punching, not for petting. 'It's all right,' I say. 'I won't hurt you. But I won't touch you if you don't want.'

That's when she falls against me, and I drop my half-smoked cigarette to draw her close.

'It all went wrong so long ago, I don't even remember,' she says. 'And now the one person who could've helped ain't here no more.'

'Was Jake with you on June twelfth?'

Her head nods a 'yes' against my shoulder, then she straightens and leans back against the painted brick of the Pop Shop. 'Night before, Kris wanted – you know. And when he started undressing me and putting his hands on me, he stopped fiddling with his belt buckle. "What's this?" he said. "You gettin' fat?" I told him it was my monthly time and I always bloat up then, didn't he remember? He said sure he remembered, but this wasn't no bloating, and besides, he hadn't seen no rags in the bathroom wastebasket for a while now.'

She checks my face for signs of – what? – disbelief, maybe, and explains. 'He didn't let me use tampons. Said the only thing going in there was him. Not one of those contraptions designed by a bunch of lesbian doctors. Anyway, that's when he pushed down harder on my belly. Then he stood back up, looking at me while I was lying on the bed. And he started fiddling with his belt buckle again, but that look on his face wasn't any kind of lovin' look. He said he didn't cotton to no sloppy seconds but maybe, just maybe, he might find it in his heart to forgive me if I told him the truth.'

I'm desperate for another cigarette, not for the nicotine rush, but for some way to occupy my hands. They've turned into tight fists at my sides as Mary Ann has been talking. 'How come he didn't think the baby was his?' I ask.

''Cause he knew it wasn't. Told me that night as he drew the belt out of its loops that he'd gotten himself a vasectomy.'

'Oh, Christ.'

'Yeah. You could say that. I didn't tell him for the longest time. I lay curled up on that bed with my eyes shut while he whaled on me with the belt. He'd done it before, but this time he used the buckle end.' Mary Ann untucks her chambray shirt from her jeans and raises it a few inches. There are crisscrossed raised scars on her belly.

'No one said anything when you delivered the baby?' I nod toward the scars. 'About those?'

'Kris told them I used to be real depressed. Said I was one of those cutters.'

'That was June eleventh?'

'That was June eleventh. Only the eleventh didn't really end. He kept going straight on in to June twelfth. All night long.' Now she smiles at me, lifting her upper lip with one chipped fingernail. 'Knocked my front teeth out. It didn't hurt – by that time I was way past hurting – but I was scared out of my pants by all the blood. That's when I told him the baby was Jake's. And that's when he stopped beating on me, told me to stay put if I knew what was good for me, and left. I heard the truck start up outside and watched it drive away through the window. When he didn't come back in an hour, I didn't know what else to do, so I called Jake.'

What she's telling me is so bad on so many levels, I don't have any words to describe it. I don't think I'll ever have them. 'You don't have to keep going, honey,' I say.

'I want to. Kris found me at the shelter in Roanoke a few days after Jake dropped me off there. He didn't say a word while we drove back home, but when we got in the trailer, he said everything was taken care of. I didn't know then he was talking about Jake being taken care of. And I didn't know then he was talking about that poor little boy named Caleb Church. So when he said the baby would be named Caleb if it was a boy, I said that was fine.'

She laughs again. 'It's best to go along with what Kris wants. Easier, you know? I asked him what he'd done and, at first, he only said he'd fixed things. Then he took my car keys away and told me I wouldn't be driving anymore. A day later, I got the news about Jake's arrest. Kris told me what had happened. Told me how that little boy cried and begged all the while he was being beaten. Told me he'd made a phone call and given Jake's description. I screamed bloody murder at him, and that's when he punched me blind.'

'I'm so sorry,' I say. The words come out, lame, limping in the air between us. These are the words you use at funerals because there's nothing else to say. These are the words people said to me when Ian was killed. These are useless words.

She looks off into the distance, checks the Timex on her wrist and shrugs. 'I could've saved Jake's life, but I didn't. Some piece a work I am, huh?'

'I don't think you had much choice.'

'No. I didn't. I still don't. Kris has my boy with him all day every day. If I don't come to the phone when he calls, it ain't me who's gonna get the buckle end of the belt. And I can't have that. Not even for Jake. If I was on my own, I'd get this all out in the open, but I have someone else I need to look out for now. I suppose that's a good thing for you.'

Mary Ann turns to go back inside, then turns toward me. Her shoulders slump with what must be the weight of the world. 'I best be getting back. It's a hard thing, knowing the truth and not being able to tell it. It's a goddamned hard thing.'

I walk around the building instead of going through the store. I don't want any of the people inside to see me cry.

Death Row Inmate #39384

'Never' is one of those words we get wrong most of the time. We all say it; we all know how to use it. I've had guys working on overhauling transmissions under a hydraulic lift say shit like: 'Hell, man, I'd never eat quiche. Fuckin' egg pie.' The couple down the street had us over once for an anniversary party – their second and their last, as it happened to go. Husband wrapped his arm around his wife and bellowed on a cloud of beer-soaked air, 'I'll never leave this little woman.' Two weeks later, he drove off. I heard he was living with a twenty-year-old pole dancer named Cookie. Probably told Cookie he'd never leave her. Probably left all the same.

Fact is, you can't never trust a word like 'never'. Except when you can.

The day I found out I had my own personal never was the first day of the trial, when Kris showed his face at the courthouse and sat one row behind me. Mary Ann sat at his right, shrunk back against the bench. She looked like she might be trying to make herself smaller, to fade in with the polished wood. I hadn't called her yet, too much else going on, but I thought there was a ray of hope. I thought I could find a way to keep Mary Ann safe, keep the baby safe, and all would be good. I'd have to come out with it all to my Emily, and coming out with it all would sting. But I'd make it up to her. I'd spend every day of the rest of my life making it up to her. Even if Em left me, I'd still find ways. And when I ran out of ways, I'd think up new ones.

Kris wore a dark blue suit – his only suit – a creased white shirt that might have just come out of a box, and a tie that some president would pick for a press conference. He looked sharp, respectable even. Kris had that chameleon kind of way about him. If we was out shooting pool, he'd roll up the sleeves of his T-shirt and put all those tats and muscles on display. If we was buying a car, he'd roll the sleeves back down, comb his hair just so, and keep the crap talk locked up tight inside his mouth. If he was sweet on a girl – and there were plenty of girls whose names didn't rhyme with Mary Ann – Kris could soften his eyes and slow down the way he moved. He could look weak or tough or angry or gentle. Today, at court, he'd picked a whole new personality.

Today, he had drawn worry on his face.

Me, I wasn't wearing a suit. Em was supposed to bring me something nice, but she'd come down hard with a stomach bug two days ago. Anyway, that's the story they told me. I got my own thoughts about what was keeping Em away.

So I sat there, me in my jailhouse denims and the faint red rings around my wrists from the bracelets I'd worn on the ride over. Handcuffs aren't supposed to hurt like that, but mine did. When you're in for kiddie-fiddling and kiddie-torturing and kiddie-killing, the screws in charge come up with all kinds of ways to make you hurt.

The judge hadn't made his way in yet, and my twelve-year-old public defender had himself in deep conversation with one of the court officials. They weren't even talking about my case, but about another one from last week. Evidently, some hilarious stuff had happened. Martin Kelleher was laughing.

That was when Kris leaned forward and laid a hand on my neck. I don't know how a person could feel hot and cold at the same time; it didn't seem possible, but that's how his hand felt. Like half of it was made of fire and the other half was dry ice. My whole body tensed.

'Relax, big brother,' Kris said. 'Just relax and listen to what I got to tell you. Cause I'm only sayin' this shit once.' That hand of his squeezed a little, and he said, 'Look at me.'

I turned.

'That's a good big brother. You always were the smart one.'

His eyes weren't those soft eyes he used when he was catting around with other women. They were hard, the pupils tiny oily dots, shiny like the metal of a switchblade. I half expected something to shoot out of his eyes and blind me right there and then.

Mary Ann wasn't so shrunk back now. She hunched forward as if she might be real interested in listening to what we had to say. I saw Kris had his right hand on the back of her neck, his thumb sliding up and down on that tender part below her jawline. His thumb moved softly like a lover's caress, but Mary Ann's pulse throbbed under the touch. She wasn't interested. She was terrified.

'I know a couple of things,' Kris said. 'For instance, I know this little girl's got a bun in the oven.' The thumb kept up its same rhythm. Up and down, down and up. 'I also know it ain't mine.' He paused, waiting for me to ask the only question a person would ask to a statement like that. When I said nothing, he went on. 'See, Mary Ann and I, we got something special. And when you got yourself something special, there ain't no reason to go on sharing that something with a snot-nosed wailer of a worm that certain folks call a baby. So I saw to fixing myself. Didn't want to do it, big brother. No sirree. A man's got one thing that makes him a man, if you see the picture I'm painting here. But I did it anyway. For Mary Ann. So we wouldn't lose that special thing we got.'

Me, I had my own opinions about why Kris did what he did. Going under the knife got him something even more special. He could ride in bareback with all those other women, never worrying about any unforeseen inconveniences. Like what certain folks call a baby. I kept quiet all the same.

'The third thing I know . . .' Kris said, turning those oily eyes left and right, checking on the room. 'The third thing I know is this. And I want you to listen real hard. I know a good husband's got things he needs to take care of. For his family, see. Even if his family is only the two of us, me and Mary Ann.' He chuckled. 'Well, now, I suppose we'll be three pretty soon, but that's okay. That's fine. I'll love the little snot-nosed worm like he was my very own. I'll take care of him.'

Over his shoulder, I could see Kris's right hand work its way down from Mary Ann's slender neck to the swell of her belly. He patted the bump there. Not a fatherly pat, but more of a that's-all-finished-and-done-with pat.

'But you know how those little ones can be. They're delicate, big brother.'

My thoughts flashed back to Ben. Ben, who was small of

stature and a giant in matters of heart. He, too, had been delicate. Then I flashed back to a time more recent than childhood, to a motel on the outskirts of Bluefield, Virginia, four months before my arrest.

It had been the worst day of my life, that day in the Pines Motor Inn, but it had also been one of the best days. It was the day I learned I was capable of being an absolute shit, a worthless soul who deserved whatever black fate might find me as the years rolled on. At the same time, it was the day I recovered something I thought had been lost forever.

It was the day Mary Ann and I made love.

No one can ever know how these things happen, how two bodies can fuse together when two minds are bent on telling them to stop. Maybe it was the dress Mary Ann wore, a bright green-and-white stripe that sang the word 'picnic'. Maybe it was the fact she was smiling, and I hadn't seen her smile since we were kids – not a real smile, not the kind that spread across her face like a butterfly and made her eyes twinkle. Maybe it was that I knew Mary Ann deserved love and hadn't had much of it in all these years with that asshole brother of mine. In any event, I'll skip the details because I ain't the kind of man who kisses and tells. But I can tell you one thing: for a few short hours that afternoon, two people on this earth were about the happiest they could be.

I can tell you something else. Illicit happiness never comes without a price tag. That kind of happiness is a commodity sold by the devil himself, and the devil always extracts something he wants. What he got from us was small at the time, and still small on the day Mary Ann called and told me, but it would grow into a monster of a problem.

'I'll pretend it's Kris's baby,' she said on the phone. 'I promise that. I'll never tell, and he'll never know. This secret's going with me to my grave, Jake.'

So much for secrets. At the time, neither one of us knew that Kris had gotten himself fixed.

In the courtroom, about a minute before the bailiff told us all to rise, Kris said again, 'Don't you worry. I'll take care of him. Or her, God forbid it's a useless piece of split-tail. Your bastard kid's gonna grow up just fine as long as you mind your Ps and Qs.'

I turned then to face him and caught Mary Ann's eyes with my own. They were pleading eyes, begging me to forgive her for telling what she'd said she would never tell. But she didn't need to ask my forgiveness. I knew my brother had beaten the truth out of her better than any of those mad Russians in the old spy movies.

Then Kris leaned in closer, hiding his lips from Mary Ann. His breath was a dirty, sour mix of last night's beer and this morning's cheap coffee. ''Course,' Kris said, running a finger along the rough line of the gray prisoner denims below my hairline. 'I guess I already took care of you.'

His hand on my neck didn't feel like a hand anymore. It felt like a collar. And when I saw his other hand resting on Mary Ann's belly, when I thought about the pain he could cause her and the baby, I knew I'd best keep my mouth shut and stick to the guilty plea.

So there it is. Now the story's out. I didn't kill Caleb Church, but I had a good reason to let everyone think I did.

CHAPTER THIRTY-FOUR

When I leave Bluefield this afternoon, I make the colossal mistake of turning on the radio, and then I make the worse mistake of not turning it off. Every single station seems to be in mid-news hour with only one piece of news worth telling. Congressional squabbles and suicide bombers and third-world natural disasters have temporarily faded into the background today, but I expect after Adrian Kopinsky rides the lightning tomorrow night, we'll all be back to our regular programming.

No one really knows where that 'famous for fifteen minutes' quote came from. Maybe it was Andy Warhol; maybe it was some guy who photographed Andy Warhol; maybe it was the brother of a guy who talked to the guy who photographed Andy Warhol. Whatever it was, short-lived fame can last for less than fifteen minutes, or it can endure for a few days. In any case, the quote is part of our national lexicon, and Adrian is living up to it. For the time being.

As I change stations, the faceless voices of those reading and commenting on today's headlines change as well. National Public Radio's *Fresh Air* is interviewing a member of Vita, who sounds mournful when she tells the host that Adrian Kopinsky lost the movement's support when she asked for death in the Bantam case. 'Our hands are now tied,' the Vita rep says. On another channel, Ted Stuyvesant, much less mournful, informs listeners that 'Kopinksy knew the law, and she went ahead anyway. All I'm doing is following the law.' On the conservative programs, outraged callers phone in, one after the other, lambasting the Remedies Act as the 'wet dream of a bunch of brainless libtards' and 'a barbarian practice that goes against everything the Bible tells us.' The moderates flip-flop between sympathy for the innocent man who paid 'the ultimate price' and a system that seems 'broken and irreparable' without actually saying anything that might set them squarely in one camp or another. And BBC World Service announces to the entire planet that 'America is no longer tipping in the direction of extreme brutality, but has fallen over the edge.'

I punch the on/off button with the heel of my hand, silencing them all, and then my phone rings.

Daniel.

'Well?' he says. 'Say you're coming back to me.'

'I wasn't sure you wanted me to.'

He sighs, and I can picture him running a hand through his hair, that tell he has of showing exasperation when he doesn't think anyone notices. 'I do.'

'I sense a "but" coming, Daniel.'

'You sense right. I want you here, but I don't want you here for another day or another week. I want you here for the long run.'

'That's what I want, too.'

'Now I'm waiting for the condition,' he says.

'Christ, Daniel. It's not about conditions. None of this is about conditions. It's about me fucking up in the worst way and not being able to take it back. Ever. Do you get that? I can't take it back.'

Now I tell him everything Mary Ann told me. I tell him about a six-year-old boy, my own boy's age, being used as a human shield. I tell him about one sightless eye and a wrist that has probably spent more time in bandages than not. I tell him Jake Milford was an innocent man.

And Daniel says the one thing I don't want to hear. He says, 'I'm sorry.'

The words have no meaning at all.

CHAPTER THIRTY-FIVE

Darkness falls when I change interstates at Charlottesville and start the last eastward leg toward home. Without a moon, the Blue Ridge mountains behind me are lifeless forms rising up from nothing. I used to love to drive out here with Ian, park the car in a lay-by, and hike among the trees. In those days, the mountains were green in summer, golden-hued in autumn, and blanketed with snow in the skiing season. Always, they were friendly mountains, but tonight they stand solemn and black, like a row of robed judges at a tribunal. I don't like these mountains or what they symbolize. They seem to be waiting for a plea while already knowing my fate.

In the physical world, only one road stretches out before me. In another world, in my own mind, the road diverges, one path to the left and one to the right. Left. Right. Left. Right. The words repeat like a drill sergeant's marching orders, and I remember a course I took in the history of language years ago in this very town.

'Left' is a dirty word in as many languages as I can think of, starting with English. Its counterpart – 'right' – is a clean word. Left means idle and foolish, right means fair and proper. In Latin, left is sinister and right is skillful. French discriminates between the clumsy *gauche* and the upstanding *droit.* There are left-handed compliments, bad dancers with two left feet, and mistresses who are left-handed wives. Practicing Muslims always eat with their right hands, and always step into a bathroom left foot first.

Left and right. The dirty and the clean. That's where these two metaphorical roads lead, and I can't see any safe middle ground, so I pull over to the soft shoulder, delaying the decision.

I have a piece of paper.

I take this out of my purse and unfold it on my lap, switching on the overhead light. It's such a small thing, so easily misplaced or lost, fragile enough to be disintegrated by a cupful of water or the touch of a Bic lighter. I could chew it, swallow it, and pass it out of me in another form. This paper is nothing.

Unless I choose it to be.

And here, I'm wrong again. I run one finger over the hotel receipt, over the place and date and name, and the paper becomes something else. It transforms from a simple accounting of facts to a road sign. I don't even have to look at it to know which direction it points.

Suddenly, I want Ian. The want is palpable and all-consuming, so strong that I can almost feel him in the car next to me, taking my trembling hand in his own. He doesn't speak; he doesn't have to. The steadiness and warmth of his hand wrapped around mine is enough.

I'm not a praying woman, never have been. I always thought if there's a heaven or a hell, they aren't places in an afterlife, but states of mind in a human being's existence. That's not what we say, of course. I've told my son and myself the same pretty lies for years now. I've told Jonathan that the neighbor's dog, a gorgeous golden retriever, is in dog heaven, somewhere over the rainbow

274

bridge. I've told myself that Ian's killer is burning in a place more terrible than a thousand battlefields. I've told both of us that Ian is in heaven and that someday, but not for a long time, we'll see him again. We'll go on family picnics and take hikes in the mountains and bury ourselves in sand at the seaside. We'll do all those things; we only need to wait a while until the time is right.

Next to me, in the empty space of the passenger seat, I think I see Ian nod. And in the quiet of the car on these dark back roads, I think I hear him tell me he's waiting.

I think I hear him say the time is now.

CHAPTER THIRTY-SIX

Daniel is standing on the porch when I arrive at his house, arms folded, brow creased, unsmiling. I think I mutter, 'Sorry,' before brushing past him to dash upstairs and check on Jonathan. My little boy is fast asleep, curled in a sleeping bag with robots dancing on it, all of them floating in space. They look like intergalactic vacuum cleaners, and the strange part is that I want to be one of them right now. I want to be anything but what I am. Even an intergalactic Electrolux.

I kiss Jonathan's forehead, smooth a stray lock of hair from his eyes, and pull the door closed until a thin ray of light from the hallway slices into the spare room. It looks like a knife blade, that light, shining on my boy's face, severing his features. The door, I decide, is better open for now.

Downstairs, Daniel is waiting for me in the kitchen with a plate of roasted vegetables and an empty bottle of wine. The empty bottle doesn't bother me. The tumbler of whiskey at his elbow and the drawn-down lines of his mouth, well, that's another story.

'I saved you some dinner,' he says, kissing me in the same way I kissed my son a few moments ago. Chastely. My God, it hurts to be kissed this way. As soon as I lean in closer, Daniel's body shifts away.

'Thanks. Have you—' There's no need to go on; the four empty plates in the sink answer my question. He and Susan and the boys ate without me.

'Susan went home after we ate. Said she'd ring you tomorrow.' He picks up his whiskey glass and starts out of the kitchen, putting more space between us. When he's at a safe distance, he turns back and points at an envelope on the dining room table. 'That was in the mail at your house. I brought it over.' For a moment, he's perfectly still, and then his hand makes its way upward, raking through his hair, speaking all the words Daniel isn't speaking. 'I'm knackered. See you in the morning.'

The sound of footsteps fades as he walks up the stairs. In the upstairs hall, the steps track from the front of the house to the back, and don't return. Tonight, apparently, Daniel will be sleeping on the sofa in the television room.

I open a new bottle of wine, pour out a glass, and sip at it, staring at my plate until the glass is empty and the vegetables have gone cold. And I think about what I want.

I want to go to Daniel's bed. I want another glass – maybe another bottle – of wine. I want to curl up inside the dancing robot sleeping bag and cuddle Jonathan. I want Ian to be alive. I want to undo everything I've done. I want all these things, and, at the same time, I really don't want anything at all except to sit here and wait for tonight to become tomorrow.

In the end, the fresh glass of wine wins the game of *I want*, and I pick up the manila envelope Daniel pointed to earlier.

Every life can be measured in some repeated appearance of certain objects, and we know those objects as we know our own bodies. A plumber will recognize his wrench from its heft and shape without having to look when his hand reaches around toward the

278

back of his tool belt. A mechanic only need glance at a tire to tell if it's under-inflated or if the treads have worn down. A lawyer? She knows paper. Most of my adult life can be measured in reams of the stuff, from heavy casebooks, to final exam bluebooks, to page after page of bar exam study guides, to briefs and motions and opinions. So when I pick up the envelope, I know there's a hell of a lot of paper inside.

The envelope stays sealed on the table in front of me for the time it takes to empty my glass and refill it. All the while, I make up stories about where it came from. I have to – there's no return address, and the postmark simply says 'Richmond'. Not a hell of a lot to infer from that. Without further clues, it could be anything from hate mail to another article looking for peer reviews. I'm going with the hate mail hypothesis. Law reviews tend to use a return address.

Then again, the envelope has weight to it, less than a book but more than a few sheets. It's either a collection of 'Fuck you' notes or the longest piece of hate mail ever written, and in my experience, haters don't usually write dissertations to their targets. Once they run out of dirty words, they're pretty much done.

So I go back to the kitchen to grab a paring knife from the magnetic strip near the oven, and then I slit the thing open with one clean stroke, pulling out the short stack of lined sheets. My name isn't on the first handwritten page. Nor is there a date or a place or anything else. The printed writing is neat and careful, the kind of lettering you might use to fill in an application form, the kind that is meant to be readable. Its neatness and care doesn't jibe with what I read on the first two lines:

Death Row Inmate #39384
If I wasn't going to die, this story would end here.

Death Row Inmate #39384

I'm no hero. I'm a killer who never got the chance to do any killing. See, I had a plan I put in place before I took Mary Ann to the Roanoke shelter. That plan, which I fully intended to carry out, was to kill my little brother dead.

But there's other reasons I know I'm not made of hero stuff.

My last night alive, for instance. If you think I'm spending these hours thinking about my boy and my wife, you're wrong as can be. All I can think about is numero uno. Me. Jake. The sorry-ass position I'm in. How I'll act tomorrow when they march me into the room with the chair. I wonder if my legs will give out on the way, and I wonder if I'll be staring down at the floor or meeting the eyes of all them whose job it is to strap me in and throw a switch. It's all about me and no one else because, tonight, I still *am*.

When I'm not writing, I lie with my hand on my heart, feeling the steady rhythm of life in my own chest. I taste salty sweat on my lip and feel the hairs on the back of my neck stand up like a dog's hackles when he senses danger. I wiggle my toes and watch them obey unspoken commands. I am, dammit. By later tonight, there won't be no heartbeat, and there won't be no new sweat, and those toes won't move again until some doctor hangs a tag on them and slams me into a refrigerated drawer. Tomorrow night, I won't be anything at all, only a memory some people have in their heads, a photograph or two standing on a bedside table. I'll be worm food for a while, and then I'll be dust, just like the Bible says.

Also, and here's another thing you need to understand, heroes don't go around fornicating with their sister-in-law and then lying to their wife's face about where they've been. They got a different word for those kind of men. Probably a whole bunch of words.

Even if I'm no hero, I'm a mostly honest man. And I had every intention of killing Kris, my own flesh and blood, to save Mary Ann from his fists and his belts and his lies. All the hard work was finished by June twelfth: the secondhand 9mm pistol was easy enough to lay my hands on (we're in Virginia, remember) and I stashed it round the back of the auto shop under a dumpster along with a spare loaded clip. For all I know, it's still there, strapped in with duct tape and hidden from view.

Time and place? Also easy. When Kris was out of work, which was most of the time now, he stayed up nights and slept through days. He might wake at noon, fix himself a sandwich and chug a beer, but then he'd be back in bed until Mary Ann came home from her job. And I didn't worry much about witnesses because I knew Kris and Mary Ann had a prime trailer spot at the far end of the park, one deaf widow ahead of them in the line and a couple of strung-out meth addicts two lots down. Besides all that, I had a silencer packed in with the pistol.

I walked through the scene about a million times, and every single time was the same. Pick up the piece and the silencer after the garage closed. Drive south through the night and wait across the street from the Pop Shop until Mary Ann came in for her shift. Drive an easy few miles to Pounding Mill. Walk straight into the trailer without so much as a knock. If Kris was up, shoot him where he stood. If he was in bed, shoot him where he lay. Then, get back in the car, reverse tracks, and go to work. Not what I'd call a complicated plot, but my brother wasn't a complicated person. Neither am I.

There'd be a phone call, maybe from Mary Ann, maybe from some hospital who tracked me down as next of kin. There'd be a funeral, and I'd put on my Sunday suit and make the drive for the service, saying a few rehearsed words about my brother that didn't have no meaning at all. I figured on a week of feeling squirrelly, but no more than that. When a loser like Kris Milford gets dead, no one spends a whole lot of time and worry digging for clues. He'd be one more gun statistic in a whole sea of statistics.

I liked my plan. I still do. I don't much care for the idea of having to take a life to save a life, but now that I know we're talking 'bout two lives needing saving, I guess it all balances out.

Problem is, the gun's out there and Kris is out there. But I ain't out there. Not anymore.

CHAPTER THIRTY-SEVEN

Well, shit.

By eleven-something, I've read Jake's diary pages three times through, and that's all I can think of to say. Harvard should rescind my goddamned degree.

I don't know how long I sit here, hands folded in my lap, eyes glazed over until the words on the pages in front of me begin to look more like Sanskrit than English. I do know that it's a pleasure not to move. Moving necessarily means moving in a certain direction, and whatever moral compass I have left is spinning so fast I can't make out which way is north.

Not that it matters where north is. I have a feeling I'm about to head south.

The man I killed died with an unspoken last request, and that's what pulls me to my feet, finds my purse and car keys, and opens the door of Daniel's house. Night has brought a chill with it, and I turn back to the hall closet for a coat. All our suitcases are standing there, one carry-on bag on top of the pile, and three printed boarding passes stare up at me with their bar codes and seating assignments. I suppose they're changeable for another flight, maybe even the Tuesday evening hop. They seem to say so, seem to say they're saving a space for me. Saving me.

Come on, Justine. Welcome to the friendly skies.

The voice that speaks these words is a dark voice, hollow and monotone, the voice of a dark being cajoling me into action. It promises life and love and safety. Like all temptresses, it doesn't bother mentioning a price – that's for later on when the deal is sealed and it's too late to turn back. It whispers *Jonathan* and *Daniel* and *England* to me, drawing out each word with an intense and eerie voluptuousness that stands the hairs of my neck on end. It's a vampiric voice, and its promises are as empty as the soulless creature speaking them.

I shut the front door and turn back toward the kitchen, heading for Daniel's junk drawer, looking for note paper, the back of an envelope, any blank space hungry for a few hastily scrawled words. Jonathan's name. Jonathan's date of birth. A pair of passport numbers, an address in London that I've made up out of whole cloth, and a signature. Back in the hallway, I tuck the consent form between Daniel and Jonathan's boarding passes, telling myself this is only a precaution, nothing more than that.

Like Jake said, it isn't a complicated plot.

When I go upstairs, Jonathan is in the same position as he was a few hours ago, dreaming with the dancing robots, floating in space and time, unworried about the future. That's all right. I have enough worry for both of us. I don't kiss him before leaving the room, not out of fear of waking him, but because kissing seems to have a finality to it that I'm not ready to accept. As I walk away from the guest room, I sense a force pulling me back, and that terrible, dark voice repeats itself.

Jonathan. Daniel. England.

My own voice is stronger. It says different words. *Undeserved. Undoable. Unjust.*

This time, I manage to leave the house, and I walk out into a night so heavy the streetlights seem an exercise in futility, unable to cut through the thick cloak covering the city. If you ask me, it's a goddamned waste of electricity. But I like it, this blackness. It suits my mood, and it gives me the freedom to prowl around Richmond collecting the things I need. Gasoline, a crappy flashlight, and that essential item I hope to find duct-taped to the underside of a garbage container. The bin, a hulking chunk of industrial steel, sits a few feet away from the back wall of Pete's Auto and Parts, a sign saying *Absolutely no oil or batteries* affixed to its side with clear cellophane tape to protect it from the weather. There's not a scrap of trash anywhere near it. No takeout napkins or straw wrappers, no crushed-up work orders, no plastic soda bottles. Pete, whoever he is, runs a tight ship.

What bothers me about this isn't the absence of litter; it's my surprise at that absence. Not being a person who spends much time loitering around the backs of auto repair shops, I've brought a certain bias along with me tonight. I expected filth in the same way I expected Emily Milford to be reading *People* magazine instead of Pablo Neruda. Like most everyone else, I expect 'country' to mean 'stupid'. It's a shitty way to think about the world, and I'm embarrassed, but not so embarrassed that I forget what I came here for.

On my hands and knees, I start the process of feeling around the underside of the bin for anything with the texture of duct tape. At first, I think it's got to be the dumbest way to attach anything to a container that's going to be lifted and tilted at least once a week, but then I remember that book those two guys wrote. *It ain't broke, it just needs duct tape. One thing a Southern boy will never say is, 'I don't think duct tape will fix it.'* I remember the Apollo astronauts fixing their carbon dioxide filters on the fly – literally. And what did they use, boys and girls? Duct tape. Maybe Jake Milford remembered that, too, and figured if it worked to save the lives of those three flyboys in outer space, it would probably hold a measly two pounds or so in Richmond, Virginia.

And it does. My hands find the package on the second side I search. The familiar slick-but-not-too-slick coating and the slightly irregular texture – not to mention the outline of a barrel and grip – all say 'neatly stowed firearm'. Not that I have a ton of practical experience with firearms. I can recite forensic details from dozens of homicide cases, and probably give a half-brilliant lecture on ballistic fingerprints, but I've never fired one of the things.

Which makes me wonder if I'll be able to start now.

A Buick rolls by on the road beside Pete's garage, its lights picking up random pieces of reflective material on the blacktop. A Sprite can. A bit of oil slick – not from Pete's, of course – Pete wouldn't tolerate oil slicks any more than he would tolerate dead car batteries in the trash bin. A foil wrapper from a long-ago-eaten candy bar. The one thing they don't pick out is me. I'm a dark shape in the night. A ghoul about to do ghoulish acts.

I wait until it passes, hoping like hell this isn't one of those well-known drug-for-money exchange sites that litter this part of the city. But the Buick doesn't slow, let alone come to a stop. It moves on, catching shiny debris further along its path, and I'm alone again.

Everything Jake said would be here is here. One Beretta 9mm, one extra clip, one silencer. I haven't the faintest clue how to put all this shit together, so I take the stash to my car, drive out of the city, and pull into the first rest stop I find. They have hot coffee and those little packages of powdered doughnuts in the vending machines, and I fork over several quarters to buy one of each. I don't really want the doughnuts, but at one in the morning, a woman pretending to eat in her car looks normal – at least more normal than a woman researching handgun and silencer assembly should any stray dog-walkers or travelers decide to pass my side of the car.

The project turns out to be kindergarten-simple: screw the silencer onto the barrel. So I do that. I also discover the magazine in it carries fifteen rounds, which I'm hoping is fourteen more than I'll need. Maybe thirteen more, because I need to be sure. I practice manipulating the safety a few times, wondering why, in all the movies I've seen, no one ever mentions the fucking safety. It's always 'Here, take this, sweetheart.' Realism would be the sweetheart taking the pistol, aiming at the bad guy, and cursing the idiot who gave her a gun without so much as telling her how to use it. I figure the cursing would happen as she lies dying in a pool of her own blood.

It's two in the morning before I'm satisfied with this DIY tuition. I return to the vending machine for another two cups of weak coffee, get back in my car, and start the night-long drive down to Bluefield for the second time in the past twenty-four hours.

CHAPTER THIRTY-EIGHT

A chilling reality hits me once I'm on the road. Earlier, I had projects: tasks to perform and things to learn. I should have relished the distraction. Now, I only have myself and my thoughts and a loaded deadly weapon as a passenger. It glints at me every time I pass under a street lamp, giving me a salacious wink, welcoming me to its cold world.

If guns could think, I wonder if they would think of themselves differently, if they would say, 'Look, I'm only an inanimate object here. Doesn't matter whether you're a hunter or a cop or a sniper, whether you run with gangs or mow down innocent kids in schools. You're the one with the twisted sense of purpose, not me. If I'm your last resort, you're the problem. So take your cold-world shit and stuff it.'

I've been worrying about this last-resort business as I drive down the highway, empty but for a few lonely truckers on a midnight run. This thing in my passenger seat shouldn't be a last resort, or any option at all. There's supposed to be a system in place, a justice machine that, once fed with data, will give the right answer. I learned from my talk with Mary Ann and from reading Jake's diary that machines have a way of breaking down.

Where was the machine when Kris led his brother Ben out

onto the ice? Where was the machine when the older Mrs Milford turned a blind eye to a bad son? Where was the machine on Mary Ann's wedding night, or, for all I know, on every night of her shitty marriage?

Oh, there's a machine, all right, but it's a man-made mechanism, only as error-proof as the men and women who built it.

I walk through the steps I could take if I trusted this machine:

Surrender the hotel receipt to the district attorney, along with a short list of phone numbers and addresses. Wait while calls are made and visits carried out. Listen to two disillusioned junior attorneys as they question their career choice, a handful of overworked cops reporting exactly how many doors were slammed in their faces, and one extremely stressed-out DA telling me that reopening the Milford case based on one piece of paper and two women who aren't willing to talk isn't on his list of priorities. That's the best-case scenario. Its opposite number – Kris Milford waking up to the scent of police on his doorstep and a six-year-old boy he's got no use for struggling in his arms – isn't an image I could live with.

Justine, the Milford pickup went wrong.
Justine, a little boy died.
Justine, if you only hadn't . . .

All those voices would come together in a screaming chorus to remind me I should have kept my mouth shut. But keeping silent is another in a long line of lousy options. I've seen Emily Milford's face and held her hand. I've looked into Mary Ann Milford's glass eye and remembered Shirley from high school, left with one of a working pair, wondering what unhappy accident might take her remaining eye. I've read Jake's diary.

Omniscience is a curse.

Even if everyone listened, if the DA reopened the case and some wunderkind of a cop managed the arrest, there's another possibility I can't live with. I can't risk Kris Milford acting out in court the same way Toby Barrett did several years ago. I can picture him standing up after sentencing – he'd get a few consecutive life sentences, I think – and rubbing salt in the wounds of Mr and Mrs Church like Barrett rubbed salt in the wounds of all those parents after he starved their children. Mary Ann and Emily would get their closure; Mr and Mrs Church would see the gates of their own personal hell opening up all over again.

I know what Daniel would say, today of all days, the eve of Adrian Kopinsky's death. Change the tickets, head to Dulles, and get the hell out of Dodge. I'm not convinced Englishmen use the term 'get the hell out of Dodge' because England doesn't have a Dodge City or a television series called *Gunsmoke*, but the semantics would be the same. Every language and every dialect in the world must have a term for putting distance between yourself and trouble, which means some eight billion people live under the delusion that trouble is a thing that exists only on the outside. Enemies on a battlefield. A burning building. Shark-infested waters. It's easy to forget the kinds of trouble that live within us, that aren't a place or a separate object – cancer, depression, ennui. Try running away from those.

If I concentrate, I can project myself into the future. It stretches out like the road before me, so bright I can pick out the details of every bump and crevice on the surface, less clear further on, and finally, a wall of blackness at the limits of my vision. But I know the road ahead has a texture that will reveal itself in time, I know its width and its lines are destined to continue in similar patterns as the ones I've already driven. After all, I'm the one who paved this road.

My future may be in England or in some other pretty place. Daniel is in the picture, as is Jonathan. There are Christmases and summer holidays, birthdays and graduations, marriages and funerals – all of life's moments of happiness and grief filling the years ahead. I can see us navigating the bumps and potholes together, see myself changing as I try on a new career.

I can also see a shadow attached to me, never fading, not even in the night. I'll feel it tugging at unexpected times – in the middle of a family dinner, as I board a flight to some vacation destination, while I'm weeding a cottage garden. It will stay with me, a constant and tireless sentinel, taking on various shapes. It might be Jake Milford's shadow one day, Mary Ann's the next. It might be the form of Jake Junior as he sits alone in a schoolyard, shoulders shaking after another playground bully reminds him he's the son of a murderer. When I finally die, the shadow will cling to me, dragging us both down, south, to where the fires burn.

And, all the while, Daniel will tell me I made the right decision. Easy for Daniel; he'll never know that shadow. He'll never die dirty.

I have an easy out – we could call it the mother of all outs – in the form of a six-year-old son named Jonathan. Whatever the road ahead brings, I can shine a light on my boy. *Here's Jonathan, the reason I kept that Milford can of worms closed. Here's Jonathan, who lost one parent already – want him to lose the other? Here's Jonathan, my bulletproof excuse for absolutely every fuck-up and misstep.*

That brings me to another problem. I could call it the Curse of the Mother. I don't know how I would have felt about young

Caleb Church's death if I had been his mother, how much that biological bond would have influenced any decision I was faced with. What I know is that I never would have sent Jake Milford to the chair if I'd known I was pregnant. What I *think* I know is that Emily, a different mother, wants to clear her husband's name for the sake of Jake Junior. Mary Ann, also a different mother, wants Kris revealed as the villain he is. But neither woman wants to orphan the child of another woman.

Maybe 'mother' is more complicated than people think. Maybe we all feel some duty to protect, whether what we're protecting is our own or not.

A tractor-trailer passes me on the right, its horn blaring in short, angry blasts. I lean onto my own horn and scream words the driver won't hear, telling him to move over and get back in his lane. He responds with another ear-splitting honk, and I realize not much more than a coat of paint separates us. I also realize I have about seven feet of clear road on my left side. Through the passenger window, I hear, 'Get off the road, you dozy bitch!' and I swerve jerkily back to where I belong, hands clenched to the steering wheel and heart racing. The tractor-trailer gives me a final blast and then separates itself from me, getting the hell out of Dodge.

I have to pull over to the breakdown lane, I'm shaking that much. There, I punch the hazard button and sit in the dark, willing my hands to stay still, sucking in breath until it stops its jagged rhythm. It takes a while to calm myself, to get my body back to something resembling a normal state. When I'm nearly there, I roll down the window and take deep, controlled sips of the night air. It feels good to be here, alone and alive, to smell the green of the fields and watch stars shine, their light unfiltered by city pollution. A part of me decides to turn around and head north again, to crawl into bed with Daniel and make pancakes for breakfast, to be the best mother I can be to Jonathan.

Another part asks a question to which I think I already know the answer: What kind of mother would I be with that shadow following me around?

In the end, I continue south.

CHAPTER THIRTY-NINE

We were assembled at Ian's house again for another Death and Drinks party; that much was the same. I was no longer a timid One-L, and I was no longer Ted Stuyvesant's date, but Ian's not-so-secret lover. My work with the Vita movement had turned me into a player at these evening soirees, and we spent a fair amount of time discussing layouts for flyers and the order of speakers at an upcoming rally in Harvard Yard, with most of the all-male-minus-one crowd deferring to me.

The skinny man was there, as he usually was, and I knew his name now. He was Phil Potts, clever, geeky, and perpetually thin as a string bean despite his constant eating. It was Phil who set Ian on fire tonight.

There were multiple ways to force Ian to turn on you. Staring blankly at the floor when he asked a question was one; muttering or misquoting was another. Phil, however, tried a brand-new method, and found that it worked.

He brought up a piece of fiction.

'What the actual fuck are you talking about, Potts?' Ian spat the words out. In the lamplight, I could see minuscule particles of spit fly from his mouth as he spoke.

'I was saying that in Agatha Christie's *Witness for the Prosecution*, we get the flip side.'

'The flip side of what?'

Phil began picking at a stray thread on his sweater and didn't look up when he answered. 'The flip side of wrongful conviction. It's a case of wrongful acquittal. The guy kills an old woman for money, uses his wife to get him acquitted, and then it turns out he's leaving the wife for a younger woman. He even tells the wife he did it and thanks her for lending a hand. So she shoots him. Or stabs him. I can't remember. I mean, the wife shoots the husband. Not the girlfriend.'

'We've got Blackstone's Ratio on the agenda and you're giving me Agatha-fucking-Christie?' Ian combed his hair back with both hands, exasperated. 'Did you find that on Lexus Nexus? Was this a law review piece that I somehow missed? Maybe a citation in a Supreme Court case? Potts, did you have a sudden attack of stupidity?'

This time, Phil looked directly at him. 'No, Ian. It's not stupid. So, per Blackstone, we'd rather let ten guilty men—' Phil glanced at me '—or women – go free instead of punishing the one innocent dude. Or dudette. But what if one of those guilty types gets off and goes and wreaks some more homicidal havoc? And what if everyone in the room knows what he's already done and what he's capable of doing next? What then? It's not like we can do a reset on the trial, double jeopardy. And we don't want to go all Philip K. Dick and lock him up for a crime he hasn't committed yet.'

Ian raised an eyebrow at this, and Phil muttered, 'You know. *Minority Report*. Anyway, law reviews and citations aside, Ian, what's our moral duty here?'

'Let the law do what the law does,' Ian said. He turned to me. 'Boucher? Want to weigh in on this bag of jurisprudential shit?' He continued to call me by my surname in these meetings. As if no one saw through the subterfuge.

I did want to weigh in. Because this was interesting, this new wrinkle Phil had brought up, even if he had floor-stared, muttered, and managed to work not one, but two, fictional references into his argument. 'Well,' I started, 'I suppose we should talk about justifiable homicide.'

Ian went red. 'The death penalty is justifiable homicide, Boucher. Don't tell me you've gone over to the dark side on us?'

I shook my head. 'Not at all. Capital punishment isn't justifiable because there's already a remedy. We lock up the convicted murderer and prevent him from committing further serious crimes. We don't need to kill him. That's superfluous. But what Phil's saying is different. It's one step past self-defense. We wouldn't lock up a man for protecting his child from an armed intruder.'

'Imminent danger. Think, Boucher.'

This time, I bristled. 'I am thinking, Ian. I'm thinking of R v Lavallee. 1990. Supreme Court of Canada, wherein the argument that battered women have some heightened sensitivity to patterns of abuse prevailed. Yes, Lavallee shot her partner in the back of the head as he was leaving the room. Maybe not imminent danger, but it was still ruled as self-defense on the appeal.' The room had gone quiet as I talked, and all eyes flicked from me to Ian and back, like spectators at some weird tennis match. 'I think there's room for argument as to Phil's example. I mean, the husband in that Christie story got what he wanted and probably wasn't going to do any further killing for money. But I could see a hypothetical situation that goes a step beyond Lavallee where the danger isn't necessarily imminent, but the homicide could nevertheless be justified.'

Phil smiled at me, gratitude in his eyes. Even Ted looked impressed.

After the crowd left, I stayed, as I usually did after Ian's drinks parties. No one raised an eyebrow. It was plain I was in love with the man as much as he was with me.

But we didn't go to bed that night, not immediately. Instead, we had our first fight, a whiskey-intensified face-off in his living room.

'It's not the same,' I said from where I was sprawled on the sofa next to the fire. 'And I'm not saying I would kill anyone. I'm only saying that I can see a justification for homicide in a very specific circumstance where the perpetrator has unique knowledge and no reasonable alternatives exist. Christ, Ian, can't you see the academic argument here? It's not as if I'm going public with it. I'm not envisioning some op-ed in the *Times* where I make the case for vigilantism.'

'We're supposed to be against killing, love. Even if the argument is academic.'

'It's not that black and white.'

Eventually, he conceded, but only after I swore up and down that I would never be the finger on the trigger. Mostly, I think, I simply couldn't imagine a situation that would warrant it.

Until I came across a man named Kris Milford.

CHAPTER FORTY

I find out this morning that it's very easy and very difficult to kill a man. I should know – I've done it both ways now. But even here, there is complexity. The first Milford brother was dispatched with the simple scrawl of a pen. Other men, who I'll never know, handled the wet work, the hard part. Only afterwards did I realize the difficulties I would face.

Killing Kris, on the other hand, is hard, maybe the hardest thing I've ever done, counter to every aspect of who and what I am. But where Jake's death sits uneasily in my mind, his brother's does not. I have no moral qualms and no regrets, nothing to haunt me. Quite the opposite, really. I almost feel like a superhero. WonderLawyer, maybe.

But, oh, this morning.

I follow Jake's plan and sit in my car across the street from the Pop Shop, sipping cold black coffee from a McDonald's Styrofoam cup and scrolling through pages of microprint on my phone to be sure I have the workings of the Beretta down to a neat science. The Beretta itself lies in the footwell on the passenger side with a spare blanket from the trunk disguising it, waiting to be called to action. Mary Ann arrives two hours after I parked, a faded ball cap snugged down tight over her forehead. The forecast calls for unusual heat today, but she's in a long-sleeved checkered shirt buttoned up all the way. It looks constricting. It also looks like it might be hiding something.

There are words exchanged between Mary Ann and her husband as she gets out of the truck, but I have to fabricate them from the downcast look on her face and the way she bites her lower lip when she reaches in and pats the boy in the back seat. Kris drives away, spinning too hard on the gravel of the Pop Shop's parking lot and kicking up dust and grit at the woman he dropped off. A hate like no hate I've ever known burns inside me as I watch, shrunk down in my driver's seat, clenching the coffee cup until it begins to crack at the rim, making little popping sounds.

Then I start the car and follow Kris Milford's truck, first along the commercial strip, then through uneven back roads, stopping well before the turn-in to the trailer park and reversing direction when the truck fades from sight.

My GPS tells me there's another McDonald's back in town, and I drive to it, picking up two more large coffees and one of those egg muffin things that taste like cardboard but that I figure (incorrectly, it will turn out) might have a chance at staying down. In the drive-through lane, I notice pancakes on the menu, and I spend the next two hours thinking about little boys.

If there's a universal truth about six-year-olds, it's that they all seem to go crazy over pancakes. Maybe it's that delicious word 'cake' that does the trick, revealing a Mom-sanctioned dessert for breakfast. I know Jonathan and his cousin love them. I'd bet Caleb Church loved them. I also have a terrible feeling pancakes aren't a regular feature in Caleb Milford's home. Not when Mary Ann has to be at work early. Her husband seems more of the beer-for-breakfast type, and he's probably just smart enough to know not to share a Budweiser with a six-year-old boy.

I think hard about Jake and Mary Ann's illegitimate son. Whatever they did in that hotel room seven years ago might be a sin in some minds, but a baby can never be a sin. A baby is a perfect thing, unblemished and clean, despite all the myths that try to convince us otherwise. On my mental list of Kris Milford's other crimes, I add shitty fathering, and glance down at the blanket-covered gun while I wait my turn in the drive-through line.

Once a few bills are exchanged for coffee and breakfast, I walk myself through the scene that will soon play out, the same way Jake had walked through it. Pick up the piece and the silencer after the garage closed. Check. Drive south through the night and wait across the street from the Pop Shop until Mary Ann came in for her shift. Done. All that remains is to drive those easy few miles to Pounding Mill and walk straight into the trailer without so much as a knock—

And here is the snag in Jake's uncomplicated plan. I have no key to the trailer.

I don't know how long I sit in the McDonald's parking lot, watching wisps of steam rise from the coffee cups in their circular holders, occasionally glancing over at the blanket in the passenger footwell, smelling the grease of fried egg and Canadian bacon – whatever that is. At some point, a sense of relief washes through me. I'll start the car and reverse course, race home to Daniel and Jonathan, and put all this hero nonsense behind me. I'll watch my plan fade with every mile I put between myself and this town, disappearing in my rearview mirror.

I put the car in gear and pull out of the parking lot, feeling better than I've ever felt. It's only when I reach the turn-off to the interstate that my thoughts travel back to that winter night in Boston when the talk at Ian's Death and Drinks party had turned to justifiable homicide.

I don't take the exit to the interstate that would return me to Richmond. I double back, turn into the Pop Shop parking lot, and walk into the store. Mary Ann stands at the register, the older couple who owns the place on either side with their arms around her shaking shoulders. The man has a phone in his free hand, and Mary Ann is pleading with him to end the call. She looks up and sees me through heavy eyes that must have cried all night.

'Get out of here,' Mary Ann says. 'I don't want more trouble. Got plenty as it is, thanks to you.'

It's then I see the gash on her forehead, an inch above her right eyebrow. It must have bled like a geyser when it was fresh but now an ugly crust has formed on it. I instinctively raise a hand to my own forehead, as if I can feel the woman's wound.

The older woman turns toward me. 'You get on out of here, girlie. You've done enough harm already.'

'I haven't—' I start, and let my voice trail off. I no longer know what I've done or what I haven't done, but I might as well take the blame for one more fuck-up in this never-ending line of fuck-ups.

'One of her husband's bar buddies saw you in the back lot yesterday. Went off on Mary Ann last night. Only this time, honey, he didn't stop with Mary Ann.'

I flinch. Not the kid. Please let it not be the kid.

I can tell from the look in Mary Ann's eyes that it's the kid.

A customer comes in, announced by the bell hanging on the door. The older man shoos Mary Ann away and says he'll take care of this. At the same time, the phone on the wall rings, and his wife answers it. I hear the customer ask for a pack of Marlboros and two Powerball tickets, so it's going to be a quick transaction. I have seconds, a minute at most.

I follow Mary Ann towards the back of the store. Part of me wants to ask her what Kris did to the little boy, but I've no time. Besides, I don't really want or need to know. 'I need the keys to your trailer,' I say.

'What?'

'You heard me.' The old man is looking at me over his customer's shoulder. 'Don't make me say it again, and don't say anything yourself.' I hold my hand out, waiting.

There's an exchange, a meeting of two pairs of eyes that each tell a wordless story. In Mary Ann's, I hear pleading. In my own, I think she must hear a promise because cold metal touches my open palm before she ducks into the back room. Without a word to the owners, I slip out. I'm not sure either one notices me.

When I reach the turn-in for the trailer park, I'm a different person inside the same body. No, that's not right. It's as if my own self has gone away temporarily, and a void has replaced it. I wonder if all killers feel this hollowness, if it's a device for separating the self from the act. The fact is, I don't know, and I've no time to get philosophical.

At the entry from the main road, there's a double row of mailboxes, each numbered and named. Milford is in the first row, second from the last, number fourteen, which means there are only thirty residences in the park. I remember Jake's diary saying something about two from the end, and I drive slowly along the road, hoping no one notices my out-of-place ride. This is the land of Fords and Chevrolets, good old Detroit rolling iron, not fancy British SUVs. I park in an empty spot not far from number twelve, pick up my blanket bundle, and start walking, smiling to the woman outside of trailer thirteen. She smiles back and returns to watering her flowers. She may be deaf, but she's not blind. And now she's seen my face.

I plod on, the bundled gun and its silencer heavy in my arms.

Number fourteen is as nondescript and homely as a trailer can be. The same truck I saw this afternoon is parked at a sloppy angle, and behind it is a Ford Focus with at least a decade worth of dirt on its windshield, mostly obscuring the FOR SALE sign. A flowerpot sits on the step, its cracked terracotta holding a cluster of geraniums that are too perfect to be anything but plastic. The screen door sags on rusted hinges, and the garbage bin, one of those 1970s metal jobs, is full of frozen pizza boxes and empty beer cans.

Did Mary Ann know what she was marrying into on her wedding day all those years ago? I doubt it. I don't think any woman would say 'I do' to this shitty offer. Her first glimpse of Kris's ugly side must have come on their wedding night, and by that time, it was too late to say 'I don't'.

Jake's simple plan was only simple on paper. Walk in without knocking, aim, shoot. In reality, I've no idea whether the dirtbag inside trailer fourteen is asleep or awake, whether he's watching television with his feet up on the furniture or fixing himself a sandwich. I don't know whether he might be holding a six-year-old on his lap while he watches *Wheel of Fortune* or *The Price Is Right* or some other daytime television rot. I don't even know the layout of the trailer.

The plan needs revising.

I stuff Mary Ann's key in the back pocket of my jeans and fix a smile on my face, ruffling my hair and pulling one shirt tail out so I look less city and more country. After a quick check that my deadly little bundle is intact – no silencer poking out anywhere, thank Christ – I walk up the steps and rap on the metal edge of the screen door.

He opens it at once.

'That Ford,' I say, putting a bit of extra drawl in my already-Virginia voice, 'is it still for sale?'

'Yeah,' Kris says. 'Three thousand.'

'Does it run?'

''Course it runs. Just don't need two cars no more.'

I pause, smiling at him and looking past his shoulder into the living space of the trailer. It's neater than I expected, which makes me feel like crap all over again. Not the neatness, but my nasty expectations. 'Got paperwork?'

Kris sighs a heavy, tired sigh, as if I've asked him for an undoable favor, like moving the earth for me. 'Yeah. Come on in. I'll get it.' He looks at the bundle in my arms when I cross the threshold. 'Kinda warm for a blanket today.'

'Baby,' I say, bouncing the bundle lightly. 'Sleeping.'

'Got one back there doing the same.' He nods toward the far end of the trailer. 'Only thing better than a sleeping baby is a dead baby, if you want my opinion. Snotty little buggers.'

That's it. That's what does it. Sooner or later, this man's rage will take another life. The moment he turns from me and takes a few steps toward a chest of drawers next to the television set – it is *The Price Is Right*, I notice – I let the blanket slide to the floor in a silent waterfall of fabric, and grip the Beretta the way all those YouTube videos showed. He must hear the safety click off, because he turns around, wide-eyed, not believing the sight before him. I don't hesitate, only squeeze. Kris says, 'Hey—'

Pop.

I squeeze again in the second before he crumples to the linoleum.

Pop.

Kris doesn't say anything more.

Law school didn't teach me shit about anatomy, but I've seen enough graphic images over the years to know that the gray sludge and blood oozing from the back of Kris Milford's head isn't compatible with life. I wrap the Beretta back in the blanket, step over the body on the floor, and go into the smaller bedroom Kris nodded toward when his head was still capable of nodding. On the bed is a small boy, thin and pale, hair tousled from sleep. I smile at him before backing out of the room and calling Mary Ann at the Pop Shop. Then I go back and wait with the sleeping boy.

Drew Carey announces from the television that 'The price is *RIGHT!*' and I think he's one hundred percent correct about that.

CHAPTER FORTY-ONE

The second the taxi pulls up alongside trailer fourteen with Mary Ann in the back, I dash out to Daniel's Range Rover, put it in gear, and let it roll forward, fixing my eyes on the road ahead. I don't know what I would see if I looked left. Maybe shock, maybe gratitude, maybe disbelief. But I have to let Mary Ann sort that out on her own, let her find the body and do whatever processing is necessary. I don't have a role to play in this next scene; I need to get into character for the final act.

And that means changing out props.

On the way out of Bluefield, I stop at a defunct roadside bar advertising what used to be its two main features: 'Beer and Broads'. Around to the back, the ugly metal box I'm looking for stands among littered beer cans and condom wrappers. I figure since an industrial garbage container was where I found the Beretta and its trimmings, one just like it is a fitting place for me to lay it to rest.

I unscrew the silencer – suppressor to all those gun nuts on the internet – slip out the magazine, and check the chamber before wiping every square millimeter down with tissues from a box in the glove compartment. This is partly for me, but mostly for Jake Milford. I don't want any fingerprints leading to him, nothing to blemish his absolute innocence, so I unload the magazine and start wiping bullets, one by one. The whole mess gets tied up in the blanket, and I heave it over the top of the bin. It makes a final clank as it falls, much louder than the soft pop that killed Kris Milford.

Pops, I think. There were two of them. And I throw up a brownish sludge of Egg McMuffin and bitter coffee. It meshes well with the other detritus on the pavement, and I let it lie. No one is going to take samples of this.

I drive off, easing into the sparse traffic that leads to the interstate, and turn into the parking lot of a 7-Eleven, readying myself for this next step towards the finale. I could wait, that's true. I could wait a few days or a week before snapping a picture of the Little Walker Motel receipt and emailing it to Carmela Petrus from a burner email account. But I think waiting would lead to other things. It would lead to forgetting. It would lead to a flight over the Atlantic and life in a country that would never extradite me. It would lead to telling myself the same lie every day: *There's always tomorrow. Always a chance to make things right.*

Personally, I think that would be hell on earth.

In the parking lot of the 7-Eleven, as a family of three comes out with a trio of Slurpees and smiles on their faces, I create a throw-away Gmail account, janedoe5934041, which, based on Google's suggestion of a seven-digit add-on, makes me wonder how many other Jane Does there are floating around the internet and how many anonymous emails fly through the ether every day. Are they trolls? Lovers? Mafiosi? Well, at least one of them is a murderer. That much I know.

Jane Doe Number five-million-and-something attaches the motel receipt to the email and writes a short note:

Suppose Jake Milford had an alibi, and an eyewitness can be produced.

I don't type anything more, no longwinded narrative that a sharp pair of eyes might associate with me. Petrus shoots back a response five minutes after Jane Doe's email flutters off into the great beyond, out there, never able to be snatched back, like a trivial idiocy tweeted years ago and resurrected.

If this is a joke, it's a bad one. Go away.

Jane Doe responds:

Not a joke.

I like this game. I like being Jane Doe instead of Justine Boucher Callaghan. Jane Doe isn't a mother, or a prosecutor, or a killer. She's no one at all.

Only one more message from Carmela comes through:

No further comments.

I make one phone call and drive on.

Carmela Petrus isn't behind her desk when the clerk shows me into her chambers late this afternoon. She's in one of the wingback chairs near the window with a book in her lap, not reading, not writing, not doing anything.

'How about a drink?' I say. 'I'll buy.'

'Not in the mood.'

'Me either.'

She glances at the phone in her lap, then turns to look out the window. I clear my throat to remind her that someone else is in the room.

For four hours, all during the drive back to Richmond, I tried to imagine what Petrus was doing and thinking. I wrote scripts in my head, narrating her reaction to Jane Doe's email. One moment, she would be carrying on with whatever the work of the day was, laughing off the idea of a crank who claimed to have new information on the Milford case. In the next script, Petrus would be doing exactly what she's doing now. Wondering. In the end, the only way to sort out these two conflicting scripts was to come here and see for myself.

'I need to talk to you,' I say.

She jerks her head around and points to the chair next to her own. 'Sit. Stay. Don't speak.'

'This won't take long,' I say, and remain standing.

'Did you hear me? I said, "Don't speak." Not a word, Justine. Not until I'm done. Now sit down.'

I do, and for a while, neither one of us speaks.

'I've been a judge for twenty-five years,' Petrus says. She doesn't look at me. Her eyes seem to be fixed on the wall of books to my left. 'My job is to read the shit on those shelves, study it, apply it, interpret it.' She sighs. 'Most of the time, I like my job. I feel good about what I do because, for a quarter of a century, the shit I've read has been good shit. Fair. I can't say that anymore. Christ, Justine, I don't know if I'll ever be able to say it again. Not after today.' She gets up from the chair and reaches for a single sheet of paper on her desk. 'I typed this out four hours ago. I figure with Roger's job and the kids finished with school, we don't need the extra income.' She laughs. 'Not that my extra income went very far on three Ivy League educations. Barely made a dent.'

'Carm, what are you talking about?'

She shrugs and hands me the sheet of paper that's her resignation letter.

'You're kidding,' I say.

'No.' Now she sits in the chair again, leaning close to me, shifting her phone from one hand to the other. 'I received some news today. No idea whether it's true news or fake news, and, if I'm honest, I don't give a shit.'

I decide to play dumb and see how this plays out. 'Is there a medical problem, Carm?'

'Not at all. According to my doctor, I'm in better shape than he is. Let's call it an ethical dilemma and leave it at that.' Petrus locks eyes with me, then checks her phone and swipes to the left. 'There. No more bad news.' She stands up, taking the letter from me, and signs it with the same flourish I've seen a hundred times before. The signature has the texture of finality, a decision made after careful consideration. 'I've been thinking about raising alpacas. Maybe a few chickens. What do you think, Justine?'

'I think that's a good decision.'

I'm only talking about the alpacas and the chickens.

CHAPTER FORTY-TWO

On the short drive from Petrus' chambers to Daniel's house, I think about Jesus. Most of what I know about the guy comes from watching those movies that play every year around Easter, so I can't say my facts are all straight, but the general theme might still hold. In order to save all of humanity, some poor Palestinian dude has to die. Why he didn't simply walk off in the direction of Roman soldiers, throw his hands in the air, and say, 'Here I am! Take me to your leader,' is something I've never understood, but I think I'm coming around.

He needed a Judas to be the fixer, and I do, too. Maybe it's hardwired into us, this inability to give ourselves up, to search for a betrayer who's willing to do the nasty work. Maybe we all need a little push.

Carmela Petrus wasn't willing. Instead of pushing, she hung up her robes and decided to start an alpaca farm. I don't know if they've got alpacas in the Middle East, but I do have to ask that perennial question: *What would Jesus do?* if Judas told the Pharisees to fuck off and started a camel ranch instead of engaging in a little PDA that night in Gethsemane. I mean, let's get to the heart of it – Jesus didn't want to die any more than I do.

So here I am, driving through Richmond in the early evening, searching for a Judas of my own, when my phone lights up with a number I recognize immediately.

'Emily,' I say.

'I got the strangest call a while ago. Been thinking about it all afternoon.' She doesn't wait for me to respond. 'Seems as if Mary Ann's problem got itself taken care of. You know, the one with the big shoulders, the pea-sized brain, and the flying fists.'

I play dumb again, as I did with Petrus. 'What did he do now?'

'Oh, he didn't do a thing. It's what got done to him I find interesting. Kris Milford is dead.'

At Daniel's house, I slide the car into a vacant spot on the street, letting it idle. 'Oh.'

'Funny how we were just talking about him yesterday morning in the park,' Emily says.

'What happened to him?'

'Well, Mary Ann ain't talking too much, but I managed to get the bare bones of the situation out of her.' Emily pauses, tells Jake Junior to go play in his room for a minute, and comes back on the line. 'It appears someone went into their trailer, shot Kris twice in the head, and that's all she wrote. Mary Ann said she took a taxi home because she wasn't feeling well, and she found Kris on the floor next to the television. That old widow, the neighbor, said she saw a woman walking around the trailer park earlier, but all she knows is that it wasn't Mary Ann. That's good, I think, that Mary Ann has an alibi. In the movies, it's always the spouse they suspect when stuff like this happens. Don't you think that's good she was somewhere else? 'Specially seeing as nothing went missing from the trailer.'

'I do.'

Emily laughs lightly. 'Not that Kris and Mary Ann had

anything worth stealing, but still. They had the TV and a few music CDs. That's the kind of thing that usually has a way of growing legs and walking off on its own.'

'How are Mary Ann and her boy?'

'Oh, they'll muddle through. Gonna come up and stay with me and the folks for a spell after the police have asked their questions tomorrow morning. Maybe longer. I can't help thinking, though, what a coincidence it is. You know, with us just having talked about it.'

She's fishing, letting the line out, waiting for me to take the bait. I don't. There's still that Jesus part of me who wants this cup of poison to pass by.

Emily tells Jake Junior if she has to ask him one more time to go to his room, there'll be trouble. He asks what kind of trouble. Emily tells him he doesn't want to know. 'I've been thinking, Justine. It's okay that I call you Justine, right?'

'Of course.'

'I think maybe in a case like this, there's a right thing to do and a wrong thing to do. Problem is, I'm not sure which is which. I may not ever be sure. What do you think?'

Daniel's upstairs window is bright, and through the shade I see my son's silhouette, a lonely outline framed by a dark rectangle. It's hard to see him this way, all by himself, but only a second later he's joined by another silhouette, Tommy, and then by a larger figure who has to be Susan, unless Daniel suddenly grew breasts and long hair. So my boy's not alone after all. He's got others in his life, family, and always will. This should make answering Emily's question easier, but it doesn't.

'I said, "What do you think is the right thing to do?"' Emily says again.

It's a question I can't answer immediately, so I look up at Jonathan in the window and think about Jake Junior. Oh, Jake will take some punches at school; a few of them might come farther down the road when he's applying for a job and sees a pair of eyes narrowing over his résumé, asking all those unaskable questions. *How far did the apple fall from the tree? Is he like his father? Do I dare invite children to the company picnic if he's going to be there?* When young Jake becomes old enough to understand, Emily will tell him the truth. She'll tell him his daddy was one of the good guys, an unsung hero in an oil-stained blue work shirt. She'll say it doesn't matter what the world thinks, as long as she and Jake Junior know what really went down.

Emily might be okay with the world believing a lie, but I'm not, even if opening this Pandora's box means she'll have to come to terms with her husband's infidelity.

That's the piece that has given me pause, knowing that telling the truth is going to hurt a decent woman. If I'm honest, I've thought about using this as my way out of the darkness, repeating the same mantra – staying quiet would be doing the right thing by Emily – so many times that I even started to believe it. I guess we all have a way of twisting the world to fit our wants, and what I want is to convince myself that knowing Jake Milford's sin is too high a price to pay for clearing his name. What lies we tell ourselves.

The truth will sting, I know that much, and it won't bring Jake Milford back to life, but I've been thinking about life differently these days. Once, I was quite sure that when life ended, there was nothing else, no white light, no pearly gates, no fire and brimstone at the opposite end of the afterworld. I still don't believe in heaven and hell, but I think we go on somehow, even if going on means leaving remnants of ourselves in the world. If there's a shred of truth to my strange hypothesis, I want those remnants to be clean and untattered.

I don't know how to respond to Emily's question, so I dance around the subject. 'If I could find a way to clear your husband's name—' I start, but she doesn't let me finish.

'We talking hypothetically, Justine? Because I'd probably give my whole life. Not my boy's, and not anyone else's, just mine. But that's so easy to say. Kinda like saying you'd never eat a snake, as Jake always said. Problem is, Jake also said you never know what you'll put up with. Rattler or copperhead might go down a treat if you're starving.' She sighs. 'I don't know what else to say.'

After a long while, I tell her I don't know either.

'Maybe let's leave it at that.'

When I end the call and kill the engine, I'm still looking for my Judas.

CHAPTER FORTY-THREE

The first words out of Daniel's mouth when I walk inside are: 'I've been thinking.'

There isn't a woman or man alive who hasn't heard those words and who doesn't know exactly what they mean in the context of a relationship. No one builds up to a marriage proposal with 'I've been thinking'. No one asks a girl to the prom with 'I've been thinking' as a lead-in. Those three words are harbingers of a change in status quo, but almost always in a negative direction.

I've been thinking . . . maybe we should see other people.

I've been thinking . . . now that the kids are grown, there's no reason to stay together.

I've been thinking . . . I don't love you anymore.

So when Daniel speaks, I steel myself for the worst.

The problem is, I can't match my expectations with the visual context in this house. The table is set for two, candles flickering in the dimmed room like tiny dancers on pedestals. An extravagant mess of flowers takes up most of the real estate on the kitchen island and another, smaller bouquet sits between our plates. The entire scene smacks of date night taken to an extreme.

'I've been thinking,' he says, 'that we're not going to mope around here like mourners all night long.' Daniel looks embarrassed, almost boyishly so. 'I mean, we could put on some horsehair and eat gruel and think about what's going on with Adrian down in Florida, but I don't see that as a way forward.' He draws me close, stopping any response I might have with his mouth until I'm drowning in the kiss.

There's nothing else in the world right now – not the flowers with their heady spring scent, not Adrian Kopinsky, not the fact that I've killed twice. There's only Daniel in this moment, and for the first time, I don't automatically think of Ian.

What a shitty way to move forward in any relationship, to search for a late husband or erstwhile lover in every kiss and embrace and sexual act. Daniel's right, I think, kissing him back, letting us explore each other. I should be looking to the future.

'Mommy's getting kissed,' a small voice exclaims from the stair. 'Ha! Caught you!'

Without letting go of me, Daniel stoops down and gathers Jonathan in one arm, raising him up until our foreheads are bent together in a familial huddle. 'Looks like I caught you, Jon-Jon,' Daniel says, and the three of us stay like this for a long time, loving one another, not thinking about anything outside of our tiny world.

It's Jonathan who breaks up this intimate party. 'I had chicken nuggets. And broccoli. And milk. And I get to watch *Willy Wonka* with Tommy and Aunt Susan while you have a date night.' He looks at Daniel. 'Did I get it right?'

'You got it perfect.'

'Daniel,' Jonathan says, 'when we move to England can I learn to talk like you?'

My eyes roll involuntarily, thinking of my little boy sounding more like the king than like himself, dropping Rs at the ends of words, putting Rs in where they aren't, and using that flat 'a' whenever he says 'pasta'. But I like the thought. It seems to be a looking-ahead thought.

'All right,' Daniel says. 'Cuddling paused for a bit while we feed your mum. Want to stay or want to watch *Willy Wonka*?'

Jonathan shoots him a look as if to say 'What kind of question is that?' and flies up the stairs. I hear him singing along from his roost on the second floor, and go back to kissing my man.

'Hungry?' Daniel says.

'Starving.'

'How about we take a supper break, then?'

At the table, I tell myself the food Daniel has made is delicious; an hour later, in bed, I tell myself we have years of fabulous sex ahead of us. When I go to check on Jonathan and the Oompa-Loompas, I tell myself this is a night like any other.

None of these lies work.

When the food and the sex and the singing are done, when I'm lying in Daniel's arms and the clock ticks its way toward midnight, there's only one truth that I know. It isn't my truth or a truth, only the truth, simple in its honesty. I've lost something precious in all the evening's pretending, and I don't even know where to start looking for it.

CHAPTER FORTY-FOUR

It was another winter night in Cambridge – so many of my Cambridge memories seem to come with snow and sleet-slicked roads – and Ian's living room was empty save for the two of us.

I had three months of classes, a few monstrous finals, and that modern torture device called the bar exam ahead of me, and I was worried. I'd enrolled in a famed seminar in prosecutorial ethics, known as 'Cooper's Crucible' by the masochistic few who signed up. Those who passed reported that sitting for the final exam was tantamount to being burned alive.

Ian only laughed at my concern. 'What do you think you've been doing for the past few years, Jussie?'

'You're not saying these parties are anything like Professor Cooper's seminar. Here, it's all drinking and bantering.'

He winked. 'You forgot fucking.'

'That, too.'

'How many old faces did you count in this room tonight?' he said.

'There was Philip. You know, the guy with the mega-metabolism who drives you nuts. And me, I guess.' It was true. Everyone who had been here on that first evening when I showed up as Ted Stuyvesant's uninvited date was history – even Ted himself. It wasn't graduation that had ended their tenure at Ian's parties. They had run away, tails between their legs. Or, as in Ted's case, they had gotten themselves kicked out for being what Ian called 'intellectual flyweights with all the integrity of a melting ice cube'.

'Exactly. Don't think this isn't any less of a classroom because the blue books were replaced with a few bottles of bourbon. Most people can't stick it out. You, on the other hand, have staying power.'

'You never made it easy.'

'Honey, the world isn't easy.' He poured himself another drink, lit his pipe, and came to sit beside me next to the fire. 'Speaking of staying power, you're off to Virginia in a few months. Otherwise known as the land of the openly carried firearm and the electric chair.'

'You know I'll be working to get rid of that second item,' I said, and smiled a coquettish smile at him. 'And you'll visit, won't you? I mean, the ads all say Virginia is for lovers.'

'Do they now?' Ian ran a finger across my lips, tracing the smile.

'Mm-hm.'

'And what do they say about it being for married couples?'

'I guess they allow them in. You planning something, darling?'

He set the pipe aside. 'Right now, I'm planning on taking you here by the fire. Then we'll talk about next steps.'

It was delicious sex, the kind of give and take that seems to go on forever, starting and stopping, slowing and quickening, until we would both fall away, too exhausted to continue, only to come back to one another when our bodies begged for more. I had loved Ian for two years, and I knew he loved me, but tonight was different. The implication of a life together changed everything.

Ian had another side to him, a side he didn't show around campus, or even at his Death and Drinks parties. I knew in these moments that I would be the only one to see that side, the only person to know the part of Ian Callaghan he kept hidden from the world.

When we finally settled down, naked limbs twisted together and glowing in front of the fading fire, he said, 'I never thought I'd fall in love with a One-L. Not even a Three-L. You aren't like the rest of them, Justine.'

'Because I don't flinch when you go all Socratic method on me?'

He shook his head. 'No. Because when I do, you don't back down. You stick to your point and prove it. Believe me, Jussie, integrity is rare in this business. Make sure you don't lose yours down in Virginia.'

'And if I do?'

Ian kissed me again and reached for his trousers, which lay in a puddle of clothes around us. He took out a small box and held it out to me. 'Tell you what. You say yes, and I promise I'll help you find it.'

CHAPTER FORTY-FIVE

I think I've found what was lost. It's only two phone calls and a mountain of willpower away.

Daniel is still snoring when I leave the bed, shrug on my robe, and tiptoe down to the kitchen. I'll come back to him in a little while for one last hurrah, then I'll go upstairs and spend the waiting time with Jonathan. Maybe we'll watch a movie, maybe cartoons. Whatever Jonathan wants is fine with me. I'll bring Pop-Tarts and juice. No coffee, though. I've already got the jitters.

The dispatcher at the Bluefield police station answers on the second ring, and when I ask for Mary Ann Milford, she puts me on hold while she checks. While a Muzak version of 'Bad Boys' plays – an odd choice for police hold music, but what the hell do I know? – I keep track of the number of times I nearly hang up. The count is at fifteen when the dispatcher's voice tells me Mrs Milford is coming out of the conference room right now and then, almost as an afterthought, wants to know who I am.

I've prepared myself for this question, and I tell her an edited version of the truth. 'I was the lead prosecutor in the Jacob Milford case and I need a quick word with Mrs Milford.'

The dispatcher seems impressed. She puts me back on hold, and the *Cops* theme starts up again, the repetitive lyrics worming their way into my head even though this version is instrumental. At the umpteenth *Whatcha gonna do?* – a question to which I really don't like the answer – Mary Ann comes on the line. Her voice has changed since we last spoke; frailty and fear has been replaced with a kind of quiet strength. I like this new rendering of Mary Ann, a twenty-something-year-old girl with a shiny life ahead of her.

'I won't call again after this,' I say. 'But I have to ask you one question.'

'I don't think I can talk right now,' she says.

'You won't need to. I'll ask the question; you tell me yes or no.'

'Okay.' I hear hesitancy in her voice now.

'If you were called to testify about Jake's alibi, would you swear he was in that hotel room with you seven years ago?'

I wait a long time for the answer, and in this time, my future divides itself into two unequal parts.

CHAPTER FORTY-SIX

In one of my alternate futures, Mary Ann's unwillingness to testify means the Milford case is as dead as its namesake. Even if I walk into Ted Stuyvesant's office, throw my hands up, and beg him to invoke the Remedies Act, it will come to nothing. I know because I'll try doing exactly that.

Ted and Joanna will work on her for weeks, calling every day at different times, rapping on the door to her house, waiting outside the school where she drops off young Caleb. By Christmas of this year, they'll still be trying, and by January, Mary Ann will be fed up enough to ask for – and get – a restraining order. No one in a red suit or with the last name of Stuyvesant will be allowed within fifty feet of her or her son, so they'll work on Emily for a few months in early spring. At some point, Emily's parents will move the entire extended family out of state. Kansas, maybe. Or Oklahoma.

As for me, I might be in London with Daniel and Jonathan for the weekend, tooling around, visiting the sights. Most of the sights, that is. Daniel will be desperate to show me the Old Bailey, but I'll decline. I think I'm going to steer clear of courthouses these days, preferring the sound of a garden hoe churning up chalky Hertfordshire earth to a gavel pounding on old wood.

Everything from my former life will be gone, erased, except for Ian, who I'll still talk to when I'm alone.

I'll tell him it all worked out rather nicely in the end. I didn't run. I didn't lose my way. Whether Mary Ann thought she owed me a favor, or whether she couldn't bear to hurt Emily, I'll never know. She'll refuse to tell me when we meet briefly for coffee in downtown Richmond for a quick goodbye and an unspoken 'thank you'. I think if Emily Milford ever notices the strong resemblance between her son and her nephew, she'll chalk it up to Milford genes.

What will be key in these private, one-sided conversations with Ian is that I'll convince myself he won't lay any blame on me, that he'll understand I tried to set things right. I'll hear the same absolution from Daniel, although we'll rarely discuss the Milford case. It might come up every few months when he notices I've gone a little red-eyed, or tossed and turned in my sleep. Each time, Daniel will remind me the Remedies Act was flawed.

Every one of the states that adopted the act will agree. I think it will be the outcry after Adrian Kopinsky's execution that convinces them – an execution that went wrong in so many ways it made the three I witnessed look like well-choreographed ballets with happy endings. There will be a flood of op-eds in the *New York Times* and the *Washington Post* calling for an end to 'Old Testament barbarism', and someone will write at least one dystopian thriller about prosecutorial accountability, which will inevitably be turned into a Netflix series that I'll never watch.

My name will appear far more often than I like in news articles and court cases. In some, I'll be the radical activist who engineered Kopinsky's death; in others, I'll be a misguided heroine with good intentions and a lousy way of executing them. Speaking of execution, the entire American populace is about to become hyper-aware of French etymology, and the significance of my maiden name – whether translated as 'butcher', 'slaughterer', or 'executioner' – won't be lost on the average fifth-grader. Daniel says it will blow over sooner or later.

I'll never be as confident as Daniel.

The average life expectancy for a woman in the UK is eighty-three years and some number of months, so I expect I'll have a solid four decades ahead of me, plenty of time to see Jonathan grow into a man, marry, have children of his own. There will also be more than enough time to entertain those visiting ghosts, the ones who point accusing fingers and curse me for coddling their killers.

But Jake Milford will never point or curse. He'll be the ghost who throws me a sad smile as if to say, 'It was as much my fault as yours. I could have come clean any old time.' Jake will make it sound like we're even, and that itself will always make me feel worse. One of us is a killer on record and innocent in fact. One of us is the opposite.

I will not regret killing Kris Milford. I think I saved at least two lives by putting bullets in that sonofabitch, and if I won't exactly feel good about it, his ghost won't keep me up at night, and he won't be pointing any fingers other than at himself. My regret, all four decades of it ahead of me, will always be knowing I was part of a system that necessitated such an outrageously illegal remedy and silenced a good man. I may be in my garden when the thought comes, I may be in bed with Daniel, or I may be stirring a pot of stew on the stovetop – 'hob', Daniel will remind me. What I know is that I'll be struck with that singular thought in every mundane moment for the rest of my days:

We could have done better. I could have done better.

***

There's another future, a different fork in the road that I'll find myself walking along when Mary Ann agrees to testify and the Jake Milford case is reopened. Ted Stuyvesant, sitting in a plush office, will look at me with wide eyes and take down Mary Ann's number as I recite it. He'll invite me to sit down, but I won't. I'll prefer to stand – standing will make me believe I still have a chance to run, even if I know there's nowhere to run to. I will, however, hold my breath while he taps the ten numbers on his phone, while he asks Mary Ann a series of questions, while he waits for answers.

I'll have hope during those brief pauses, but with each nod of his head and each new note he writes on his legal pad, another slice of that hope will vanish.

Ted, or someone in his group – perhaps the woman from the playground that is home to miniature painted animals on springs – will make two more phone calls: one to the district attorney's office and one to the police. They'll watch me carefully as we wait, checking for the slightest movement or gesture that might telegraph a failure to cooperate. I'll remind them I came in on my own, but their eyes won't leave me until two men in uniform arrive and ask me to put both hands behind my back.

So starts this other path, much shorter than its alternate. It won't have any twists and turns, no spur-of-the-moment detours to London or Bath for sightseeing trips. Instead, it will be perfectly straight, leading to a singular destination with plenty of signposts along the way to remind me where I'm headed. There's no turning back on this path, and no pausing to take in the view – not that a narrow cell in Block D of this correctional center an hour northwest of Richmond will offer a view of anything other than a dry, brown patch they call the recreation yard.

Daniel will visit me, of course. He won't be happy, but he'll visit, telling me I look too thin and bringing me coins for the vending machine. The two problems with the vending machine are that it sells nothing but fried corn products and that I don't have priority, so by the time I push through my coins, all I've got to choose from are Fritos and Fritos, so I'll pass on both and get thinner. He'll never stay long on these visits, partly because of the time limit, mostly because each visit takes something out of him that he won't get back.

When Susan comes with the boys in those first days I'm allowed contact visits while the necessary paperwork gets pushed from one desk to another somewhere in the capital, she'll shake her head as if by constantly moving it to the left and to the right she can negate reality. But she won't say an unkind word, not even as she takes one signed form after another – my will, the deed to my house, a pile of stock transfers and bank authorizations – and slips each piece of my former life into a courier bag. They'll become her life now, and Jonathan's.

On my last day, someone will ask me if I want a chaplain. Another someone will give me a meal request form, apologizing if my first choice isn't available. A doctor will come in to poke around for plump veins and check my heart rate. I'll be frightened and tired and unable to eat the salad I ordered. Then, the warden will arrive to tell me it's time.

There will be a gurney and technicians and bright lights, but the only color will be the red of the phone on the wall. It might ring, circling me back to the fork in the road where that other path starts. It might not.

All I'll be able to do is wait.

Death Row Inmate #39384

I learned the meaning of hell when it all started. Hell is waiting.

Hell is waiting for a jury to decide your fate based on evidence you're damn sure is missing some crucial piece you can't tell them about. Hell is waiting to see your wife on a Thursday morning — even if you're behind a filth-smudged glass screen. Hell is waiting to hold your boy again, to throw a few balls in the backyard or sneak him a Happy Meal from Mickey D's when his mother isn't looking.

Mostly, hell is waiting for a phone to ring.

There was a knock on my cell door a few minutes ago, and it opened a crack. The chaplain came in, took a seat without asking, and told me he was ready to hear my confession. I had one, but it wasn't the kind he expected. My confession is in these pages, and I hope the chaplain sees they make their way to the right hands. He said he'll do it, and I suppose I have to trust his words.

He's nodding at the stack of papers as I write these final lines, holding out his hand. That means my work's done.

All that's left is the waiting.

ACKNOWLEDGEMENTS

Fifty percent of my thanks go to editor-extraordinaire Cicely Aspinall and the entire team at HQ stories. The other half go to my husband, whose lawyerly insight made this a better book (although any errors are my own). The final fifty percent are for all the men and women who have stuck by me though the dark times and offered torches to guide my way.

That's more than one hundred percent, but I have a lot of thanks to give.

ONE PLACE. MANY STORIES

Bold, innovative and
empowering publishing.

FOLLOW US ON:

@HQStories